BURIED BENEATH

BURIED
BENEATH

BURIED BENEATH

DEBBIE BALDWIN

Columbus, Ohio

Buried Beneath

Published by Gatekeeper Press
2167 Stringtown Rd, Suite 109
Columbus, OH 43123-2989
www.GatekeeperPress.com

ISBN (hardcover): 9781662918674
ISBN (paperback): 9781662918681
eISBN: 9781662918698

"Try to be a rainbow in someone's cloud."
-Maya Angelou

To the women of Wednesday night, my rainbow.

CHAPTER ONE

The small cabin sat nestled in a clearing in the snowy wood. Smoke puffed amiably into the starry sky.

The setting might have inspired Robert Frost but for the rotting roof and supporting wall threatening collapse. The crumbling chimney sat at a Seussian angle, and most of the windows were boarded up.

Then, of course, there were the men inside.

Dressed in winter camouflage, Camilo Canto moved silently through the wet snow, approaching the house from the side. He was the newest member of the team, but with each day that passed and every op they ran, Cam grew more certain that leaving the CIA to join Bishop Security was one of the best decisions he had ever made. In eight short months, he had found a home and had slammed the door on the demons of his past undercover work.

If only those demons would stop knocking.

Cam stepped on a twig, the small snap like an explosion in the quiet. He was distracted, and it didn't matter if he was a SEAL, an undercover officer, or a Bishop Security operator; distraction could get you killed.

Before they boarded the jet in South Carolina, Cam had received word from the CIA that someone had called the cell phone belonging to Cam's cover identity, Miguel Ramirez. The call had not connected and had come from an untraceable burner phone. It was a nonevent—no message, no caller to identify—and yet it needled him. It was the country code where the phone call originated that spurred his disquiet: Crimea.

There was one man who might have called him from that part of the world. Cam didn't have friends in the CIA, but Raymond Greene came close. He and Raymond shared a common interest in a very uncommon criminal. Greene knew Cam was out of the CIA, which only made the phone call more confounding. If it even was Greene who had attempted to contact him.

A voice in his ear forced Cam into the here and now. "Cam, what's your twenty?" Miller "Tox" Buchanan, their team leader, spoke in an even voice.

"About thirty yards to the north. I have a clear view of what looks like the kitchen. No activity." Cam refocused—if there was one thing he could do without hesitation after living for more than two years as his cover identity, Miguel Ramirez, it was compartmentalize.

"I thought Vermont was supposed to be quaint, like where they tap maple trees and churn butter and shit. This isn't one bit quaint." Hercules Reynolds, their sniper, spoke into the comm from his perch in a White Poplar. "Very un-fucking-quaint."

"Fuck off, Herc. At least you're in a tree. I'm stuck in an ice swamp," Jonah "Steady" Lockhart muttered from thirty feet below Herc's roost. Steady had earned his nickname on his SEAL squad for his ability to keep an even keel under the most trying of circumstances. Despite the griping, today was no exception.

The crunch of tires on gravel had the men snapping to attention. "Incoming." Looking through binoculars, Leo "Ren" Jameson spoke from behind a tree to Cam's left. Ren was short for Renaissance Man. Leo Jameson was officially their medic; he also possessed an encyclopedic knowledge of topics ranging from astrophysics to zoology.

Bishop Security had been contracted to locate and rescue the daughter of a prominent insurance executive. Amy Rafferty had been driving from Bloomington, Indiana to Colorado to meet up with friends for a ski trip when she went missing. Her car was located at a truck stop outside of Lincoln, Nebraska. The FBI was only too happy to hand over the case. Their list of investigations into killings and abductions potentially involving long-haul truckers was so long, the agency had an entire database dedicated to it.

The evidence—security footage and some blood droplets at the primary crime scene—had led the team to Alfred Winston Bell. Bell was a forty-three-year-old trucker with a string of offenses, including public indecency and peeking while loitering—a lawyerly way of saying he was a peeping tom. It appeared Mr. Bell had decided to take it up a notch. Unfortunately for him, he chose the wrong girl. Amy Rafferty's father was an influential businessman with a network of connections that looked like an airline route map.

A rusted-out pickup rumbled up the drive, pulled onto the grass, and stopped with a sputter. A tall man with a beer gut jumped down, then turned back to the cab to grab four pizza boxes and a six-pack. He entered the cabin through a side door.

"Is that Bell?" Herc asked.

"Negative," Steady responded.

Cam crept through the wet snow to a closer tree, confident in his ingrained training. He had served as a SEAL with most of these guys before leaving the Navy to work for the CIA. He spoke softly into his comm. "I've got three men in the cabin. I don't have a visual on the girl, but Asshole Number One brought four pizzas when he came in, so it's a safe assumption there are more people in there."

"Unless Tox is in there," Steady ribbed. "Four pizzas would be about right."

Tox fired back, "I'm currently in a warm, dry van getting some very provocative texts from my wife, but by all means, you boys keep up the trash talk." Tox was a newlywed. He had fallen in love on an op last spring, and the six-foot, five-inch warrior was like putty in his new wife's hands.

Steady and Ren both groaned from their positions in the icy snow.

"Got a visual on the girl," Herc said, staring through the scope of his rifle. "She's in an upstairs bedroom. Looks like she's alone."

"Tox, Asshole Number Two just polished off the fifth of Wild Turkey they've been passing around. I'm going to move to the window," Cam said.

"Good copy. Any of these assholes our guy?" Tox asked.

"Negative. Moving in now," Cam answered.

"We've got you covered. Chat's on your six," Ren added.

Andrew Dunlap moved into position, his dark skin and bald head masked by the night. The guys on his SEAL squad called him "Chat," a facetious nod to the fact that he was a man of few words. His instincts, however, were razor-sharp—when he did speak, they listened.

"Right behind you, Cam," Chat spoke into the comm. "Looks like Asshole Number Two is going outside to use the facilities, and by 'facilities,' I mean tree."

"Neutralize and move in. Nathan wants to avoid a body count on this one. The local sheriff is a friendly, but he hates paperwork," Tox instructed, referring to their boss, Nathan Bishop.

A minute passed, the silence cut by the drunken man's crunching footsteps in the snow, and then by Chat's neutral words, "Asshole Number Two is hogtied and napping."

Steady whispered, "Chat and Cam, take the back. Welcome Wagon is coming in through the front door." Cam watched Steady, with Ren at his back, make a low run to the entrance.

"Copy that," Cam acknowledged. Then, with practiced movements, he and Chat darted to the unlocked rear door.

If a mini-fridge, a hot plate, and a card table qualified as a kitchen, then the kitchen is where Cam spotted Asshole Number Three standing with a slice of pizza in each hand and a look of confusion on his face. Cam dropped him with one punch. Chat restrained the unconscious man with zip ties, and they continued into the cabin. By the time Chat and Cam got to the main room, Steady and Ren had taken down Asshole Number One.

A dingy back hall led to opposing bedrooms and either a very narrow staircase or a very wide ladder that went to a loft above the front room. Cam took point. The step-rungs groaned their protest as he climbed. When his head cleared the second floor, he immediately spotted the girl. Appearing unharmed, she was sitting on the side of the bed shivering in jeans and a T-shirt. When she looked up at him, he recognized Amy Rafferty from the photo her parents had provided. The picture... That's when he remembered. They also had a photo of the perp. None of the assholes downstairs matched the description of their suspect, Alfred Winston Bell.

When Cam looked at Amy again, she was indicating frantically with just her eyes that someone was behind her. He reached for his sidearm, but not before the man himself, Alfred Winston Bell, popped up from the far side of the bed on his knees, pump-action shotgun pointed directly at Cam's head.

Cam was torn between cursing himself for the rookie mistake and trying to recall some sort of Catholic invocation from his childhood when he heard the tinkling shatter of glass. Alfred Winston Bell fell forward onto the bed. The back of his head did not follow. Amy released a pent-up scream and raced to her rescuer. Cam moved her against the wall, cleared the room, and crossed to the window where he spotted Herc in the tree, sighting Cam through the scope of his Remington. Herc lifted his head and gave a thumbs up. Cam nodded his thanks and turned his attention to Amy just as Chat, with Steady on his heels, leapt up into the loft.

"Amy Rafferty?" Cam held her upper arms gently as she nodded confirmation.

"You're safe now," he reassured her.

She took in their tactical gear and face paint. "What are you guys? Commandos or something?"

Cam explained, "We're security specialists hired to get you out."

Amy started to shake. Chat threw an emergency blanket around her shoulders and spoke softly. "Your parents are nearby waiting to bring you home. Ready to go home?"

She gripped the edges of the silver blanket and nodded again through her shivers.

Ren called up from the bottom of the stairs. "Local law enforcement is en route with an ambulance. Tox is going to sort it out. Her parents are meeting us at the hospital in Stowe."

Twenty minutes later, Cam stood in front of the cabin and watched the commotion. Tox was shooting the shit with the sheriff while two deputies loaded the three assholes into the back of a police cruiser and a body bag into the coroner's van. Chat climbed into the ambulance with Amy. Steady and Ren flanked Cam and clocked Herc as he swung down from the tree, long gun in its soft case over his back. He joined the group with fist bumps for the team.

Steady pointed to Cam. "You may not be the new guy anymore, but you're still buying the beers."

Cam smacked Herc on the shoulder, and they turned as a group to head to the van. "Yeah, sure. I guess you clowns have earned a free beer."

Cam joked and trash-talked with the guys as they left, but in the back of his mind, that phone call to his old CIA cell phone continued to plague his thoughts.

CHAPTER TWO

Ten nautical miles off the coast of Sevastopol, Crimea
November 21

The Maestro bobbed peacefully in the heart of the Black Sea. At a mere twenty-four meters, the flybridge pocket yacht was luxurious but unobtrusive—megayachts were not an uncommon sight in these waters.

Clad in an impeccably tailored Armani suit, The Conductor sat alone at the head of a lacquered cherry wood dining table and cut into a rare filet. Juices flowed onto the plate surrounding the complements to the meat—beet salad and seasoned potatoes.

Standing at attention in the corner of the room, a leggy assistant, in a green dress just long enough to be within the bounds of propriety, eyed her boss with obvious interest. Nothing would come of the invitation. It wasn't the assistant's employment status or appearance that precluded consummation; it was the simple fact that desire alone was enough to keep her loyal. Sex was a weapon for The Conductor; better to conserve ammunition when one could.

Strains of Prokofiev filled the small room, the music both invigorating and soothing. It was a far more pleasant sound than the crunch of bones and the cries of pain from the interrogation taking place one deck below.

Over the past several hours, a bloody-knuckled man had appeared at the doorway three times and uttered only two words each time: *still nothing*. Nevertheless, the information would be obtained. The truth agent and roughing up were simply the prelude. It was time for the finale.

When the meal had been consumed and the plates cleared, the assistant sauntered to the table and placed a single photograph on the gleaming wood. In the picture, a smiling, dark-haired girl of about six or seven held the hand of a woman on a tree-lined street, a school bus in the background. The street sign on the corner read "Birchwood Lane." Pleased, The Conductor slipped the photo into a pin-striped pocket.

"The CIA can teach you all the resistance tactics they want. There's no defense against love."

Raymond Greene didn't have long to live. Raymond knew it, and The Conductor knew it. Drugged and pummeled, the CIA officer sat tied to a chair, staring at the opposite wall. Greene hadn't uttered one word. Admirable.

Not one to mince words or waste time, The Conductor grabbed a folding chair from against the wall, opened it, and took a seat directly in front of Greene, whose eyes widened slightly in recognition.

"Officer Greene, your country is grateful for your service. So what do you say we end this suffering?"

Greene remained stoic, returning his gaze to the far wall, but The Conductor felt the aura of defeat blanket the man; he was waiting for the other shoe to drop.

"Two people are going to die as a result of this encounter. One of them is you. The question is, who will be the other. Will it be the man whose name you refuse to tell me? Or..."

Holding the photograph up for Greene to see, The Conductor sounded like a game show emcee introducing a contestant. "Will it be Lily Marie Pope? Lily lives with her mother, Teresa Pope, at 4214 Birchwood Lane, Springfield, Kansas. She is a first-grader at Parsons Elementary and loves soccer and Peppa Pig."

It was then Greene broke. The Conductor waited.

"You'll leave her alone?" Greene spoke to the floor.

"Like I never knew she existed."

Eyes squeezed shut, chin to chest, Greene's words were barely audible. "His name is Miguel Ramirez."

"That's his alias. What do they call it at The CIA? His *legend*? I want to know his real name."

"Miguel Ramirez. That's all I know." Greene bit out, tears dripping down his face.

The Conductor stood and patted the man's shoulder, then instructed, "William, arrange for the execution of Lily and Theresa Pope."

"Wait!" Greene shouted.

An underwater silence blanketed the room. Then Greene groaned, "His name is Camilo Canto."

"He is hunting me, yes?"

Greene grunted his affirmative.

"What evidence does he possess?"

Greene's voice dripped with venom. "He has a log of detailed notes and a video of a meeting on this ship in Morocco."

After giving a slight nod to the man in the corner, Greene's captor stood and left the room.

After waiting in the hall for the sound of the suppressed round, The Conductor walked the narrow passage of the yacht and entered a stateroom akin to a hotel penthouse. The office was luxurious and masculine, with rich burgundy walls and dark maple wainscoting. Paintings of ships at sea and photos of sport fishing decorated the walls and bookshelves. A humidor sat at the corner of the desk. On paper, the yacht belonged to a Russian oil exporter, a family friend. No one tracing the vessel's ownership would find any meaningful connection—if anyone ever got that far.

Now to the matter at hand. This type of situation was part and parcel of this business. The secret was stamping out the small flames before they grew into wildfires. This wasn't the first time an American CIA officer—or SIS or Mossad or the SVF—had poked a nose into the myth of The Conductor: a lone oligarch who held the reins of all international black market shipping. It was, however, the first time an operative had discovered any sort of *proof*. Camilo Canto most likely didn't even realize what he had. If that video saw the light of day, the entire house of cards could collapse. Camilo Canto had sealed his fate when he recorded the activity on *The Maestro* that day; he would soon be nothing more than a plaque on the wall at Langley.

The Conductor stared out at the calm, dark water of the Black Sea in contemplation. This world of international trafficking was not unlike a symphony. The politicians were the percussion, banging fists and pounding desks—law enforcement, the woodwinds: subtle and pervasive. The smugglers were the brass: bold and obvious, and the logistics were the strings, winding through every movement, every measure with beautiful complexity. And there, at the front of the stage, leading them all from sonata to rondo, was The Conductor.

Camilo Canto. He should have been eliminated a year ago with a bullet between the eyes. Now, the entire situation had to be handled with the utmost care. People died or disappeared every day in this world, but a CIA officer was a different story. The dead man down the hall would already be a catalyst for suspicion—no need to add to that. The spy couldn't be killed until the evidence was found and destroyed, and Canto's demise had to be far, far removed from the myth of The Conductor. With Canto otherwise occupied, the journal and the video could be located and eliminated. Fortunately, a delightful way to divert suspicion had already presented itself. Camilo Canto, a.k.a. Miguel Ramirez, was going to put his stud services to use on Mallorca. On top of that, he was also going to take care of a particularly irritating problem that had sprouted—pulling two weeds with one yank, as they say.

A rustling in the adjacent bedroom and a flash of green fabric fluttering to the carpet seemed to indicate the long-legged assistant was showing some initiative. Well, it had been a long day; perhaps a little relaxation was in order. Soon, the baton would tap the music stand, and The Conductor would make the musicians play.

CHAPTER THREE

Griffin Island, South Carolina
November 25

Camilo Canto sat on the deck of the beachfront bar and sipped a Modelo. Despite the slight chill in the autumn air, two bikini-clad women were frolicking in the surf. He wasn't egotistical enough to think this little show was for him, but it was clear he was the most likely prospect when he looked around the deck. He was visualizing his usual come-on when a large body blocked the view.

Jonah "Steady" Lockhart set a beer and two red plastic baskets overflowing with clam strips and fries on the table and took a seat.

"*Hermano*, there are two other chairs here." Cam gestured around Steady to the women who were now trying to remove each other's tops.

"Suck it up. I'm just as pretty to look at." Steady winked.

Cam scanned his friend from his mop of sandy blond hair and lively green eyes down to—"That shirt is blinding me. What is that thing?"

Steady glanced down at the turquoise Hawaiian shirt exploding with pineapples and parrots. "I think it was my grandpa's." He grinned around the mouth of his beer bottle. "Found a whole box of them in the attic."

"Wear that to The Sand Bar tonight. The glare should send the ladies right to me." Cam popped a french fry in his mouth.

"Yeah, yeah. We need to eat and get to the hardware store and the lumber yard. Ren and Chat are meeting us at two," Steady replied.

Steady had taken over the beach house where he had grown up summering. As Cam understood it, no one in the family had used it in years, and Steady's parents had been content to rent it out. When Steady announced his return to the region, his overjoyed parents offered up the place without having to be asked. Last season, back-to-back tropical storms had done their worst, and the house was in disrepair. Fortunately, Steady had several able-bodied volunteers at the ready.

"How is there no Home Depot?" Cam complained.

"Small town living, my friend. This ain't Miami." Steady stretched his arm over the empty seat to his right and tipped back in his chair.

"No shit," Cam agreed.

"And there is a Home Depot. It's just…" Steady gestured vaguely inland, "yonder."

The Bishop Security team had officially made the move to South Carolina with great success. What the area lacked in box stores and Chinese restaurants, it made up for in charm and seclusion. On top of the picture-perfect setting, their offices were beyond anything the men could have imagined. Nathan Bishop had renovated an old elementary school and turned it into a state-of-the-art facility. From the outside, the building looked like an expansive colonial home. Inside was something else.

Steady polished off the last fried clam, wiped his fingers with the flimsy paper napkin from the stainless steel dispenser, and stood just as an unusual triple ping emanated from Cam's phone.

"Shit," Cam muttered.

"What's up?" Steady asked.

"Nothing. Loose ends. I need to make a call. Why don't we split up? You hit the lumber yard. I'll get the supplies at the hardware store and meet you back at the house."

Steady polished off his beer and dangled the empty by the neck between his fingers. "Sometimes I think you spooks use the 'I need to make a call' line to get out of doing shit you don't want to do."

Cam just shook his head, amused.

"All right. You go 'make your call,'" Steady air quoted. "I'll haul the wood."

Cam headed for the side stairs that led from the deck to the parking lot. "I'll pick you up on the side of the road. That Tonka toy you drive will probably collapse under the weight."

Steady waved him off, then seemed to rethink. After throwing some cash on the table to match what Cam had left, he looked to the side parking lot and eyed his Jeep. At a glance, the old Wrangler looked like it had been stripped for parts. He ambled up to Cam and put the phone on speaker as he placed a call. Herc answered without greeting.

"Let me guess. You need my truck." Hercules Reynolds was a former marine sniper and current Bishop Security operator. At the moment, he was breathing hard, and the wind was louder than his voice.

"Where are you?" Steady asked.

"Running on the beach. Where are you?" Herc answered.

"The Shack."

"Dude, this chick just pulled her friend's top off. *Awesome*," Herc exclaimed.

Cam looked to the water, and sure enough, one of the frolicking women was running away from the water, waving a scrap of pink above her head while the other was laughing and covering her bare breasts with her hands.

"Where *exactly* are you?" Steady asked.

"What the fuck are you wearing?" Herc replied.

They finally spotted Herc standing on the beach behind a closed lounge umbrella.

"Vacation attire." Steady smoothed his hands down the front of the shirt.

Cam could see Herc's gagging gesture.

"Got half an hour to help me haul some lumber?" Steady asked.

"Sure, man," Herc replied.

"Where are you parked?"

"Public lot half a click south. I'm going to invite these ladies to The Sand Bar tonight, and I'll meet you there." Herc gestured with his thumb toward the women.

Steady toasted his acknowledgment with his empty beer bottle then tossed it in the trashcan and headed to Herc's truck.

"You want a lift?" Cam asked.

"Nah, the public lot is right there. See you in a few, brother." Steady waved over his shoulder as he walked off.

Cam split off, heading to his SUV. This was the second alert from the CIA in as many weeks—first that strange hang-up phone call from Crimea and now whatever this was. He tightened his grip on the phone. Would his Agency work ever really be over?

Scanning the parking lot, Cam's gaze paused on a blue Ford Explorer with a distinct splat of seagull poop on the hood. He'd noticed the same car in town the day before, not following him, just parked nearby. He hadn't looked at the vehicle with suspicion, simply wondered idly why the person hadn't cleaned the bird shit off the hood. Like most Teamguys, Cam was fastidious and organized. He kept his car clean. Resuming his pace, he climbed in his 4Runner and pulled out of the lot.

Cam drove inland for a mile or so, then pulled over onto the impromptu shoulder. Just as he was about to enter the number, his phone rang.

"Hey, ma," he greeted.

"I love that I can just pick up the phone and call my son, and he actually answers." His mother's melodic voice floated across the line.

Cam chuckled. "The new job is working out great."

"Abuela is going crazy for your first Christmas home in ten years. You'll have an entire new wardrobe, and her garage looks like she won a game show." His mother's words danced over the line.

Between the Navy and the CIA, Cam hadn't spent a December in Miami in over a decade.

"Oh jeez, tell her to stop. I don't need all that stuff," Cam protested.

"When has that ever stopped her?" his mother asked. "Remember when she bought you two bicycles that year?"

"In case one got a flat." He smiled at the memory. "Yeah, I remember."

"She's at least letting me handle the menu and the cooking." His mother was more than a good cook in a "my mom's a good cook" kind of way. She was an actual chef.

"Don't start talking about your food, or I'll pull onto the highway heading south right now."

He could feel his mother's pleasure through the phone.

His father's familiar baritone came over the line. "Your mother's been trying out new recipes in anticipation of your arrival. I think I've gained ten pounds."

Cam's dad had either just walked into the room where his mom had the phone on speaker, or he had been listening the whole time.

"Hey, dad."

"It's my son! With a clear connection and a phone call that lasts more than ten seconds."

"It's good to be back in the States," Cam affirmed.

His mother laughed. "You've got ten years of hugs to make up for."

"Ma, I've been home. It's not like I was abducted by aliens for ten years and was suddenly returned to Earth."

"I know, but this is Christmas," his mother insisted.

"I get it," Cam said.

"And the way these kids are growing. You won't recognize your nieces and nephews."

His father added, "The mayhem gets crazier every year."

Kate Canto spoke to her husband. "Jamie and Theo set up a skateboard ramp in our driveway."

Cam's dad's voice was muffled. "Maybe you and I should take a little vacation to prepare for the onslaught."

"Oh, that's a perfect idea," his mother agreed. "Let's go to that art fair in St. Petersburg I was telling you about."

Cam shook his head. His parents tended to get lost in their own world.

"Mom? Dad?"

"We're here!" His mother returned her attention to her son. "We can't wait to see you, my heart."

"Love you both. See you in four weeks," Cam said.

"We love you, too, son," his dad replied.

Cam ended the call, set the phone into the cradle on the dash, and embraced this feeling of... joyful frustration. Most thirty-five-year-old guys would have ground their teeth at the thought of a chaotic family holiday, but this was what had been missing from his life. After eight years in the Navy and another three with The CIA, screaming children and bickering over nonsense seemed like heaven.

After forty years of marriage, his parents were still deeply in love. Theirs was a fairytale romance. In 1980, Cam's father, Aarón, had been interning at a Miami law firm when he met a group of lawyers for lunch at a local bistro. Seated at the crowded table, Aarón had glanced past the half-wall that separated the kitchen from the dining room and locked eyes with the most beautiful woman he had ever seen. Equally smitten, the woman—the chef—shot him a warm smile, and thirty minutes later, she was helping the waitress place their lunches on the table. Aarón circled her wrist with his hand. He didn't pull her or grip her; he simply touched her. When she met his distinctive gaze, he said, "I'm going to marry you."

"Kate," she clarified. "I'm going to marry you, Kate."

He was already in love. "Kate."

"Why don't you take me on a proper date first?" She patted his shoulder and continued serving the food.

Six weeks later, they were married.

For better or worse, Cam's parents' example had an unintended side effect: he refused to settle for a relationship that paled in comparison to his mom and dad's. He didn't expect the lock-eyes-and-instantly-know-she's-the-one lightning bolt, but he did need... something. He had come to refer to it as his dad's "zing test." Cam didn't know what that zing was, but he figured he'd know it when he felt it. And until then...

He started to merge back onto the road when he remembered why he had pulled over in the first place. Leaving the phone in the holder, he entered the number. Just as the call connected, Cam glanced out the window. The same Ford Explorer with the bird crap on the hood drove by at about ten miles below the speed limit. That was one sighting too many. Cam switched the phone to camera function and snapped a picture of the plate. The voice on the line prevented further speculation.

"*Operator.*"

Cam stated his username and unique code.

"The phone assigned the following number received two text messages in the past twenty-four hours. They have been cleared, and the messages are available to access."

"Acknowledged," Cam confirmed.

The call ended with a soft beep.

After leaving the SEALs, Camilo Canto had been recruited by the most elite and covert division of the CIA as a Non-Official Cover, or NOC, officer. The Special Activities Center/Special Operations Group (SAC/SOG) conducted highly classified paramilitary and covert ops. Prior to his departure from The Agency, Cam had spent nearly a year in Suriname in the employ of the notorious arms dealer, Dario Sava. Sava's obsession with the now-wife of Bishop Security leader, Nathan Bishop, had brought Cam to his current job.

Nathan Bishop had contacted Cam—who was embedded in Sava's organization as Miguel Ramirez—for information to help protect his wife from the madman. Once Dario Sava was dead, Cam maintained his cover for another year hunting down weapons and intelligence Sava had sold. Cam had intercepted a Javelin en route to Boko Haram in Somalia and recovered stolen research on silencing blade vortex interaction in U.S. helicopters. He had also gathered intelligence on an elusive underworld figure known as The Conductor.

The Conductor.

Cam had firmly believed no such man existed. He was a myth cobbled together by internet trolls, media extremists, and conspiracy theorists. The notion that one man controlled all international black market shipping was, well, it was preposterous. Yet the more Cam moved through the underworld, like Dante exploring the circles of hell, the more he began to notice a pattern. Export methods were too similar, logistics too uniform, procedures too sophisticated for the gunslinger smugglers and ham-handed traffickers he came across. A theory began to form.

Why couldn't one man consolidate the criminal shipping enterprise? People certainly did it in the legitimate private sector. It was an idea that his superiors had considered and dismissed, but Cam wasn't so sure.

Telling no one, for fear of being accused of running down rabbit holes, Cam—operating as his cover identity, Miguel Ramirez—began keeping a log of leads, shipping schedules, persons of interest, and financial transactions that pointed to one master puppeteer. After six months, the journal looked like the ravings of a lunatic. Still, he continued to make entries, documenting the tenuous threads that supported his theory.

Then, on a balmy afternoon in February, in the coastal city of Rabat, Morocco, he had captured video of a weapons smuggler he was tracking boarding a yacht. It wasn't an unusual sight; underworld buyers and sellers met in locations ranging from back alleys to palaces. It was the name of the ship, however, that caught Cam's attention: *The Maestro*.

The following day, Cam had met with his contact, a fellow NOC officer named Raymond Greene, and to his surprise, Greene had similar suspicions. Cam shared what he knew, including the meeting on *The Maestro*, and he and Greene agreed they would continue to gather information. They were a long way away from approaching their superiors with anything more than conjecture. After chasing shadows to Marrakech and Ibiza, Cam temporarily abandoned his search for The Conductor.

Three weeks later, Cam had come across a small village burned to the ground by a drug cartel. He had been feeling the crush of this work, and that was the final straw. He had wanted to make a contribution, to help the powerless, but not at the cost of his sanity. He was tired. Tired of espionage. Tired of being so damn alone. Tired of giving his body and his mind and his soul to combat a never-ending stream of violence and corruption. Then and there, amid the smoldering rubble and corpses, he had called Nathan Bishop and accepted his job offer. The Conductor may be real, but someone else could hunt him down.

The moment he had stepped into Nathan Bishop's office in New York, and Nathan had greeted him with an extended hand and a *welcome to the team*, he knew he had made the correct decision. Everything about the job felt right, most of all, the camaraderie.

Cam and Steady had been on the same SEAL team but in different platoons, so they hadn't worked together often or had the same deep bond as Steady and Cam's other new coworkers, but they all knew each other; it was a small community. The Teamguys at Bishop Security certainly all knew how he got his nickname, "JJ." They called him *El Jefe de Jodor*: the nonsensical Spanish was intended to translate to "the boss of fuck." He had certainly earned it. At six-one, with a thick head of auburn hair and the striking golden eyes he'd inherited from his father, Cam never suffered from a lack of female attention. The moniker, however, was a burden he was all too happy to shed in civilian life. Like many military nicknames, "JJ" was not something he wanted to explain to his mother.

He continued on the main road away from the beach, over the low bridge to the mainland, and headed to Bishop Security. In his work for the CIA, he had traveled from Amazonian jungles to Mediterranean cartel compounds to East African smuggling outposts. Looking out the window, he took in the marshy South Carolina lowland; this would be his home for the foreseeable future. Cam didn't think anything had ever looked more beautiful.

CHAPTER FOUR

Sa Calobra, Mallorca
November 25

This was certainly not the Mallorca of British royals and German billionaires.

Evangeline Cole released a contented sigh as she took in her surroundings. The cave dripped and breathed, a living thing growing and changing over millennia. Stalactites lined the walls like a picket fence of human femur bones, warding off trespassers far more effectively than the signs on the narrow strip of beach.

Evangeline glanced back at her Zodiac, the November rain pelting the rubber boat in a steady stream. Then she turned to the mouth of the cave and ventured into the belly of the beast. Mindful of the calciferous rock formations biting from above and below, she switched on the flashlight and followed her remembered path.

This particular network of caves ran for approximately forty kilometers along the north-central coast. The Mallorcan government had done an exceptional job preserving ancient sites, and this area was doubly fortunate due to its inaccessibility. Cliffs above provided scenic overlooks for hikers and sightseers, and neighboring towns

with larger beachfronts snagged tourists. The appeal of adjacent lo-
cales and the stern warnings to keep out of this area had combined
to keep her little cove relatively unnoticed.

Evangeline, "Evan" to her friends, scanned the walls and cave floor
as the dark space grew more confined. She shook off the feeling of
foreboding. She was supposed to be here. Well, not *supposed*, but she
was allowed to be here. Maybe not technically *here*, but she could undoubtedly talk her way out of a confrontation by explaining that she
was part of the team excavating the newly discovered ancient Talaiotic
burial site nearby. Fifteen kilometers qualified as "nearby." Right?

When Evan had taken a break from excavation to kick a soccer
ball around with a group of local kids, they had informed her of their
discovery. Like young boys everywhere—although on Mallorca, it was
certainly more of a possibility than most places—they dreamed of
finding buried treasure and routinely poked around in the labyrinth
of caves that wove beneath the island. They had found something that
had the hairs on Evan's arms tingling—small rock formations deep
within the system. The boys had pointed to a short stack of stones at
the official dig site and explained in their native Mallorcan Catalan
that they had seen similar rock piles in two small interior caves.

Without explanation to her colleagues, Evan had piled the boys
into an ATV and driven them to the location. They had taken her as
far as the first opening and explained the route. Then she dutifully
drove them back and gathered a few supplies. Evan had returned
in her Zodiac for purposes of convenience and efficiency, not, she
silently insisted, secrecy. So here she stood once again, staring at the
small opening the boys had cleared, one of three she would need to
crawl through to get to the location they had described. Pushing
irrational images of blind beetles feasting on her flesh and phan-
tom hands pulling her into the abyss, she dropped to her knees and
crawled through.

While not unexplored, this smaller space was certainly not in any guidebook. The confined entrance allowed almost no light into the interior chamber. Deep puddles on the floor indicated that the incoming tides were still a threat. Evan scanned the area with her flashlight, the beam chasing an elusive whisper. She took tentative steps avoiding the irrational urge to jump at every errant sound.

The next, even smaller opening appeared man-made and led to a hallway-like cavern, long and narrow. The rock formations closed in like prison bars, and Evan had to turn to the side at points to avoid disturbing them. Beyond the beam of her flashlight lay stygian darkness. Between the wind and the water, the cave almost seemed to moan. She imagined the walls expanding and contracting like lungs on a breath. Evan took a moment to gather herself as the eerie setting rattled her sensibilities. *Great. Next, the bulb in the flashlight will flicker like I'm in some old-school horror movie.*

The passage hooked to the left, and, as the boys had indicated, a small knee-high passthrough was located near the end on the right— beside it, a small pile of stones the boys had wisely left untouched.

It was indeed some sort of marker. It was not, however, Talaiotic. The ancient people who had lived on Mallorca during the second millennium B.C. had used surface rocks to form small pyramids to mark places of significance: burial and ceremonial sites. These rocks were calciferous, from the cave itself, as if someone had knocked out pieces of the cave wall to create an indicator. The rocks had eroded, nearly melted into each other as years of water had melded them into an ice cream cone of an object. Despite the clear evidence of time, Evan estimated these markers had been there merely hundreds, not thousands, of years.

Evan sent a prayer of gratitude that the boys had not only noticed the little formation but left it alone. How many boys exploring a cave would have simply kicked a pile of rocks aside in their excitement to investigate? The boy she spoke with was a budding archaeologist; his parents worked as mappers at their dig site. He had sensed the significance of the marker, but his mother and father had dismissed it when he had shared his discovery. They were not the least interested in crawling around in a dark, wet cave to investigate something they correctly assumed was not relevant to their project. Evan, however, was an ambitious graduate student hungry to do precisely that.

She had a theory. One she had yet to share with her doctoral advisor. Evan had joined the team a year ago. Prior to that, she had pored over the research and discoveries from the Talaiotic population center and wrote her Master's Thesis on the original 2013 excavation in Valldemossa. The dig now extended to four other sites along the northern coast of Mallorca. Evan hypothesized that the ancient civilization's coastal homesites were not only strategic for defense against Sea Peoples and Phoenician invaders but also because the Talaiotic men were seafarers themselves. She wasn't alone in her theory—a sword discovered several years ago made from metals not readily available on Mallorca had spawned a cadre of archaeologists who pursued the possibility. In the absence of evidence supporting seafaring, the number had dwindled. Evan wasn't so quick to dismiss the idea. She planned to use her downtime on the excavation to examine areas of note and find the evidence she sought. She didn't need to unearth the maidenhead of a ship; the slightest thing—a foreign coin, a reference in an etching—could be of monumental significance.

Hence her current predicament.

Apparently, she did not have the proportions of a twelve-year-old boy. She twisted her shoulders and forced herself through the small opening—flashing only briefly to the impossible-to-suppress image of a baby being born—tumbling into the lower chamber and landing on her backside in a puddle. She frantically reoriented herself and scanned the small space with the light. The Mallorcan cave systems had dozens of underground lakes, some of them quite large. She needed to make sure her next step didn't plunge her into a watery void. Regaining her footing, she was relieved to confirm the water was merely a shallow pool.

Evan wasn't prone to drama. She never looked at a mole or a freckle and planned her funeral, never panicked about upcoming exams. If, however, she were to ever stray to the neurotic, this would certainly be a worthy situation. The chamber was low and cramped, about the size of a small root cellar, and the rock formations were slowly encroaching on the space. Across the short distance, she spied another of the mysterious markers. This one had sprouted a small stalagmite. Evan did a rough calculation. Stalagmites grew at approximately half a millimeter per year. This little fellow was just shy of a foot, putting the marker upon which it grew at approximately six hundred years old. Definitely not Talaiotic, but unquestionably noteworthy.

She made her way the six or so paces to the far side and knelt to examine the next marker, her flashlight creating a tunnel of light in the pitch. This grouping was also composed of rocks from the cave wall and stacked in three. She cast the light around. The wall of stalactites at the back originated from the cave ceiling. A rock shelf jutted out in one part, causing the stalactites to form about a foot away from the back wall and creating a sort of natural cage. She peeked through the curtain of rock and discovered a section of the rear wall had been caked with gravel and silt, sealing off a passage in a manner that appeared to be man-made. Slipping behind the stone balusters, she ran her hand over the area, only to find the earth had hardened over the centuries. Despite an overwhelming urge to kick at the homemade clay, she remembered her role. As an archaeologist, she couldn't merely karate kick a wall; there were procedures to follow. She needed her tools, better lighting, and a game plan.

Evan was slowly backing out of the narrow space between the stalactites and the back of the cave when a thunderous clanking from the other side of the wall had her shrieking and careering into the rocks. She spun and fell to the hard ground, banging her head on the limestone.

Sprawled out on the damp ground, she groped for a handhold to right herself. Once she regained her presence of mind, she paused. The clamor, the unmistakable sound of metal colliding with metal, had come from the other side of the rear wall she had been inspecting. She tossed a beam of light that way. The noise had ceased. Perhaps this small chamber abutted a more frequented cave. There were entire tours of Mallorca dedicated to spelunkers and sightseers. Some caves were cathedral-like spaces, upwards of fifty meters high.

Climbing to her hands and knees, Evan focused on the task at hand: extricating herself from this rock formation and making a plan. As she brought her feet beneath her, something near the wall caught her eye. She realized she had fallen into the marker, upending the stack of rocks. The stalagmite that had sprouted from it now lay broken on the cave floor. She pushed away some damp earth from the base rock and saw two small metal objects. They appeared to be links from a chain, just two substantial, rectangular gold links that sat resting on the limestone, which would have been concealed by the rocks set atop them. In the absence of an evidence flag, she grabbed a small paper bag from the side pocket of her pants—like a grandmother with butterscotch candy, she always had them—filled it with dirt to weigh it down, and set it next to the chain links.

She carefully retraced her steps back through the labyrinth until she emerged into the large primary cave. Despite her (nearly) unwavering sense of calm, she allowed herself a small sigh of relief, only to gasp the air back into her lungs when she spotted a hulking man with a large black umbrella inspecting her little Zodiac.

Evan weighed her options. While she had no intention of hiding her discovery, she wasn't yet ready to show her cards. Moreover, while indeed an authoritarian presence, there was no indication that this man was, in fact, an official of any sort. So she ducked out of the cave and hurried up the beach out of his line of sight. About forty yards away, Evan turned back to the man and waved both hands over her head to signal him.

"Hey! That's my boat!" She ran toward him, making sure to obliterate the footprints she had left coming out. Still, she maintained a safe distance; Evan didn't like to be touched, a condition that was doubly true in this instance. She skidded to a stop ten yards from the menacing figure. She could have probably gotten away explaining she was part of Dr. Omar Emberton's archaeological contingent, but she was hesitant to reveal that information. So, she played the ditz.

"Restricted area," the man boomed above the rain patter in broken English.

"I'm sorry, okay? I was trying to go meet some friends for a hike, and the stupid thing started sputtering and making all kinds of noise." Evan gestured to the Zodiac.

His only response was an icy stare and a clipped, "You. Go."

She had a director's-cut version of her sorority-girl-beach-breakdown story, but the man was giving her an out. On top of that, he clearly wasn't with the Mallorcan authorities or Spanish military from the naval base on the northeastern tip of the island—time to go.

The man continued to examine the Zodiac. It was a military-grade vessel and stocked with supplies. Rather than attempt to explain her definitely not-ditzy cargo, she hopped in the boat, started the motor, and pulled out of the cove.

His cell phone rang as he watched her depart.

"Sí."

Evan spied him over her shoulder as the man turned his back to continue the conversation. When he tossed his hand to the side in a careless gesture, she assumed she had succeeded in convincing him she was a lost tourist and quickly made her escape. In addition to the commotion she had heard in the adjacent cave, the strange markers, and the little piece of chain hidden within, this man's presence on the beach was yet another question in a remarkably confounding expedition.

CHAPTER FIVE

Cam sat on the bed in the guest apartment of Bishop Security. He was looking forward to moving in with Steady when the house was finished, but he had to admit it would be hard to leave these temporary quarters. The new offices were like a spec op's wet dream. From the tech to the training facility, from the war room to the gun range, if it could be conceived, Nathan Bishop had implemented it. If the Naval Special Warfare Center and the Ritz Carlton had a building-baby, it would be the Bishop Security office.

He took a moment to prepare himself for the shift into Miguel Ramirez's world. It had been his cover for over two years, and the transition back to Camilo Canto had taken some time. When he was on assignment, there was no other reality. His life depended on it. He was Miguel Ramirez from a small village outside Bogota. He smoked pot, used cocaine, fucked women, and was particularly good with a knife. He did what he was told to do without question or hesitation.

That reliability and obedience had granted him access to intelligence that struck a blow to trafficking operations and terror groups around the world. Cam was proud of the work he had done. Although somewhere, deep inside, he was ashamed of it too, ashamed of Miguel Ramirez. He reminded himself of the big picture and the good that he had done. Nevertheless, the work had left scars. Cam hadn't sacrificed life or limb, but he had lost a lot on those assignments.

He opened the secure laptop, followed his old instructions, and accessed the texts.

It was Luis, a coworker of Miguel's from Dario Sava's outfit.

Alguien te está buscando.

Someone is looking for you.

Shit. Had he still been at The Agency, this would have been good news. He had stood out in Sava's organization. At first for his size; later, he had garnered Dario Sava's attention because he was reliable and an exceptional fighter—not a Special Forces fighter, a street fighter. Nevertheless, men like him were a dime a dozen in that world and treated as such. Why would someone be looking specifically for him? The alarm bells clanging in his head made it difficult to continue reading.

In the final text, Luis gave him a meeting location and time.

When Cam began his assignment as Miguel Ramirez, his jefe, Dario Sava, was an arms dealer who worked with calculated precision. Bringing down the Sava empire had been the culmination of two grueling years. For Cam, the satisfaction was immeasurable. A year ago, the thought of infiltrating another organization would have been exhilarating. Now? The pursuit would come from obligation rather than desire.

At the bottom of the laptop screen, a message from his former handler flashed. Cam sighed heavily and dug out the old cell phone to charge it. Occasionally, non-official cover (NOC) officers held on to their devices for as long as a year for this very reason. He stared blankly at the phone, knowing he couldn't walk away from whatever this was.

Reaching into the case for the charger, his fingers brushed a leather-bound notebook: his notes on The Conductor. He withdrew the journal and flipped through the pages. Anyone who came across it would think Cam had gone off the deep end. The scrawl looked like the musings of a madman. However, upon closer examination, Cam saw that his notations, facts, and threads of thought held merit. Seeing his words on paper brought his thoughts to Raymond Greene. Had Greene placed that phone call to his CIA cell phone, and if so, what was he going to say? Perhaps simply placing the call was warning enough. Maybe it was nothing, but the text messages coming on the heels of that call from Crimea where Greene was stationed were enough to give Cam pause.

He decided to jump in the shower while the phone charged. He wanted to be clear-headed when he placed the call to his former handler.

Cam tapped on the open door of Nathan Bishop's office. His boss looked up from his computer and waved him in, pointing to the coffee pot on the bar. Cam declined the offer and took a seat in one of the taupe suede and chrome chairs that faced the desk.

"I may have an issue. It's probably nothing, but I wanted to keep you in the loop. The good news is your clearance is high enough that I can do that," Cam said.

"What's up?" Nathan checked his personal cell then set it aside.

"One of Dario Sava's old enforcers, a guy named Luis, texted Miguel Ramirez's phone. Said somebody is looking for me, for Miguel," Cam explained.

"Specifically Miguel Ramirez?" Nathan asked.

"That's what he said."

"That makes no sense. I mean no offense, but you were no doubt put in that role in Sava's organization because those men are easily replaced and unnoticed." Nathan drummed his fingers on his desk.

"Exactly. So I figure it's one of two things. Someone is trying to backtrack through Sava's organization to find the mole. There's no way any other players saw Sava go down and didn't suspect an informant." Cam leaned forward and laced his fingers between his knees.

"Agreed. What's Option B?" Nathan asked.

"A couple of the guys Miguel got close to were poised to grab a piece of the pie the minute things went south with Sava. If one of them wants to start assembling soldiers..." Cam shrugged, letting Nathan finish the thought.

"That person might reach out to his old crew."

"Got it in one." Cam nodded.

"What did your former handler have to say?" Nathan asked.

"He said it's my call."

"And what do you say?" Nathan steepled his fingers at his chin.

Cam's eyes met Nathan's. "Something tells me I should follow up on this."

Nathan leaned closer. "Cam, one of the main reasons I hired you is that your instincts are strong. Hell, you wouldn't have lasted in the field if they weren't. I'd be one hell of a hypocrite if I told you to ignore them now. We've all torn apart a lot of haystacks over the years. What's one more?"

Cam rethought the offer of coffee, stood, and crossed to the sleek machine. He filled a mug from the fresh carafe, his back to Nathan, and spoke. "There's something else."

Cam returned to his seat. He took a cautious sip of black coffee, set the mug on the edge of the desk, and gathered his thoughts. On a deep breath, he withdrew the worn leather journal from the pouch of his hoodie, thumbed the cover, then slid it across to his boss.

Nathan picked it up and turned to a random page. "What's this?"

"Have you ever heard of The Conductor?" Cam asked.

Nathan didn't hide his surprise. "Aside from the rumors floating around the Intelligence community, I actually have. It was several years ago. I had just left the Navy. My father wasn't the most scrupulous of businessmen. He was caught up in a Senate investigation for an off-the-books weapons sale. He was drunk one night, ranting about being extorted and that a senator had thrown him to the wolves. I was just about to leave him to his ramblings when he grabbed me by the shoulders and said, 'He's in The Conductor's pocket.'"

"Who?" Cam asked.

"I assumed he was talking about the senator leading the investigation, Harlan Musgrave. I did a little poking around after that. Didn't find much. From what I can discern, The Conductor is a myth." Nathan flipped to another page.

"I think he exists," Cam said.

Cam waited for Nathan to scoff, but his boss simply pressed on. "And this book? It documents your reasons?"

"Yes. Senator Musgrave is mentioned in there as well." Cam pointed to the journal.

"Really?" Nathan sat up in his chair.

"He was staying at a hotel in Athens at the same time the yacht I suspect The Conductor operates out of was anchored there. I know it's a little thin." Cam wobbled his hand.

Nathan turned a page. "Don't dismiss your hunches. Yes, it's a wild proposition, but certainly not impossible or even improbable. I, for one, have seen too much crazy to dismiss the theory of an experienced operator."

Cam's relief at Nathan's support propelled him. "It's all in there. Common procedures, the same men I've seen at meet-ups with different smugglers with no obvious overlap, shipping routes, customs protocols."

Nathan nodded, still buried in the journal. "You've gathered a tremendous amount of information."

"And possibly proof," Cam said.

The declaration had Nathan looking up.

Cam pointed to the book. "In the binding is a flash drive. It's a video clip. I was tracking an arms dealer in North Africa. I filmed him boarding the yacht I mentioned docked in Rabat. The ship departed, and my target was never seen again."

"How is this proof?" Nathan challenged.

"The name of the ship was *The Maestro*. I think it belongs to The Conductor," Cam explained.

Nathan's eyes widened, and he felt along the journal's spine, detecting the outline of the device.

"So, what are you thinking?" Nathan asked.

Cam ran a hand over his stubbled jaw. He had skipped shaving in anticipation of returning to the field. "It's not like The Conductor haunts me. I don't need to bring him down personally, but I *know* he exists. And I suspect some very powerful people are covering it up. I would have liked to at least have gathered enough intel for law enforcement to investigate. Shit." Cam laughed. "I don't even know what Luis wants, but maybe this is a chance for Miguel Ramirez to take one last look around. Either way, I don't think I can turn my back on investigating whatever Dario Sava's men are up to now."

Nathan set the book down and folded his hands across the cover. He met Cam's determined gaze with a look of pride. "I guess it's settled then. I know this is a solo op, but the team is here if you need us."

"There's one other thing." He pulled out his phone. "I've seen this car three times in the past forty-eight hours. Nothing overt. It just always seems to be where I am." He passed the phone with the photo displayed to Nathan.

"Get it to Twitch. Let's see what the plates turn up."

Cam nodded. As he stood, he noticed his boss recheck the screen of his phone. "Expecting a call?"

"Sorry about that. Emily's due next month. Apparently, it's no less nerve-racking the second go. Emily was early with the boys, but this one? I have a feeling our daughter is taking her time."

"Daughter?" Cam repeated.

"It's a girl this time. Emily wanted to find out. She's not big on surprises."

"Got a name picked out?" Cam asked.

Nathan came around the desk to walk with Cam out of the office.

"Yeah, but I'm nervous about it." Nathan shoved his hands into his pants pockets.

"Nervous?"

Nathan stopped at the doorway and spoke in a low tone as if this information were more classified than the material they had just been discussing. "Emily wants to name the baby after Twitch."

"Twitch Bishop?" Cam grinned.

"*Her real name.* I warned Emily, Twitch doesn't ever use her name, doesn't answer to it, and very few people outside of this office even know it, but Emily insists it's perfect."

"What's her name?" Cam asked.

Nathan rechecked his phone. "You'll find out in a month or so."

Cam shook his head through a laugh, and both men headed for the exit.

Cam climbed into his 4Runner, both relieved by and grateful for Nathan's support. He didn't have that kind of leeway in his former job, and the encounter left him feeling confident in his decision to join Bishop Security. He started the car, then, out of habit or paranoia, checked his surroundings. Despite his renewed sense of determination, a looming sense of dread lingered.

CHAPTER SIX

Valldemossa, Mallorca
November 26

Evan sat on the narrow balcony off her bedroom in the charming stucco finca she shared with her advisor, Dr. Omar Emberton, and the two other graduate students working at the dig site. She and the students each had a bedroom on the second floor, while Doctor Emberton occupied a small apartment on the main level. The rain had abated, leaving a dark sky and heavy air in its wake. An olive grove slept at her feet. Beyond, a meadow led to low hills. Evan knew, in just a few short months, this same view would burst with electric orange poppy blossoms and vibrant green olive branches. The current landscape was muted but no less spectacular in her eyes, the browns and darker greens far more complex and foreboding.

The view took her back to her childhood home in northern California. Her father was a vintner of some renown, and they had lived on the family vineyard in Santa Rosa. The view from her bedroom window, rows and rows of tangled grapevines lapping onto low rolling hills, was different in both topography and vegetation. Still, it held the same juxtaposition of magic and disquiet.

In the spring, Mallorca was a fairytale. In November, it was a Gothic novel.

A bottle of sparkling water sat next to her tablet and attached keyboard on the small round table, the blank document, a white void, beckoning her to transcribe *something*: a thought, a theory, a conclusion, a course of action. Thus far, she could only contemplate the things that had bothered her about the excursion: the markers from the wrong era, those strange chain links, and of course, the frightening man.

In her mind, Evan had named him Diablo; it seemed to fit his demeanor, his subtle but malevolent accent, his threatening stance. He certainly wasn't law enforcement, which begged the question: what was he doing in that remote cove dressed very much like her in cargo pants, military boots, and a slicker?

She dutifully noted her observations on the document then paused as she considered her next steps, the cursor blinking impatiently while she thought. What had caused that loud clanking noise? What were the tidal restrictions? How would she gain access to the sealed-off cave? When and with whom should she share her discovery?

First things first.

She needed to return to the caverns with the proper equipment to break through the last cave's sealed opening. She typed as she formed a plan of action. She had to extract the gold chain links from the limestone marker for testing. Her skin prickled as she imagined a great discovery. Not a cache of treasure or an ancient tomb, she pictured just the slightest clue: another breadcrumb on the trail of her search to prove the ancient peoples she was there to study were seafarers. On a dig in Djibouti, her doctoral advisor at Stanford discovered a bone that proved a prehistoric mammal species had a vestigial gizzard, changing an entire evolutionary chart. Her job was all about tiny needles in very large haystacks.

Evan wasn't discouraged by the more recent objects she had found. If anything, they proved that this cave system had been accessible centuries earlier. And who knew? Perhaps those small piles of rock would lead her to something extraordinary.

"Anybody home?"

She recognized the voice of her mentor and pulled back the curtain to reveal her location. "On the balcony, Doctor E."

Dr. Omar Emberton parted the sheers and squeezed around Evan to take the other seat at the table.

He pulled his glasses to the end of his nose and assessed her over the rim. "You don't appear ill."

She chuckled. "Not ill. Some kids pulled me aside the other day and explained they had found markers, similar to those at our excavation site, in a cave on the coast. I went to check it out."

"And?" Emberton pressed.

Evan wanted to put this conversation off until she had something more noteworthy to report.

"The markers the boys found are interesting. Definitely not Talaiotic. I'm guessing Moorish, probably Fifteenth Century. I'd like to follow up, but it's not related to our project."

Doctor Emberton circled his fingers on the glass surface of the table, paused in thought. "Take another day or two. See if you can determine if the markers lead somewhere. You'll have a devil of a time in those caves. The limestone practically dissolves."

She agreed. "The markers have badly deteriorated. I'm dating them based on a stalagmite that had formed on one of them."

"I see. Well, it's a fascinating period on Mallorca—the Moors fleeing crusaders, hiding treasure. Did you know there are supposedly over a hundred shipwrecks in these waters?" He gestured vaguely in the direction of the Mediterranean. "And just a few years ago, some farmers found a stash of gold coins in a cave near their property."

"I read something about that," Evan replied.

"My point is we have a rather exciting excavation we're exploring, but if I've learned anything in my years, it's to follow the clues history puts out. I'd be very interested in knowing what you discover. I'm descended from the Moors after all." He rose from his seat.

"I'll spend a day or two poking around. I don't want to leave you shorthanded, and I need the Talaiotic research for my dissertation." Evan stood with her mentor.

"Very good. I'd like to see you hooded this year." He patted her shoulder, referencing the ceremony in which Ph.D. candidates were conferred their doctorates and received a hood for their gowns.

"So would I." She smiled up at the man she respected beyond measure.

Omar Emberton parted the drapes and made his exit, leaving Evan to plan for another adventure in the caves.

CHAPTER SEVEN

South Island, South Carolina
November 26

Standing on the dark sand, Steady looked up at the beach house. It was still in disrepair but much improved after a day of intense labor with his makeshift construction crew. The stilts had been reinforced, and the shingles and shutters repaired. The deck was still a hazard, and the sliding glass door frame was boarded over, but in a few weeks, the place would be palatial. He turned back to the ocean, pleased with what he and his brothers had accomplished.

Telescope in hand, he trudged across the damp sand toward the surf. They were finally getting a clear night, and he was eager to do some stargazing. It was one of his fondest memories with his dad growing up. Each May, before they left Charlotte for the shore, they would spend time determining interesting and anomalous astrological phenomena and when they would occur. Then, throughout the summer, they would set up the telescope and canvas chairs on the beach and bring a bag filled with whatever treats they could swipe from the kitchen. They'd sit and talk until the start of a meteor shower or a planetary alignment. His father worked crazy hours and traveled extensively for his job running the family business, a small chain of boutique hotels. There were weeks during the school year that Steady rarely saw him. So those nights on the beach just sitting and talking to his dad—the telescope incidental—meant the world.

It wouldn't be fully dark for another hour or so, but Steady spread the tripod and planted the telescope in the sand. He had plenty of time to heat the casserole Maggie Bishop—Herc's grandmother and the unofficial den mother of Bishop Security—had dropped off for him knowing his kitchen currently consisted of a microwave and a minifridge. Steady figured he would include a kitchen renovation in the repair work—in for a penny, in for a pound and all that.

As he turned to head back to the house, the headlights of a car pulling into the driveway next door caught his attention. This small strip of beach houses was active in the summer, but the places were far enough apart that it never felt overrun. This time of year, it was a ghost town.

He heard the muffled slam of a car door, and a moment later, a light came on in the home. More out of curiosity than suspicion, Steady aimed the telescope toward the house and bent to look through the eyepiece. When he spied the outline of a woman in a duster and beanie entering, he immediately jerked himself to standing. *Eyes on the sky, creep.* He knocked the heel of his hand against his forehead and headed back to the kitchen.

An hour later, Steady once again stood behind the telescope and pointed the lens skyward. He was just about to see what magic the heavens held when the low thump of bass had him looking up the beach. A football field away, every light on the first floor of the neighboring house was on, and Steady caught a flash of hot pink through the sliding glass doors that separated the living space from the wraparound deck.

The music—he thought it was classic Ramones. Suddenly the temptation was too much, and he swiveled the telescope toward the house and leaned down to take a look. Well, *call it what it is.* He bent to *peep.* There, in the large family room, a tiny slip of a woman was dancing around, more like jumping around, to the music wearing a T-shirt and boy shorts. Her clothes, however, were not the flash of pink that had caught his eye. That came from her head. The dancing girl had *hot pink* hair.

Could this get any weirder?

Then, as if the universe answered his question in the affirmative, the pink-haired woman jumped her way over to a whiteboard, erased a section of a complex formula, and began rewriting it. Nothing in the night sky could compare to what was going on in that house, and Steady watched like his orbital bone was glued to the eyepiece. Until a voice sounded from behind him.

"Whatcha doin?"

Steady shot up, upending the telescope, and spun to face Cam, smiling like the kid who found the last Easter egg, hands in his pockets rocking back on his heels.

"Oh, eh, hey, Cam," Steady said.

"Spot any heavenly bodies, Stead?"

Steady shot both hands to the top of his head.

"Fuck, I know, but seriously, it was too much. She's cranking music and dancing in her underwear, writing math formulas on a whiteboard."

"Got a hot-for-teacher thing?" Cam quirked a brow.

"Doesn't everybody? We all had that spank-bank teacher in middle school." Steady kicked the sand.

"Mrs. Jones." Cam sighed wistfully, then paused, rubbing the back of his neck. "Huh."

"What?" Steady asked as he righted the telescope.

"I just realized she married a SEAL. Maybe that's what got me interested in the Navy, not all that service and honor crap." Cam looked up at the sky.

Steady chuckled as he ran a hand through his hair. "Shit, is everything we do just to get laid?"

"Nah, I took out the head of Shining Path with the RPG he thought he was buying. That was for Uncle Sam." Cam looked to the ground after the uncharacteristic disclosure, then circled back to the situation at hand. "So, is she hot?"

"So hot I want to walk over there and propose." Steady threw his hand toward the house.

Cam stepped to the telescope, and Steady obliged, tipping the main tube toward him. Cam adjusted the focus. "Well, she's gone. The whiteboard is there, though. That's not a math formula. It's a chemical formula. There's molecules and shit."

At Steady's raised brow, Cam shrugged. "Mrs. Jones taught science."

Both men laughed, and Steady redirected the telescope toward the sky. "There's a meteor shower tonight. Starts in about twenty minutes. Beer's in the cooler, and Maggie dropped off some snacks." Steady pointed to the supplies on the blanket.

"Sweet." Cam parked next to the food as Steady snagged them each a beer and took a seat on the blanket.

"So no luck at the bar last night? I saw you sneak out solo." Steady grabbed a handful of the seasoned popcorn.

Cam took a pull on his beer. "Wasn't feelin' it, you know?"

"Not even a little. I'm pretty much always feelin' it. Shit, I'm spying on my neighbor." Steady swung his beer bottle toward the other house.

Cam laid back, resting his head on his forearm. "I guess I've just been a little off lately."

"Dude, you were pretending to be someone else for what? A year?" Steady asked.

"Two," Cam replied.

"Cut yourself some slack. My dad always says you gotta be comfortable with you before you can get comfortable with anyone else," Steady commented absently.

Cam lifted his head. "Yeah, that's... yeah. Good advice."

Steady rested his forearms on his knees and looked out at the water. "Of course, I never liked you much on the Teams. Swooping in and stealing all the ladies. Maybe this new you will be a little more magnanimous."

"Oh, damn." Cam pointed toward the house they'd been scoping out. "She's naked coming out of the shower."

Steady turned so fast the open beer fell from his hand and erupted at his feet.

"Psych." Cam laid back, his hands locked behind his head, and grinned.

Steady dumped the foamy beer in the sand and fished another out of the cooler. "Asshole."

CHAPTER EIGHT

New York City
December 2

Cam got out of the Uber and scanned the block. He didn't know Spanish Harlem well, but he knew one of his former colleagues in Dario Sava's organization, Luis, had moved here after Sava's death to live with his cousins. Cam didn't even want to guess at the nature of his current employment. Luis had instructed Cam to meet him at a bar called El Vaquero. Cam rounded the corner onto 115th street and spotted it. Two Latin men were smoking out front listening to a third man playing a guitar and singing. Cam pulled out his wallet—*Miguel Ramirez's* wallet—and dropped a few bills into the musician's open guitar case, nodded to the men, and pulled open the door.

It took a second to adjust to the lighting—or lack thereof. A half-lit neon Corona sign buzzed over the pitted bar to the left, and a handful of round tables filled the remaining space. Luis was sitting at the back table with a white guy with blond hair Cam had never seen before. The man wore an expensive suit and had the bearing of an operator. Despite the alarm bells clanging in his head, Cam shifted his mind to his cover, Miguel Ramirez, crossed to the table, and took a seat.

"*Eres el pendejo que me está buscando?*" *Are you the asshole who is looking for me?*

"You are Miguel Ramirez, correct?" the blond man asked.

Before Cam had confirmed his identity, the door opened, and two more white guys entered and hovered by the entrance. Cam silently cursed.

Luis answered for him, "He's Miguel."

The man withdrew a thick envelope from the breast pocket of his jacket and tossed it across the table.

Cam went to take the money, pulled a bill from the stack, and held it up to the light. At the same time, Luis withdrew a syringe from his jacket and swung it. Cam felt the prick of the needle in his neck and grabbed Luis's forearm as he compressed the plunger. Cam jumped from his seat, knocking his chair over in the process. He rammed Luis's head into the table then stumbled to the filthy floor. Luis held his bloody nose, snatched up the envelope of money, and ran out the back.

Cam tried to stagger to his feet as the two men each took an arm and hauled him up. He reached for the cell phone on the table but fumbled, and the device clattered to the floor with a crack. One of the men holding him raised a booted foot and crushed it.

It didn't matter. The phone was an untraceable burner Twitch had given him for the New York trip. When the front door to the bar opened, everything got very bright, then very black.

——————— ◆ ———————

The buzzing cell phone had The Conductor setting aside the well-worn copy of Tolstoy's *Master and Man*.

"You have news." It was not a question.

The voice on the other end did not bother with a salutation. "*Your puppets are dancing.*"

The Conductor waited in silence.

"*As you suspected, Camilo Canto, a.k.a. Miguel Ramirez, is no longer with The CIA. He's working for some bodyguard business in the States. We provided the information as instructed. Luis Flores made contact, and Canto was acquired in New York.*"

"And Señor Flores? Is he still with us?"

"*I took the liberty of trimming that loose thread,*" the voice on the line explained.

"Very good. You've done well."

"*Thank you,*" the voice replied.

"Keep me apprised."

Now, with Camilo Canto otherwise occupied, it was time to uncover the CIA officer's secrets.

CHAPTER NINE

Washington, DC
December 2

The distinguished Senator Harlan Musgrave rapped his knuckles on the file in front of him.

The old, pine desk was modest, dwarfed by the size of the office. It had been his grandfather's desk from his childhood home on their family farm, and Harlan Musgrave made a big show of telling the story to visitors and colleagues. *Never forget where you come from. The strength of the tree is from the roots.* He said it so often that his assistant, a sycophant named Arlo, unconsciously mouthed the words in awe as his boss spoke them. It was a lie, of course. The closest his grandfather had ever come to a desk was standing before a judge.

He glanced out the window at the low buildings, a blanket of gray promising snow. It was beautiful. It wasn't merely harsh winters and time that had buffeted the eighteenth and nineteenth-century architecture; like the people of his adopted town, the buildings had been sullied over the years by crime and corruption. He placed his palm flat on the glass, secure in the knowledge that he had contributed substantially to the adulteration.

Musgrave stood and began to pace across the cavernous office. He was a big man in every sense of the word, tall and broad, loud and imposing. He had a limp from an old football injury that he exaggerated when it suited him, but now he wore through the carpet with a steady stride.

He paced when he had a problem. And The Conductor's most recent request was indeed a problem.

Drugs, weapons, women, antiquities, hell, if a goddamned Indonesian white cockatoo was being smuggled in a drainpipe, The Conductor knew about it. And collected. No one, *no one,* moved illegal goods without going through him. And if they tried, The Conductor arranged for one of the customs agents or CIA officers in his pocket to get a well-deserved bust, which also served to make his people look good.

Power and connections had enabled Musgrave to line his pockets for decades. Bribes, blackmail, graft: nothing was beneath him. It wasn't, however, until he crossed paths with The Conductor that he realized he had merely been dabbling.

Perhaps *crossed paths* was not the correct term. He had never actually met The Conductor, never even laid eyes on the man. Communication was handled through assistants and assistants to assistants. Even the one time he had been invited onto the yacht, *The Maestro,* he hadn't had the pleasure of an introduction. For twenty hours, he had indulged in every vice the mind could conceive—and even a few he had never imagined. He mingled with models and celebrities and partook in sex and drugs as casually as playing a deck-top game of shuffleboard. When the time came for business, two executive assistants sat with him at a small conference table and outlined expectations and compensation. No phones or electronics of any sort were permitted at the meeting. Harlan correctly surmised that, like him, The Conductor wasn't foolish enough to presume he was above the law, that his money, ruthlessness, and power had moved him beyond the wingspan of justice. Quite the contrary. Law enforcement evolved as quickly and momentously as crime. The Conductor, with meticulous care, never revealing himself, never trusting *anyone,* operated in the shadows. He hadn't evaded law enforcement and government probes by being careless. Musgrave looked on The Conductor with the kind of awe usually reserved for the looks he received from others.

Harlan almost laughed out loud. No one in his world had the slightest suspicion of the dark depths he plumbed. They certainly wouldn't dare to imagine an association with The Conductor. After all, The Conductor didn't exist. Harlan made sure of it. The Conductor was a myth, a dark web fairytale, a conspiracy theory, and Harlan Musgrave was paid handsomely to ensure that's how it stayed.

To date, The Conductor's demands had been expected and reasonable, but this most recent request would prove to be a bit more of a challenge. No matter. He may have even relished the opportunity to show The Conductor his power.

Camilo Canto.

Discovering the identity of a NOC officer was next to impossible, but The Conductor had done it. Now Musgrave had been tasked with locating a piece of evidence the spy may have stashed anywhere in the world. That was a bit of a challenge. This spook, Canto, had dirt on The Conductor that must be found and destroyed. The "destroyed" part was easy. It was the "found" aspect of the assignment that was vexing. The best Musgrave had managed up to this point was having Canto followed.

A soft knock on the thick door interrupted his contemplation. His assistant, Arlo, held the exterior knob and leaned into the room. "Senator Musgrave? The Subcommittee on Crime and Terrorism meeting starts in fifteen minutes."

The senator pasted on a grin. "I'd forget my shoes if my feet didn't freeze. Thank you, Arlo. I'll head over shortly."

Arlo returned his boss's smile and retreated.

Musgrave ran a hand across his smooth jaw, dreading what he was about to do, but there was no way around it. Failing The Conductor was not an option. He returned to his desk, grabbed the cell phone he used for such matters, and placed the call.

CHAPTER TEN

When a shadow fell across his desk, Nathan Bishop looked up to see Miller "Tox" Buchanan eclipsing the overhead lighting. He shoved his hands in his pockets, looking uncharacteristically uncomfortable.

Nathan set down Cam's leather journal. "Everything okay?"

"Got a sec?" Tox asked.

Nathan gestured to the suede and chrome chair opposite his desk, and Tox folded his six and a half feet into it with surprising grace.

"How's Emily?" Tox drummed out a rhythm on the arms of the chair.

Nathan checked his phone then replaced it face down on the desk. "Still a few weeks out." He leaned forward on his elbows. "What's going on?"

"So, uh, we pulled the goalie," Tox said.

"What does that mean?" Nathan asked.

"It's a hockey metaphor," Tox explained.

"For…?" Nathan prodded.

"The female reproductive system." Tox's face reddened.

"Ahh." Nathan nodded his understanding.

"The goalie being birth control, the net being Calliope's uterus, the stick and the puck—"

Nathan cut him off, "Yeah. I got the picture. Congratulations, man. That's great. Jack and Charlie need some younger kids to corrupt."

Tox half-laughed. "The thing is, nothing's happening."

"What do you mean?"

"She's not pregnant yet." Tox threw up his hands.

"Well, how long ago did you… 'pull the goalie?'" Nathan borrowed Tox's metaphor.

"The honeymoon." Tox bugged out his eyes, emphasizing the situation.

"That was two months ago," Nathan stated.

"Exactly. You get it."

"Tox, I realize I'm not the typical case when it comes to fertility, but from what little I know, two months sounds like nothing." Nathan entered something on the search bar on his phone. "Says on WebDoctor that the average length of time is six months to a year."

"A year!" Tox leapt to his feet.

"You've got to relax. It'll happen when it happens," Nathan soothed.

"You sound like Calliope." Tox sank back down.

"Is she concerned?" Nathan asked.

"Calliope? Fuck no. She's so fucking Zen about the whole thing; it makes me want to put a fist through the drywall." Tox ran a hand over his stubbled head.

Nathan finally released the laugh that had been building. "You know I'm not a Zen guy, but in this case, she's right. Don't invite trouble. Hell, it's no imposition to keep trying."

The thought lit Tox's face. "Yeah, that's true. I do enjoy the trying."

Before Tox could lift himself from the chair to leave, a frantic knock on Nathan's open door had both men looking up. Nathan looked across the room and spotted Twitch holding her laptop and shifting her weight from one pink Converse to the other. "Something's not right, boss."

"What's up?" Nathan gestured to the other seat.

"We know Cam went to New York to try to get some intel on who was asking about his old identity," Twitch said.

Nathan nodded along. Tox listened.

"And we know he was planning to meet with his former handler after that to determine how to proceed," she continued.

Taking the remaining chair, Twitch set her laptop on the opposite side of Nathan's desk and typed as she spoke. "According to Sofria, Cam hasn't contacted his handler." Sofria Kirk was a CIA analyst who had helped them in the past. She and Twitch had become good friends.

"I don't think that's cause for panic," Nathan said.

"But this is." She rotated her computer screen so Nathan could see the grid with the blinking dot. "Calls don't go through, but the tracking chip is functioning."

Twitch had installed a modified tracking chip on all Bishop Security phones that continued to send a signal for up to two weeks after a phone had been disabled.

"According to this, Cam, or at least his phone, is still in Spanish Harlem at the bar where he was supposed to meet that Luis guy… four hours ago," Twitch explained, her concern evident.

Nathan texted the Bishop Security office in New York. After dispatching two men uptown to assess the situation, he set his phone on the glass-topped desk and rubbed the bridge of his nose.

"There's no indication he's been blown. The communication was with Miguel Ramirez. For all we know, he met with his contact and went willingly to another location. Whoever it was may have insisted he leave his phone so he couldn't be tracked," Nathan offered.

"I also got the info on that license plate," Twitch added.

She reached for her laptop. Nathan had come to think of it as her security blanket as well as a tool of her trade. She brought up the information.

"The Ford Explorer belongs to a small security firm in Charleston. From the website, it looks like they mostly do event security and some P.I. work. They also need a cybersecurity expert because their firewalls are nonexistent."

"Any idea who hired them?" Nathan asked.

"I know the who but not the why. Or if Cam was even their target." She ran her fingers across the keyboard. "The firm currently has three active clients, two out of Charleston and one out of Washington. The DC client is listed as John Smith. Payment was wired from the bank account of Harlan Musgrave."

Tox sat up in his chair. "Senator Harlan Musgrave?"

Twitch held up her hand. "The job was terminated yesterday."

Nathan reached for the landline on his desk. "We need to speak with Cam's handler."

"Um, I'm assuming you don't just call the CIA's main number and *press two* for handlers," Tox remarked.

Nathan chuffed. "Not quite."

He picked up the handset and dialed. Then put the phone on speaker.

"*DDO Sorensen's Office,*" A pinched voice announced.

"Is she available? Nathan Bishop calling."

While Nathan waited for the call to connect, he watched Twitch do a quick search. Her eyebrows shot to her hairline. Jennifer Sorenson was Deputy Director of Operations for National Clandestine Services at the CIA. In government acronym speak, the DDO of NCS.

"*Hi, Nathan. How are you?*" Jennifer Sorenson greeted.

"Good, good. And you? How's Dave?"

"*He's great. Loves the new job. Has that baby made an appearance yet?*"

"Christmas, we think." Nathan unconsciously checked his cell phone.

"*What's up?*"

Nathan explained the situation with Cam to the DDO. Sorenson had come up through the ranks, so she understood, as only a former undercover officer could, the red flags that were flying. She arranged for Nathan to meet with Cam's former handler. After ending the call, he directed his attention to Twitch.

Twitch smirked. "Friends in high places, huh?"

Nathan shrugged. "I knew her at Dartmouth. You'd never peg her for a spook. Probably why she was so good at her job."

Nathan's father had helmed a prominent private defense contracting company, and his Uncle Charlie, who routinely helped them out, was a former Secretary of Defense. Nathan may have had a troubled childhood, but his family connections had their advantages.

Nathan continued, "I don't know what his handler is willing or able to share. Twitch, you are our best asset for information gathering. Start digging. We know this has some connection to Dario Sava because Miguel Ramirez was his cover for that op, and for the year after, hunting down Sava's associates. Do whatever you have to do. We aren't at DEFCON 5 yet, but I want to be ready."

"Copy that, boss." She grabbed her laptop and stood. Nathan thumbed the worn leather journal on his desk.

"Anything else?" she asked.

"Bring Finn into the loop on this," Nathan said. "I don't know if he's even reachable right now, but he's privy to information no one else will have." Finn McIntyre was a Teamguy and currently working for the CIA in a role similar to Cam.

Twitch hadn't mastered the poker face of the men in the office. She scowled.

Nathan sighed. "Look. I don't know what went on between you and Finn, and I don't want to know. Your personal life is your business."

Tox signaled his agreement by holding up both hands in an I'm-staying-out-of-it gesture.

Twitch nodded.

"However," Nathan continued, "your work life *is* my business. If Finn can help, you need to set aside your differences."

Twitch swallowed thickly. "Of course, I'll get on this right now." She turned and hurried out. Mumbling her discontent, she ducked around Steady, who was standing in the open doorway leaning against the jamb.

"Tell him *hi* for me," Steady quipped.

"What? How?" Twitch looked at him, puzzled.

"You only mumble to yourself when you have to deal with Finn." She turned on her heel and fled the room.

Steady directed his attention to Nathan, who had returned to his computer. "Any developments?"

Nathan tilted his head, bemused.

"Twitch filled me in when I was in her office. Actually, she was talking to herself, but I got the gist. Cam's MIA?"

Steady entered and flopped into the chair that Twitch had vacated. Nathan scrubbed a hand down his face then filled in the blanks. "It's impossible to investigate this with the layers of secrecy involved. I spoke with the DDO. She set up a meeting with Cam's former handler on Friday. Feel like taking a quick trip to DC?"

"Absolutely. Nathan, do you know what Cam was doing for the year after Sava was killed?" Steady asked.

"Only what wasn't classified. It's pretty clear he was chasing down Sava's merchandise," Nathan replied.

"I think he was chasing down a person, not a weapon," Steady said.

"What gives you that impression?" Tox asked.

"You know Cam. The guy's a vault. You could pump him full of scopolamine, and you still wouldn't get anything out of him." Steady crossed an ankle over his knee.

Nathan nodded.

"A couple months ago, I asked him if he liked living here after his European tour." Steady continued, "He said he loved it here, but any place was better than running around the world chasing a ghost."

Nathan sat back in his chair and ran his hand over the journal containing the notes Cam had compiled on The Conductor. "I'll fill you in on the flight."

"Copy that."

Steady and Tox stood to leave just as Nathan's cell phone trilled. Nathan shot to his feet and answered before the completion of the first ring.

"Hey, Emily. What's up?" After a moment, he eased back into his chair.

Nathan glanced up and saw Steady and Tox waiting, eager for news. Nathan shook his head in the negative and continued talking. "I don't know if the guy at the sandwich shop can make a Reuben like Carnegie Deli, but I'll figure it out."

Tox jerked his head to the door, and Steady waved over his shoulder as they left.

CHAPTER ELEVEN

Miramar, Mallorca
December 3

Cam's first thought when he awoke was, *what the fuck did I drink last night.* A small man with a jackhammer was going to town on his brain, and his mouth tasted like an old sock. The cloying scent of Stargazer lilies in the vase next to the bed was making him sick. He rolled away and nestled into the luxurious bedding, lowering his head to block out the sliver of sunlight peeking through the drapes.

He tried unsuccessfully to clear his head, his consciousness fighting a losing battle with the bed. He remembered walking into the bar in Spanish Harlem, meeting with a man. Before he could analyze the situation further, he was asleep.

An hour later, Cam opened his eyes to a glorious morning. Sun poured through open french doors, and a breeze tinged with the scent of the sea billowed the sheer curtains. He sat up fighting nausea, noting he was wearing a new plain white T-shirt and boxer briefs. His head was still in a fog as he glanced around the luxurious room with blurry eyes. It was on the main floor, and glass-paned doors led to a flagstone terrace where a table was set with a silver coffee service, a bowl of glistening sliced fruit, and a pastry tray. Beyond the patio lay a lush lawn leading to a vineyard and neat rows of orchard trees. He furrowed his brow; he could be gone from this place in an instant, but curiosity kept him rooted in the room. There were two open doors: one led to a walk-in closet at least half the main room's size and filled with men's clothing. On the opposite wall, double doors led to a marble-tiled bathroom. In his fieldwork, Cam had experienced the full lavatory spectrum; this one buried the needle. On the far side of the jetted shower and soaking tub, a retractable wall was open, and the space extended out to a Marbella stone deck and rectangular swimming pool.

Then, as if his mind had completed the fantasy, the head of a woman appeared from the water, coming up the submerged concentric steps at the near-end of the pool—head, shoulders, breasts, stomach, and mile-long legs. Gloriously nude, glistening water sluicing down her blonde hair and bronzed body, the woman walked straight toward him. She stepped into the open bathroom and plucked a sleek robe from a hook but didn't put it on; she dragged it behind her as she continued toward him. All Cam could do was sit in the massive bed and watch.

"Hello, Miguel. It's been a long time."

Her words had Cam jerking his eyes up from her flawless body to her bewitching face. Yes. Even through the haze, he knew that face. He had been with a lot of women over the years, and while he had felt no deep connection to this woman a year ago, a man didn't forget Gemini March. Even if the sex had been forgettable, the pages of fashion magazines and designer ad campaigns were an ego-boosting but regrettable reminder. Her temper tantrum over the hotel's available selection of champagne at 3 a.m. certainly didn't help. Cam was wary of the temptress before him, but Miguel Ramirez would have no such reservations. With his head still heavy on the pillow, he licked his lips.

She spoke with the confidence of a woman who had never been looked upon and found lacking. "Cat got your tongue?"

He thought about pretending not to know who she was, but his face had given him away. Instead, speaking in thickly accented English, he went with the truth.

"What the fuck is going on?"

She laughed then. "So much. Don't worry, Miguel, it's all good."

"Where am I? Because I know I wasn't good enough on earth for this to be heaven." Cam licked his lips.

She giggled. "*We* are not far from the place we first met. Do you remember, Miguel? Do you remember my shoes? My dress?"

Oh, he remembered.

"Because I do. I remember grabbing fistfuls of that auburn hair and licking the tattoo of the cross that I know is on your back." Her face morphed into an affected moue. "And I remember waking up all alone."

"Ibiza?" he guessed.

"Close. We're about ten kilometers outside of Palma," she replied.

"Mallorca?" Cam confirmed.

She clapped little, girly claps, the robe resting over her forearm.

Cam scanned the room again, then returned his gaze to Gemini's perfection. Had he been abducted by a supermodel? God, it sounded like the title of a bad porno. Something was going on, and he intended to find out what. "Why?" he asked.

He attempted to sit up, but dizziness overtook him.

Gemini donned the robe but didn't tie it, then sauntered over to him. She leaned over and placed her full lips to the shell of his ear. "Because today is your lucky day." She moved her face an inch in front of him. "When you're up and changed, my cousin would like a word."

Cam couldn't miss the sudden ice in her voice.

"Your cousin?" he repeated.

She gave a hum in confirmation. "Atlas March."

Slowly the pieces were fitting into place, but Cam couldn't make out the picture that was being revealed. "Atlas March is your cousin?" Now he remembered. Atlas March was the head of a mining conglomerate based in Mallorca.

He was also on the CIA's radar for some suspicious activity when he had lived and worked in Colombia.

A sultry smile touched her lips. "Mmm-hmm."

She crossed the room and struck a seductive pose in the doorway, the open robe exposing a swath of tan, lustrous skin. "I'll see you for lunch by the pool." And with that promise, she was gone.

Cam flopped back on the bed and ran a hand down his face muttering a string of Spanish expletives that would have his grandmother swatting the back of his head.

He had met Gemini March just over a year ago at a club on the neighboring island of Ibiza. He foolishly had chased a lead on The Conductor and had been left high and dry waiting for an informant who had either been killed or had never existed in the first place. Just when he thought the night was a complete bust, in a hail of camera flashes, in walked Gemini March.

He didn't know much about the cousin. Atlas March had taken over the March Conglomerate last year when the senior March, Ulysses, if Cam remembered correctly, died in a suspicious plane crash.

Maybe Cam simply didn't want to face the fact that a spoiled, possibly unhinged princess had kidnapped him in the hope of making him her lover, but something deep in his gut told him there was more going on than the state of play indicated.

CHAPTER TWELVE

Built in the mid-sixteenth century for a valued advisor of King Philip II, the March family estate, Villa Marzo, sat on just over ten thousand hectares on a high plateau between Port des Canonge and Valdemossa overlooking the Balearic Sea. Over the centuries, various occupants had added and changed the original home—wings and cloistered walkways grew from the central structure like limbs. As a result, the pale stone estate sprawled amid olive and fruit orchards and grazing fields like a giant reclining in a meadow. The current occupants, the new head of the March Mining Conglomerate, Atlas March, and his cousin, Gemini, a famed fashion model, rarely spared the palatial interior a glance, so accustomed to opulence that it seemed almost mundane.

Joseph Nabeel sat at the dining table that seated thirty and watched his new boss over the edge of *The Financial Times*. Atlas March was picking through a fruit platter with a fork, inching undesirable slices of papaya and pineapple to the edge of the plate. Joseph returned to his newspaper.

With the senior March's untimely death, the bylaws of the privately held company clearly stated the blood relative with the largest percentage of holdings would take over as Chief Executive. That person was Atlas March. Within a week of Ulysses's funeral, Atlas had moved into the villa, redecorated the master bedroom, and taken over March Mining's Mallorca operation. After three decades, Joseph Nabeel had a new employer. That was a year ago.

In the intervening months, Atlas had been applauded by the international community for converting the mining operation from the environmental blight, brown coal, to copper. Environmentalists may have hailed the young CEO as a visionary, but Joseph was well aware the refitting of the mine served more than one purpose for the cagey young man.

Joseph had been the loyal adjutant to the company's founder, Ulysses March, for nearly thirty years. While Ulysses was no angel, he at least conducted himself with a refinement that suited his position. Atlas, on the other hand, was a spoiled upstart with little concern for the consequences of his actions.

The silence in the room was rent with an ear-splitting shout.

"You *idiot!*" Gemini March charged into the room, picked up the fruit platter, and dumped it into her cousin's lap.

Atlas shot to his feet. "God damnit, Gemini!" The resemblance between the cousins was obvious; they both shared the same narrow upturned nose, cerulean eyes, and blond hair. The effect, however, was quite different. The refined features gave Atlas the look of an aristocratic prig, while Gemini had a face that felled men the world over. She could have any man she wanted, but she only wanted one.

"I asked you to go pick up Miguel Ramirez. Not drug him and abduct him!" she shouted.

"You asked me to get him. I got him. What's the problem?" Atlas ran a napkin over his ruined suit.

"Well, for one thing, you've managed to squeeze every drop of romance from the situation. The man can barely lift his head!" She looked around for something else to throw at him.

"Relax, darling. It was just ketamine. Give him a couple of hours, and he'll be *lifting his head* just fine."

Joseph continued to observe. For the most part, Gemini hid her loathing well. She had adored her father, and he equally prized her. She didn't give a fig about the company, but Joseph knew Gemini suspected Atlas March had had a hand in her father's death.

"All you had to do was tell him Gemini March wanted to see him." She balled her fists at her side. At the far end of the table, Joseph braced himself. Gemini had a temper and a half, and he had a feeling she was just getting started. "A year, Atlas. I've been looking for him for a year! I finally track him down, and he's so out of it he can barely speak."

Atlas wiped away the last of the fruit and retook his seat. He spoke with deceptive calm. "Let me make something clear to you, cousin. March Mining is mine. This house, which is owned by March Mining, is mine. The jets, the cars, the yachts are mine." He refolded his napkin and set it beside his plate. "A week ago, you asked me to do you a favor. A week ago, you told me that a man you thought could be "the one" needed to be flown from the States to my home.

"But guess what, princess? Unlike most men who blindly obey your orders, I had some questions. So I looked into this Miguel Ramirez." Atlas brought the Brunello Cucinelli leather portfolio at his feet to the table, snapped open the latch, and withdrew a file.

"Do you know who this man is? Do you know what he does?" he pressed.

"He's a businessman." Gemini busied herself, pouring a glass of orange juice from the pitcher on the sideboard.

"He's not a fucking businessman, Gemini. Miguel Ramirez is a lieutenant for an arms dealer. Well, he was anyway. His former employer, Dario Sava, was killed last year. This is no Armani-wearing, snort-a-line-at-a-party asshole. You have brought a very dangerous man into my home."

"Well, technically, *you* brought a very dangerous man into our home." She gave him a mock toast with her drink.

"This is not a joke, Gemini. This man is a brute." Atlas banged a fist on the file.

Her voice turned sultry. "I'm well aware."

"Oh, for God's sake. He lit your fuse for one hot night, then vanished. I hate to burst your bubble, but that happens all the time."

Gemini snapped, "Not to me, it doesn't."

Joseph continued to observe the pair, saw the moment Atlas realized he needed another way to push her buttons. Probably wise. Atlas wouldn't get anywhere insulting her allure; Gemini knew better.

Atlas didn't look up from the paperwork that had stolen his attention. "Maybe he should come work for me. I could use someone with his… qualifications."

"No." Gemini turned to face her cousin.

"Why not?" Atlas continued to flip through the pages.

"I don't want him working in some filthy mine." She wrinkled her nose. "I just wanted to bring him here for a getaway. For a reunion. You've botched my entire plan."

"If I want him to work for me, he'll work for me. You don't make the decisions about my business. Are we clear?" Atlas said.

"Perfectly." Gemini huffed her reply, but as she turned her attention to Joseph, he saw the Mona Lisa smile ghost her lips. Gemini was a master manipulator. She had wanted Atlas to hire Miguel Ramirez, and she had not only done it, she'd made him think it was his idea.

"Joseph, good morning. I'm sorry I didn't say it earlier. I was… distracted. You know how long I've been looking for Miguel." She bent down and pecked her late father's loyal assistant on the cheek.

"Well, the heart wants what it wants, I suppose." Joseph patted her hand.

"Yes. You understand." Gemini rested a hand on his shoulder.

"May I see the file? I'm curious about this young man of yours." Joseph folded his newspaper and set it to the side.

"He's dark and dangerous. Atlas better not make a miner out of him. I think I would lose interest immediately." She gave a dismissive wave to her cousin.

Atlas stood and walked the length of the table. He handed the file to Joseph but spoke to his cousin. "Not everyone who works in a mine is a miner."

Joseph cleaned his wire-rimmed glasses with a handkerchief, replaced them on his nose, and opened the file. "Gemini, this man is a criminal."

"I know. Isn't it exciting?" She beamed.

Joseph eyed her over his glasses. "I feel obligated to discourage you from pursuing a relationship with him."

"A year, Joseph. I have been looking for him for one year."

Atlas took the chair next to Joseph and lit a cigarette. "Perhaps he didn't want to be found." He puffed a smoke ring across the table.

"I'm sure he didn't want *some people* to find him, and I'm also sure that list does not include me," Gemini insisted.

"How did you suddenly discover his whereabouts?" Atlas prodded. "I imagine men of his *ilk* are probably very good at disappearing. Or dying."

"The planets finally aligned. Out of the blue, someone I employed to find Miguel managed to track down a former colleague who was able to get a message to him." Gemini plucked a grape from Joseph's plate. "What can I say? It's fate."

Atlas grunted his disbelief.

Joseph continued paging through the file. He held up a grainy color image and inhaled sharply. Miguel Ramirez was undeniably handsome with an imposing build and chiseled features, but that wasn't what had elicited the gasp. "Those eyes," Joseph said.

"I know. Isn't he magnificent? He's like a Latin lover fantasy come to life." Gemini kissed Joseph again. "I'm off. While Miguel recuperates, I can get some work done."

Atlas laughed. "What could you possibly have to do? Practice your runway walk? Post tips for applying mascara?"

Joseph felt Gemini's grip on his shoulder tighten to the point of pain. "What I do is more work than you could possibly imagine."

In hopes of avoiding another confrontation, Atlas lifted both hands in surrender, the cigarette like a small white flag.

Gemini turned and stalked out.

"I have some thoughts." Joseph paged through the file.

"I'm listening," Atlas replied.

"I think you should hire him," Joseph advised.

"I was joking, Joseph. That was for Gemini's benefit."

"I'm aware of that, but think about it. This man, Miguel Ramirez, was one of Dario Sava's men." Joseph ran his finger down the papers. The infamous black market broker was well known to both men.

"Your point?" Atlas countered.

"He's been vetted. For the right price, he would be a loyal and capable employee. Sava dealt with betrayal or incompetence swiftly." Joseph withdrew his pipe and a bag of tobacco from his breast pocket and filled the bowl as he spoke. "This family has always operated in the gray, but where your uncle was a diplomat, you are a warrior." He patted down the leaves and struck a wooden match. Atlas inflated at the compliment. "This man, Miguel Ramirez, could prove to be quite an asset. No reason not to take advantage of Gemini's flight of fancy. She has plans for him; why not make some of your own?"

Joseph puffed on his pipe, absently tapping the closed file.

Atlas sat back and brushed the velvet upholstery of the armrest, watching the fabric's color change with the back and forth motion. "And what if he is not... amenable to these plans?"

Joseph countered, "Read the file, Atlas. The man is an urchin, an enforcer. He was living on the streets before coming to work for Sava. You think you can't convince him to come live in the lap of luxury with a beautiful woman in his bed?" Joseph folded his glasses and replaced them in his breast pocket, pushed back his chair, and stood, patting his employer on the shoulder with fatherly affection as he left. "I'm sure you've successfully negotiated deals with far less to offer."

Joseph stopped at the room's entrance and looked back. Alone at the table, Atlas placed one finger on top of the closed file and slid the papers in front of him. Pleased, Joseph continued walking. Miguel Ramirez was about to experience an abrupt change in circumstance.

———————— ◈ ————————

Joseph Nabeel ate up the lawn in long strides. Golf carts were scattered throughout the March estate, but Joseph chose to walk the kilometer or so to his quaint guest house, just as he had for the past twenty-two years. He idly wondered if he would still be living here when he would require such a conveyance.

He depressed the latch on the unlocked door and entered the lavish guest cottage that had been his home for two decades. After following his ingrained routine—hanging his trench coat on the coat rack, flipping through the stack of mail his housekeeper had left on the small pillar table by the door, and pouring himself a small measure of sherry—he surveyed the surroundings. His outward calm belying the excitement bursting from within.

Joseph Nabeel was a man reborn.

In the name of his many endeavors, he had foregone marriage and family, had led a solitary life. Instead of friends, he had staff. Instead of children, he had Gemini March. He had grown tired. Tired of a search that never seemed to yield rewards. Taking his drink, he made his way to his study. At the doorway, he stared at the ancient map that lay on the weathered desk.

Crossing the room, he opened the top drawer, withdrew a pair of loose, white cotton gloves, put them on, and took a seat. His hands and eyes moved reverently over the drawings and landmarks depicted on the centuries-old parchment. Time had altered the shoreline and terrain of Mallorca, but Joseph had spent a lifetime studying everything from sea currents to volcanic activity. The landscape had a familiarity to him that no one else possessed, as if the eyes and thoughts, even the very souls, of his ancestors lived within him.

Over the centuries, many men had attempted to find the place indicated on this map. The piece of parchment itself now spread before him was worth over a million euros. After studying every nuance of the page for nearly a year, Joseph believed he had discovered the error the cartographer—or, more likely, a lowly sailor—had made.

In 1478, the caravel ship had made a rushed departure from Algiers, the Moorish king desperate to escape with his prize before King Ferdinand's Spanish crusaders arrived. They had sailed through the night in a violent storm. Joseph was convinced that the ship had been blown off course. What was marked on the map as Ibiza—actually Yebisah, the Arabic name from when the Moors controlled the island through the thirteenth century—was actually a jutting tip of the Spanish coastline. Thus, the point where the ship ran aground in Mallorca had been miscalculated by over thirty kilometers.

Joseph relished the image of infidels and claimless treasure seekers scouring the caves near Palma when, by his estimation, the location was just east of Banyalbufar in the honeycomb of caves carved into the limestone cliffs.

Despite his revelation with the map, his search had yielded nothing. The Panther's Eye remained undiscovered.

As a small boy, Joseph had been hypnotized by the story. Each year, during Ramadan, after they had broken the fast and prayed, one of the village elders would gather the children and share the lore. The others had whispered and giggled, but Joseph had been snared.

He knew even then that the story was meant for him, that Panther's Eye was to be his.

He had worked two jobs to pay for his schooling at the University of Cairo. Then he had received an offer of employment that was both profitable and prophetic: March Mining. Ulysses March had just started his business when Joseph came to his side. Joseph's work had included the immoral and even the criminal, but he was well-appreciated and better compensated. More importantly, he had ample time to explore the arcane caves and underground passages of Mallorca in search of his prize.

And that's what he had done for more than two decades. He had found breadcrumbs through the years; he had even discovered a stash of Moorish coins and silver from another ship and another time. He had been on the brink of abandoning the hunt. Joseph was not a religious man, but two nights ago, he had knelt and prayed to whatever god would listen. He had begged for a sign. And like a dying man resuscitated, he was brought back to life. He withdrew the photograph from his suit pocket and placed it on the desk. The moment he beheld the golden eyes of the man, he knew. It was his sign. This man had *panther's eyes*.

When a soft knock came at the door, Joseph stood to assist his man with the tray. After the servant had poured the mint tea into the handleless decorative cup, Joseph dismissed him and set the food aside. He walked to the window cradling the small teacup in one hand, the photo of Miguel Ramirez in the other. A smile touched his lips.

CHAPTER THIRTEEN

Miramar, Mallorca
December 3

Cam stood in the open doorway as Atlas March sat behind his desk, one hand spread on the surface, attempting the knife trick and paying no heed to the mahogany he was marring. Cam knocked.

Atlas summoned him in without looking up. "Come."

Adopting the persona of Miguel Ramirez, Cam walked five steps into the room and remained standing. He knew better than to do anything beyond what was instructed.

"Damn this thing," Atlas groused. "How do they get the knife going so fast?" He looked up then and scanned Cam from head to toe. "I'll bet you can do it," Atlas challenged.

"I used to do it on a plank of wood on the street in my village for coins," Cam responded.

Atlas tossed the knife end over end, and Cam caught it by the blade. He grabbed a magazine—a foreign issue of *Vogue* with Gemini March on the cover in a massive ball gown—from the coffee table in a small seating area and tossed it on the desk. Then he placed his left hand flat on the cover and began slowly moving the tip of the knife from one gap between his fingers to the next in a familiar rhythm. It didn't escape his notice that each jab of the blade created a tiny stab in the image beneath his hand. After completing the pattern twice, he sped up, the hand wielding the knife moving like lightning. He finished with a final plunge into the magazine, leaving the knife protruding from the center of Gemini March's head, and calmly turned his attention to his one-man audience.

"You've killed my cousin," Atlas smirked.

"Apologies, señor. I thought it was better than damaging the wood."

Atlas scoffed. "There are a thousand magazines and a thousand desks."

Cam nodded, still standing.

"Take a seat, Miguel." Atlas gestured to the two green leather chairs that faced the desk. Cam sat. "Tell me about your work for Dario Sava."

Cam shrugged. "I did what I was told."

"And what was that, exactly?" Atlas pressed.

The lack of reply answered the question.

"I see." Atlas nodded. "And you were given responsibilities? I mean more than just cleaning up messes."

"Yes."

"One of Mallorca's most successful industries is copper mining. I own the largest mining operation in the region. March Mining is global, but the headquarters is here in Palma. I also own the shipping company that handles exports."

That got Cam's attention.

Atlas continued, "I had urged my uncle Ulysses to purchase a shipping company when I ran the Colombia mining operation, but he felt it was unnecessary. I disagreed. Now, I make the decisions. It was a substantial initial investment, but it's already paying off."

Atlas pulled the knife from the magazine and set it to the side. "I have a position for you—security to start. If you prove yourself, we can take it from there. There is some job mobility, but not just yet. I don't know what sort of, eh hem, pay scale you've had in the past, but I think you'll find the salary competitive. Certainly, the benefits, you know, health insurance and no constant threat of death, will be enticing."

Cam's lips twitched in a calculated move.

"When I'm confident where your loyalties lie, there will be opportunities."

"I am loyal to the man who signs the checks," Cam replied dryly.

Atlas nodded, satisfied. "My cousin brought you here for a re-union. Apparently, you made quite an impression. I'm sure I can put her impulsiveness to good use, and I can assure you none of the rats scrambling to the top of the trash heap in your former career can offer you the same."

Cam leaned in slightly, the only indication of his interest, but Atlas noticed.

"Tomorrow, I'll take you on a tour of the mines. I can show you the operation and explain your duties. I can assure you it's an entic-ing offer for a man with your..." He scanned Cam from auburn head to booted toe. "Abilities."

Cam shifted. Something was tainting the air between them. A trap? A setup? He didn't know what it was, but he smelled it.

Atlas picked up the knife and ran his finger along the blade. "You want to know why you."

Cam nodded once.

"Well, that is an easy question to answer, but not for me. Gemini gets what she wants, and she wants you. Why? I can only speculate," he drawled.

"Sí. Yes, sir."

"She has a proposition of her own for you," Atlas continued. "Take the morning to explore our island. Palma is within walking distance, but you're free to take a Vespa or a car. The beaches are beautiful, but unfortunately, it's the wrong time of year for sunning."

When Cam's eyes widened, Atlas continued.

"You may leave if you like, Mr. Ramirez. But I promise you, you'll not find an offer as lucrative or appealing. I assure you, it's in your best interest to remain with us for the time being."

CHAPTER FOURTEEN

Palma, Mallorca
December 3

December was the off-season on Mallorca with good reason. Despite the unseasonably warm 72 degrees, the air was thick, and low clouds moved across the sky, intent on blocking the sun. A few hardy souls were out to read in peace or jog or play with their children; there would be no sunbathing today.

Cam wandered along the path above the water. Cliffside terraces were dotted with chaise longues and closed orange beach umbrellas. Charming stucco buildings sat cradled in lush foliage. Waves lapped the shore in a hypnotic rhythm. This island was idyllic. It was also torture.

He worked his way down a series of wide stone stairs and found himself alone on the small swath of nut-colored beach. His trainers left deep divots in the damp sand, and a clammy breeze ruffled his dark hair.

He sank onto an abandoned beach chair and stared out at the calm water. The cloud cover had darkened the small waves to an eerie green. Forty yards out, a swimmer wearing a black wetsuit and a pink bathing cap with a snorkel and diving mask attached stroked across the bay. He dropped his gaze to his sneaker-clad feet, hands dangling between his legs, and contemplated his next moves.

Cam drew a circle in the sand between his feet and stifled a laugh. If thirty-six hours ago, someone had told him he'd be transported to an island paradise and forced to resist the advances of a supermodel...Cam scolded himself. His cover identity, Miguel Ramirez, would already be wearing a condom; he would look at this opportunity— every aspect—as a windfall.

Gemini March was undeniably beautiful. He had pulled out all the stops to seduce her when they had met a year earlier. He had been in a nightclub on the neighboring island of Ibiza, hot on the trail of a weapons trafficker who was planning to sell a handheld Javelin to an East African insurgent leader. Dressed in all black, in a suit with no tie, Miguel Ramirez looked exactly like what he was, an ominous underworld figure.

Gemini had entered the club, and every head had turned. Her blonde ponytail was restrained in a thick jeweled cuff. Dressed in a blood-red slip of silk, shimmering spike-heeled gladiator sandals that wound up to her knees, and a stark ruby choker, she looked like a slave girl fantasy come to life. Miguel Ramirez sat in the back corner of the VIP section, nursed a rum and coke, and watched the coterie of men try, and fail, to make headway. God, she was spectacular: red lips, red nails, that red jeweled band around her neck. Yet Miguel had simply spun his glass, watched, waited. Finally, she rose to her full height—Cam estimated 6'2" in the stilettos—and pranced over to him.

"Who are you waiting for?" she demanded.

"You," he replied.

"You're right about that." She shot him a sultry smile.

"Good." He stared up at her.

"Well?" She placed a hand on her hip, the action hiking her red dress to indecent heights.

"Take off your shoes." Miguel met her blue gaze and didn't miss the quick breath she had drawn at spying his golden eyes.

"What?"

"You heard me," he said.

After a moment's hesitation in this little battle of wills, Gemini placed a jeweled toe on the chair between his legs and began unbuckling the shoes. Then she switched feet and repeated the action, finally standing barefoot and dangling the sandals from her fingers before tossing them into the corner. Miguel then stood, took her hand, and led her to the floor for the first dance of the evening.

The erotic memory produced nothing but frustration in his tired body, and Cam shook his head in annoyance. He had gone to the mat, rather the mattress, for his job in the past, but now... He wasn't fully immersed in this world. He was in a dangerous limbo between Cam Canto and Miguel Ramirez, and it was a gray area that could get him killed.

He scanned the horizon, searching for what? A sign? An explanation? Nothing to see but the intrepid swimmer.

Her shriek pulled him from his thoughts, and he saw she was thrashing and bobbing in the bay. Without thought or hesitation, Cam stripped down to his boxer briefs and raced into the water. As he swam effortlessly toward the woman in distress, he saw the issue. A fever of stingrays was circling the woman as she held onto one leg and tried to swim away.

He switched to breaststroke to create less disturbance in the water and skirted the magnificent beasts, popping up in front of the woman and eliciting another scream. She jerked out with her good leg, nailing him in the upper thigh with her heel. She had missed his most vulnerable region but still managed to deliver a painful blow.

Cam shook off the cramping pain and focused on getting her away from the stingrays before she agitated them further.

"Hold onto my back," he ordered.

She complied without protest, and Cam quickly stroked them back to shore.

Stingrays rarely stung humans, but it happened, and the toxin could be deadly if not treated immediately. With two graceful dolphin kicks, Cam propelled them into the surf, spun the woman around in his arms like a bride, and rose from the foam.

"You're a seal," she murmured, her head resting against his chest.

"What did you say?" Cam nearly stumbled at the comment.

"You swim like a seal." She hissed at the pain.

Ah, a seal, not a SEAL.

Once on land, Cam held the woman in his arms and bounded up the series of steps. Recalling the fish market he had passed on his walk to the shore, he raced back and located the deep outdoor sink attached to the back of the shop. After plugging the drain with the rubber stopper and filling the basin, he plunged her injured leg into the hot water. Her cry of pain was stifled as she vomited down his bare chest. Cam wiped her mouth with his thumb.

"The hot water breaks up the toxin and slows the spread, but we still need to get you to a hospital."

"Oh, God. This hurts like a mother." She moaned.

"People compare the pain to childbirth, so hurting like a mother is pretty accurate." Cam gave her a crooked grin.

"Thank you for helping me, but if you crack another joke, I'm going to punch you in the nose," she threatened.

"You might punch me in a second anyway because I want to see if I can pull the barb out. Sometimes, it's too deep, but if it's sticking out, I can get it." Cam waited for her permission.

She nodded, the fogged dive mask still covering her face bobbing up and down on her head. Cam steadied her on the edge of the industrial sink and pulled a long tan leg from the scalding water. He stared for just a beat at her painted pink toes before rotating her already swollen ankle. Below the edge of the wetsuit, the stinger protruded just slightly from the puncture, but it was enough. Fortunately, it was relatively short, about an inch and a half in length, and Cam employed the ripping-off-the-bandaid method pulling the jagged shard from the base of her calf. She cried out and, almost involuntarily, whirled her arm around, landing a surprisingly accurate blow to his right eye. Then she passed out.

The fishmonger poked his head out the door, assessed the situation, and returned with his phone. Moments later, as Cam cradled her cap-covered head, the whining hee-haw of an ambulance sounded in the distance. He extracted the snorkel from the rubber ring on the side of the dive mask and set it on the back ledge of the sink, leaving the fogged mask in place—better that she didn't get a good look at him. Moreover, nothing could compare to the rescue fantasy he'd conjured in his head. He'd leave it untarnished for reenactments on lonely nights—long legs and pink toes and a faceless beauty. He'd edit out the puke and the soon-to-be black eye.

The ambulance pulled to a stop, and the paramedics hopped out. After confirming the diagnosis, they immediately injected her with what Cam assumed was the standard administration of a tetanus shot and an antibiotic. He explained as best he could in rudimentary Catalan—his Spanish was fluent, but Cam knew the locals chafed at the usage—that he did not know the woman and had merely pulled her from the water when he saw her struggling. Nevertheless, the two men insisted on his contact information.

That gave him an idea. He quickly scribbled the number of Miguel Ramirez's cell phone back at his apartment at Bishop

Security. The CIA monitored all calls to that phone. If someone from the hospital happened to call, The Agency would be alerted to his whereabouts. The medic took the slip and turned to help load the unconscious woman into the back of the ambulance.

Just as she was about to disappear from view, she shot up on the gurney with a gasp and ripped the mask and cap from her head as if they were choking her. A massive tangle of dark hair was matted to her head, and her face bore the impressions of the mask. She made a panicked sweep of her surroundings, but before her wide eyes landed on him, she retched, and the paramedic placed a kidney-shaped dish under her chin. Her face contorted in pain and mortification as she emptied the remainder of her stomach into the bowl. Cam stood in the alley, watching, and, as the second paramedic pulled the rear doors closed, she lifted her hand without looking up and flipped him the bird.

Cam cupped his hands around his mouth and shouted, "You're welcome!" as the ambulance pulled away.

Still grinning, Cam scooped some water from the basin and washed the mess from his chest. With proper treatment, she would fully recover by the end of the day. Reining in his revelry, he ran through the events that had transpired, noting that he hadn't done anything that a regular guy who knew how to swim and had some basic first aid wouldn't do. He acknowledged that Miguel Ramirez probably would have lit a joint, sat back, and watched her thrash. Even so, no one had been paying attention, and even if they had, it wasn't too out of character. He dove in the water to help a beautiful woman. What guy wouldn't? Granted, he was assuming she was beautiful, all evidence to the contrary.

He thought about his dad's "zing test." He hadn't felt a shock or a jolt. There was no tingle or zap. Rather, he felt something else, something he hadn't felt in so long, something so foreign, that it took him a moment to identify it. After a dozen years fighting wars in one form or another, Cam found himself standing in his underwear in a rutted alley, staring at a rusty sink filled with bloody water and puke, and feeling… peace.

A peace that was shattered a moment later when he noticed a man standing in an alcove half a block away watching his every move.

———————— ◆ ————————

Evan walked gingerly toward the exit of the Palma hospital, feeling a bit like a callow tourist. She was wearing hospital scrub pants over her swimsuit and a pair of flip-flops a nurse had given her. The sting-rays had startled her, and, rather than remain calm and continue swimming, she had thrashed and flailed, inciting their aggression. The doctor had treated her injury successfully, and she should fully recover in a matter of days.

The doctor also encouraged her—in English that was surprising-ly good and annoyingly parental—that she should be sure to thank the man who helped her to shore, as he had, in all likelihood, saved her life.

She toyed with the little slip of paper the paramedic had placed in a plastic drawstring bag with her mask and swim cap. Evan was uncomfortable playing the victim; it was a role she swore she would never play again, but she owed this man her thanks. God, he had charged into the cold bay without a wetsuit and swam through the angry rays to rescue her. What's more, she had felt safe in his arms. She limped over to the reception area to ask to use the phone but thought better of it, not wanting to speak to the man in the middle of a crowded hospital. Returning the scrap of paper to the bag, she made a mental note to call when she got back to her room. Her to-do list was getting long. In addition to tending her wound, she had to call Dr. Emberton and explain what had happened. Then she needed to formulate a plan to return to the caves and figure out the meaning of those markers. She wasn't on Mallorca to embark on some Fifteenth Century treasure hunt, but she had tugged at a thread, and she was determined to unravel the mystery.

With her rudimentary plan in place, Evan hobbled to the exit and hailed a cab.

CHAPTER FIFTEEN

Bishop Security
Somewhere outside Beaufort, South Carolina
December 3

The team sat at the granite-topped racetrack table in the large, glass-walled conference room of Bishop Security.

Tox leaned forward on his forearms and intertwined his fingers on the table. "Let me get this straight. We are saying that an unknown subject tracked down Miguel Ramirez's friend Luis, who then texted the phone Cam used as Miguel Ramirez, claiming," he looked at the sheet that listed the transcribed texts, "someone was looking for him?"

Nathan nodded. "Correct."

"So, I'm assuming Cam had some unfinished business with these men?" Chat looked to Nathan.

Nathan met Chat's knowing gaze. "He had unfinished business. We don't know with whom."

Nathan picked up Cam's leather journal. "These are Cam's notes, observations, and theories concerning the possible existence of The

Conductor, a lone person or entity that controls nearly all global trafficking."

No one spoke.

"Twitch has scanned the journal and uploaded it to your secure Bishop dropbox. No one above him at The Agency lends any credence to this. But I'm not ready to dismiss it. Before Cam went MIA, he was being followed by men hired by Senator Harlan Musgrave."

"Musgrave has a good reputation," Ren said.

"True, but he did business with my father, so he can't be as clean as he appears." Nathan crossed his arms over his chest. "I put out some feelers with some of the less than upstanding associates of Musgrave's and my father. Let's see if anyone knows what Musgrave is up to."

"And these 'less than upstanding' people are just going to volunteer this information?" Tox asked.

Chat answered. "Having Nathan Bishop owe you a favor is good incentive."

Nathan crossed his arms across his chest. "I'm willing to work in a gray area here because we need to know Musgrave's interest in Cam, and we need to know now. Because if it's connected to Miguel Ramirez's disappearance—"

"Then Cam's cover has been blown," Ren stated.

"Exactly," Nathan confirmed. "At this point, all we know is that Musgrave hired a local security firm and that Cam spotted their car on three separate occasions. The job was terminated the day Cam went to New York."

"That's two coincidences too many," Tox said.

"I agree." Nathan tapped the spine of the journal on the table. "But until we get more intel, we can't proceed."

Chat steepled his fingers. "I'm assuming you have a plan."

"More than one, depending on how things play out over the next couple of days." Nathan spun his chair slightly to face Tox."Is your brother in the States?"

Tox's twin brother Miles was a fixer who worked for everyone from underworld figures to politicians. He operated using the alias Caleb Cain. Despite a dark past, Miles had proved very helpful to the team.

"New York. He's there for a couple of weeks for a job." Tox held up a hand. "I don't ask."

"Good. I may need a favor." Nathan turned to Twitch. "Any word on Finn?"

"I've contacted him through the usual channels, but so far, nothing."

"We could use his input."

"I'll keep trying, but you know Finn." Twitch finished quietly, "He's impossible to reach."

CHAPTER SIXTEEN

Belgrade, Serbia
December 3

Finn McIntyre leaned against the wall in the fetid alley, hidden behind a stack of crates. He took a hit of a joint and blew the smoke toward the black sky. A rat scurried across his boot. He checked his watch, listened. Nothing yet.

In twenty minutes Leonard Pippen, the CIA officer embedded with the U.S. embassy as a cultural attache, was due to meet Milo Sivik at the back door of the bar across from where he stood. Pippen was planning on making Milo an informant.

Plans change.

Milo Sivik was the worst kind of scum, a pedophile, a rapist, a trafficker. Pippen was willing to overlook those transgressions because Milo had access to a very big fish—his cousin Hugo was high up in Gabriel Lorca's drug cartel, and the CIA needed intel.

In his three years working as a NOC officer for the CIA, Finn had seen a lot of bad, had done a lot of bad. Operating undercover as an enforcer, he executed Gabriel Lorca's orders with brutal efficiency. But this, *this* he could not abide. He could not work for an agency that paid money to and overlooked the crimes of Milo Sivik. Yeah, he knew all about the greater good.

Fuck the greater good.

A tin can went clanking down the alley. Finn tossed the joint and poked his head around the crate. A shadowed figure moved toward him. Milo always arrived early, wary of an ambush. Short and round, Milo lured children by dressing as a clown. As a result, he always smelled of grease paint and candy. The smell made Finn sick. Everything about Milo made him sick.

Finn whistled, and Milo spun around to face him. He started for his gun, then relaxed when Finn stepped under a low-hanging light.

"Jesus, Scarface, you scared the shit out of me," Milo snapped in a hushed voice.

Half of Finn's face had been ruined after an explosion while serving with his SEAL squad. Working in the cartels, he had been called Scarface in a dozen different languages.

"What are you doing back here, Milo?" Finn asked.

"Just passing by. Thought I'd grab a beer before I go home." Milo thumbed over his shoulder toward the back door to the pub.

"Looks like you're meeting someone." Finn stepped forward.

"Nope. Just taking a shortcut." Milo shot a nervous glance down the alley.

"Taking a shortcut or stopping for a beer? Which is it?" Finn prodded.

Between his cartel connections and his new CIA gig, Milo felt untouchable. "Maybe both. Maybe neither. It's not your business."

"Pippen isn't coming." Finn tipped his head to the end of the empty alley.

Milo's eyes grew comically wide. "You know? You're a fucking spook?"

"Not after today." Finn pulled the magnum from his holster and blew a hole in Milo Sivik's head. He stood over the body and gave it a kick. "Better than you deserve."

Headlights lit the scene, and Finn held up a hand to block the glare. He heard car doors open and footsteps. Even in silhouette, he recognized Gabriel Lorca.

"Scarface, you beat me to the punch." Lorca stood flanked by two lieutenants and two bodyguards.

Unsure how the situation would play out, Finn remained silent.

"Take his tongue." Lorca, Finn's current boss and the head of the largest drug cartel in Eastern Europe, instructed. "That's what we do with rats."

Finn knelt down and pulled a vicious-looking knife from his boot. With a deft slice, he cut Milo Sivik's tongue out and tossed the piece of pink flesh to the ground.

"I received word Milo was going to betray us." Lorca stared at the body, unmoved. "The CIA isn't the only one with moles."

Finn wiped the blood from the blade on his pant leg and sheathed the knife.

"I arranged for two people to learn that information." Lorca withdrew his weapon and screwed on the suppressor. "You." He pointed the gun at Finn. "And you." He turned the weapon on the man at his side and pulled the trigger. Lorca turned back to Finn. "You were the one who acted."

Lorca holstered his gun and held his gloved hand out to Finn. "Thank you, my friend. Your loyalty will be rewarded."

"Thank you, el Jefe." Finn shook Lorca's hand.

"What do you need? Money? A car? Name it." Lorca stepped past the body and stood with Finn.

"I need time," Finn said.

"Explain," Lorca insisted.

"My girlfriend is pregnant. I want to go to Mexico City to be with her," Finn lied smoothly.

Lorca nodded. "You love this woman."

"Yes. Very much."

"Good. That's good. Come back when you're ready. I owe you." Lorca met Finn's gaze. "That's no small thing."

"Thank you, el Jefe. You're very generous." Finn turned and strode down the alley at an even pace, walking out of a world where the villain rewarded him for doing the honorable thing, and the heroes would punish him.

Just as he was about to reach the street, Lorca called out to him. "Did I kill the right man?"

Finn turned around and, after a moment, replied, "I hope so."

CHAPTER SEVENTEEN

Miramar, Mallorca
December 3

Cam entered the villa salty, itchy, and exhausted. A butler met him in the front hall with instructions to change and meet Miss March on the east patio. Cam lumbered past the grand staircase that bisected the central gallery and wandered back toward his assigned quarters on the main floor. He mapped the floor plan as he moved through the home, noting the large living room with a portrait of Gemini, standing with her head turned in profile, wearing a strapless black gown. The painting bore a striking resemblance to Sargeant's Portrait of Madame X. He passed a library, solarium, and billiards room before crossing into the more utilitarian section of the house, noting a storage room, a catering kitchen, a mudroom, and servants' quarters. In his bedroom, he spotted the clothing laid out on the bed and brushed past it without a second look. No one had dressed him since he was a small boy. Opening the bathroom door, he flashed to the memory of Gemini March floating up out of the pool and across the room like a goddess in an Olympian palace.

On paper, it was the sexiest thing most men could imagine. Why it left him feeling decidedly *turned off*, he had no idea. He stepped into the massive spa and had to admit, even in his wildest imagination, he couldn't have conjured such a place. Everything from the walls to the counters to the floor was marble, iridescent grey with subtle veins of gold. Inspired by the region's Turkish-style baths, the rib-vaulted ceiling and built-in benches that ran across the wall were reminiscent of a lavish hammam. After that, the twenty-first century took charge. From the steam room to the soaking tub, Cam could have lived in this room and been a very happy man.

He stepped into the open jetted shower and scrubbed the day from his body. As the lather ran down, his thoughts wandered to the woman from the ocean. He touched his tender eye, relieved she hadn't blackened it. She had punched him, kicked him, puked on him, and flipped him off. Yet, when he pictured those damn pink toes and the desperation with which she had clung to his back as he swam them to safety, well, the shower took a bit longer than planned.

With a towel low on his hips, Cam paused at the ensemble on the bed, a cream linen suit, blue button-down, and woven loafers. He huffed. *Ensemble.* That's precisely what it was. Without a second thought, he moved to the closet and retrieved a pair of dark wash jeans and a long-sleeved gray T-shirt. He knew how to handle Gemini March, and he'd be goddamned if someone tried to dress him like he was a toddler getting ready for school.

Miguel Ramirez was a yes-man. He did what he was told when he was told. But the one thing Miguel Ramirez and Camilo Canto had in common: nobody told them what to do in the bedroom. Ever.

Thirty minutes later—and twenty minutes after he was instructed to arrive—Miguel Ramirez sauntered barefoot onto the east patio. The elegant space was surrounded by a waist-high limestone balustrade that in the spring would be obscured by vines bursting with gem-colored blooms. To his right, a path opened to the pool and an expansive, impeccably manicured lawn. A mirroring walkway on the left led to the front of the villa. And in the center, Gemini March sat at a round glass table laden with fresh fruit, cheeses, a Spanish-style baguette called pan de barra, and a whole lobster sitting atop a steaming bowl of paella.

Cam noted Gemini's look of disapproval at his clothing before her face morphed into a cover-girl air of pleasure and seduction. She looked like she wanted to eat *him* for dinner and knew exactly where she wanted to start.

"Hello again, Miguel." She plucked a strawberry from the fruit plate and made a show of taking a bite.

Cam strode to the table, took a seat, and began filling a plate, taking mouthfuls of food directly from the platters as he loaded up. Behind him, a servant appeared with a wine bucket.

"Champagne?" Gemini nodded to her glass, and the young man filled it with the Roederer Cristal Rosé.

"Beer," he commanded, mouth full.

She stiffened but nodded to the servant, who hurried off.

"So... I imagine you have questions." Gemini toyed with her champagne flute.

Cam merely shrugged. "What's to question? A job, a nice place to stay." He met her gaze then as he cracked a lobster claw with both hands. "You."

She paused a strawberry at her full bottom lip. "Aren't you wondering why you?"

Cam extracted the claw meat and ate it in one bite. Then he sucked the juice from the pad of his thumb as he shamelessly stared at her flawless breasts beneath turquoise silk that failed to mask her pleasure at his perusal. "No."

She shivered at his confident reply. "That night on Ibiza was…" She searched for one word that could accurately describe their encounter. When she couldn't find one, she settled on "unforgettable."

He met Gemini's gaze then, knowing exactly when to play into her hand. "Yes, it was."

"What were you doing in the club that night? Who were you waiting for?"

Cam chewed thoughtfully. Then his golden eyes met hers with a predatory gaze. "You."

Her full lips tipped. "Right answer."

She plucked a mussel from the paella and fingered the morsel in the shell. Gemini March was not yet willing to cede control. "I'm eager to see if the present is as satisfying as the memory, but our reunion must be postponed."

The news that delayed their rekindling excited her. Cam waited, slowly chewing his food.

"I have been selected as one of *Couture Magazine's* Most Beautiful People on Earth. It's a distinction I've wanted for three years, and it's not something one declines." She scanned his body. "No matter how tempting the reason."

"They chose correctly."

"Thank you, Miguel. I don't fish for compliments. They simply jump out of the water and land in my lap. But it's nice to hear your lover finds you desirable."

Cam met her gaze. "*Desirable* isn't the word I would use."

Gemini flushed from her cleavage to her ears. "I leave tomorrow morning. I'll be gone for four days. But we have tonight."

Cam stood and rounded the small table. Towering over her, he ran the back of one finger down her cheek. "I'm not fully recovered from the drugs, but I have many ways to bring you pleasure we have yet to explore. Tonight will be for you, *querida*."

He held his hand flat, and she slipped hers into his palm. Banishing every shred of Camilo Canto from his mind, Miguel Ramirez led her into the bedroom.

CHAPTER EIGHTEEN

Miramar, Mallorca
December 4

A soft knock preceded the door's opening, and Cam lifted his head from the intoxicating pillow to spy a young man in black trousers and a short white jacket holding a breakfast tray.

"Good morning, sir."

Cam hadn't been asleep, but he sat up and stretched. After leaving Gemini, he had gone straight to his room, mapping out scenarios and exploring possible ways to contact his team. More than once, his thoughts had strayed to the woman he had pulled from the ocean. Everything about her rescue had been painful and unappealing, and yet, something about her—that strange mix of feistiness and compliance made his blood pound. As quickly as the images appeared, he dismissed them. More pressing issues were at hand.

"English?" Cam questioned.

"Sí. Yes," the boy corrected himself. "Mr. March insists on English."

"Well, good morning then," Cam said.

"I have the breakfast, and I will clean the room while you dress." He gestured with his head toward the bathroom.

Cam signaled his agreement by throwing back the covers and swinging his long legs over the side of the bed. "What's your name?"

"Tomás."

Cam rubbed a hand down his face. "You're straightening the room? There are maids all over the place."

Tomás busied himself, setting the tray laden with fresh fruit and pastries on a table by the doors leading out to the terrace. "Miss Gemini," he mumbled, "she doesn't want the women in the room."

Cam rolled his eyes and pushed to his feet. "All right then."

As he reached for the bathroom doors, Tomás added, "Mr. March will be ready to leave at noon. You are to meet him in the front hall."

Without turning back, Cam acknowledged, "Thanks, Tomás."

Cam started the shower and surveyed his surroundings. The retractable wall was closed, but he could see the pool and property beyond through the large windows. At the edge of his sightline, he could just make out the trunk of a limousine, heavy with luggage. He blew out a sigh of relief.

Gemini March was trying to master him, and her attitude strangled his arousal. For Cam, it wasn't about dominance and submission or winning and losing. When it came to sex, he wanted a partner, not an opponent. Gemini was a competitor, and she wasn't about to concede defeat in this war of wills. The thing she failed to realize was that Cam wasn't even on the battlefield.

He had been granted a four-day reprieve from her seduction. When the time came, he would play his part. Until then, he had ninety-six hours to figure out if there was more going on here than an overindulged woman in need of stud services. This was the part of the world where he had last had a lead on The Conductor. Cam didn't have the first clue where to begin, so he'd do what he always did. Pay attention.

Cam was dressed and ready when Atlas March sauntered into the front hall at ten past noon; another man, older and smartly dressed, was a half a pace behind. Atlas gave two firm claps and gestured to Cam. "Punctuality. Excellent, Miguel."

Cam remained impassive. Working for his former employer, Dario Sava, the penalty for tardiness was a beating, usually administered by him. Men were never late twice.

"Miguel," Atlas continued, "this is Joseph Nabeel, my second in command. You will defer to him in all matters."

Cam gave an abrupt nod in acknowledgment.

Atlas thrust an index finger into the air. "To the car."

Cam sat up front with the driver and observed the route as they cut across the island. The trill of a cell phone in the back of the town car broke the silence. Atlas listened to the caller and replied, "Wait until I get there."

He ended the call and spoke to Joseph. "A woman has been poking around in the caves near the shoreline. One of the guards thinks he's spotted her little boat again."

Atlas sent a text, then informed the driver of the change in destination, and the car continued on.

Their first stop was a low cliff overlooking a small cove about ten kilometers from the March villa. Another car pulled up behind them, and two mine security guards stepped out. Atlas exited the sedan, and Cam followed.

Atlas spoke as he walked to the overlook. "Joseph, in his infinite wisdom, has this shoreline regularly patrolled. March Mining owns the mineral rights all the way to the water. We want to guard our interests but also keep people safe. There is no limit to the dangers in those caves. Ah, Franco was right. There she is."

The small Zodiac puttered around an outcropping of rocks and headed toward the secluded shore. The woman piloting the craft gave a tentative look around, then focused on the beachhead. Suddenly, Cam recognized the woman he had pulled from the ocean the day before. Her slight limp as she pulled the boat to shore confirmed it.

Atlas was nearly outraged at the sight. "That woman has returned." He raised a hand to the two guards flanking him, and both men withdrew their sidearms from their holsters.

In an uncharacteristically forward move, Cam raised a hand. "Sir, allow me. It is not necessary to shoo away a fly with a cannon."

Seemingly pleased with his initiative and the metaphor, Atlas extended his arm to allow Cam to impress him. "By all means, Miguel."

Cam knew the woman would not recognize him. She had been delirious, and her dive mask had been fogged. Moreover, when he had rescued her, he had been Cam, a charming, kind-hearted good Samaritan. Now he was Miguel, a callous, menacing enforcer. A man even Cam himself didn't recognize when he looked in the mirror.

As he made his way down the sandy path, he knew the exact moment she spotted him. Before his very eyes, she transformed from a determined, competent professional into a naive, ditz. She spun her ponytail around the tip of her finger and turned in a slow circle as if lost.

When his feet hit the flat of the beach, she pretended to see him then, her face forming a comically exaggerated expression of relief. She waved both arms over her head like she was signaling a plane.

"Hello! Hello! Hola!!" She pronounced the "h" in *hola*. "Can you tell me how to get to Port de Sóller? I think I'm lost." She spun around again for good measure. Cam fought the urge to laugh. *Miguel*, however, was not amused.

She stopped her twirl and faced him. Her cocoa-colored eyes widened, and she took a half-step back. Cam was used to the kaleidoscope of emotions swirling across her face—dread, apprehension, fear.

He walked over to the Zodiac and looked down, spying a professional-looking pack, a flashlight, a first-aid kit. The woman wasn't here to sunbathe.

Cam spun to face her. "This beach is restricted. Go. Now."

He watched as the eddy of emotions swirled and drained, leaving one: fear. It peeked out from behind her mask of self-assurance, but it was there.

"Okay, okay. Jeez. You guys aren't big on hospitality," she mumbled.

Cam stepped forward to match her retreat. He was a mere foot away when he explained, "Parts of the island are dangerous, chica." He touched the placket of her blouse, and she recoiled. "Now, thank me for keeping you safe, then go."

"Um," she hesitated.

He took a half step closer until they were toe-to-toe.

"You heard me," he said.

"Thank you?" she squeaked.

"You're welcome, mouse. Now go before a cat comes and eats you."

Without a word, she spun on her heel, hurried to the Zodiac, and shoved it into the water. She attempted poise, but her fear had her stumbling as she threw herself into the boat. As she piloted out of the bay, she turned back to Cam and yelled her thanks again—while flipping him the bird.

For the second time.

The March Mining operation was nestled deep in the Tramuntana mountains in the northern part of Mallorca. The main office was in a

Mediterranean-style building on a tree-lined street in Palma. At the actual site, a renovated farmhouse served as the foreman's home base and business office. Low grass, brown for the winter, blew gently around the quaint structure. A blanket of dormant poppy fields lay in the distance. Only the stacked interlocking "M"s above the door, the March Mining logo, gave any indication this was a place of business.

The sedan coasted to a stop in a paved parking area, and Atlas, Cam, and Joseph emerged.

Men milled about, some eating lunch, some laughing and talking on a smoke break. Two Andalusian mares frolicked in the field, the sounds of machinery merely a distant grumble. It was... idyllic.

Cam had a hard time imagining anything nefarious going on in this utopia. Hell, he had a hard time imagining a mining operation here. When he thought of mines, he pictured the coal mines from his high school history classes—men with dirty faces and troubling coughs pushing coal carts and riding in deathtrap elevators deep into poorly ventilated shafts. This place was a pair of animated birds away from mining paradise.

A hundred yards behind the farmhouse office, the entrance to the mine was large and well lit. Broad stairs led into a cavernous mouth, and men filtered in and out in gray coveralls with white helmets. Off in the distance, terraced land led down to an open quarry.

Cam was taking it all in when Atlas slapped a hand on the roof of the car and announced, "Welcome to March Mining."

Under normal circumstances, Miguel Ramirez would remain silent, perhaps acknowledge the declaration with a nod, but Cam sensed Atlas March's need for validation, so he spoke up. "Very good."

Puffing at the affirmation, Atlas continued. "Just wait, Miguel. There's more to see. Much, much more."

Entering the converted farmhouse, Cam was impressed with the state-of-the-art equipment. One section was set up to oversee health and safety; the mines were outfitted with security cameras, emergency tunnels, and devices to monitor oxygen and carbon dioxide levels. Another area was administrative, and another—based on the satellite imagery of shipping and trucking routes—looked like logistics.

Atlas stopped to question something he saw on a monitor, and Joseph indicated Cam should move to another area. "Security is this way." They moved into a large room that Cam imagined must have once been a dining room. The setup was equally impressive. Two men sat at L-shaped desks with three monitors on each.

Joseph continued the tour. "Security cameras are located at various checkpoints in the tunnel systems. There are also emergency phones and safety boxes throughout, containing everything from first aid kits to fire extinguishers. If a box is opened, a notification comes here, and the foreman dispatches security to investigate."

Cam listened along. Joseph gave him a probing look. "I don't imagine you have any experience with this sort of thing."

"I do," Cam countered. "Señor Sava's compound was well-guarded. I handled security when it was required."

"I see." Joseph nodded, impressed. "I get the feeling many of your talents have yet to be revealed."

Before Cam could contemplate the comment, Atlas joined them. "Ready to tour the mines?"

"Yes," Cam replied.

Atlas led them into the mouth of the mine, and again Cam marveled at the clean, bright space. As if reading his thoughts, Atlas remarked. "It gets a bit more claustrophobic the farther we go. Some of the tunnels are quite narrow."

They stepped into an elevator just slightly smaller than a standard building elevator and descended. "You can walk this way as well; the tunnels lower in elevation as they move away from the mountains. The elevator is just faster." Atlas commented.

Cam carefully mapped the maze they walked as Atlas and Joseph pointed out oxygen saturation devices and security cameras as well as the safety boxes and emergency phones Joseph had mentioned earlier. Atlas spoke with pride about ore extraction and new methods of transport. Cam couldn't muster the enthusiasm Atlas seemed to expect, but he rationalized that Miguel Ramirez was nothing if not inscrutable. Finally, they rounded a corner and arrived back at the elevator.

"Here we are." Atlas dusted off his hands. "So, Señor Ramirez, have I impressed you?"

"More than impressed," Cam replied.

"Excellent. Let's head back to the villa for a late lunch." Atlas clapped him on the back and walked into the elevator car, Joseph falling in step.

"Sir," Cam halted the men, holding the door open with one hand. "If it's all right with you, I'd like to stay and observe, maybe look around a bit."

Atlas grinned, "Of course, of course. Take all the time you need. Keep track of where you are; I don't want to discover you lost and starved in a week. To the left, toward the shore, are currently unused tunnels and storage. Keep to the right, and you'll see a lot of work."

Cam stood stoic as the elevator door slid closed and, like the smoke from a magician's flash paper, all that remained of Atlas March's presence was a cloud of expensive cologne.

Cam turned and headed left. Something he had seen on the tour had the hairs on the back of his neck standing up. He wound through empty shafts, passing a break room and a storage room that was actually a cave. They must have broken through into a cave system while excavating the mine. A few yards past the storage area, a tunnel was chained off. A sign hung from the middle:

No Entrar. Perill.

Do Not Enter. Danger.

Cam wouldn't have looked twice, but for the man he had seen look around carefully, then duck under the chain and disappear. Shielded by the break room door, their group had gone unnoticed by the man, but Cam had noticed him. Stepping over the barricade, Cam wandered through the empty tunnels until he came to a locked steel door, a digital keypad on the wall.

Turning back, he filed the information away, made note to keep an eye on that area, and continued exploring the mine. Hopefully, there were no more surprises.

CHAPTER NINETEEN

Sa Calobra, Mallorca
December 5

Evan had waited, bobbing in the bay behind an outcropping of rocks. When the men drove away and the guard who had reported her left to patrol another section of the shoreline, she stashed the Zodiac, grabbed her gear, and disappeared into the caves.

She would have thought familiarity with the confining space would have eased her irrational anxiety. Turns out, not the case. Knowing a pitch-black stalactite cage lurked at the end of her path did little to soothe. Nevertheless, determined, she crawled through the last opening, yanking her canvas supply duffle behind her. Skirting a puddle, Evan settled next to what she had surmised was a small sealed ingress marked by one of the low stone stacks.

She tackled the marker first, a miniature snowman of limestone rocks melded by water and time. Separating the small middle piece from the base, Evan once again discovered two gold chain links. They could have been part of a substantial necklace or a chain from a lock. She carefully marked and bagged the pieces. Next, she addressed the closed hole in the cave wall. After taking photographs and measurements, Evan withdrew a small geological hammer from the duffle and gave the surface an experimental tap. She brushed away the detritus, checking for more chain links or other concealed objects, and continued.

———————— ◆ ————————

Cam turned down another dark hall and found himself back in the old storage room. Well, not a room but a cave. The mine shafts occasionally intersected with the dozens of cave systems that crisscrossed the island. Cam stifled a shudder. He wasn't claustrophobic or afraid of the dark, but this dank space with rows of limestone formations that dripped like rabid jaws was downright creepy. He mapped the room's layout, the one egress, and items of note. Through experience, he knew that anything could have significance, from the crate marked "demolition" sitting by the entrance to the small stack of rocks by the back wall.

Out-of-commission coal carts lined one wall like errant grocery carts in a parking lot. The men probably used them to transport heavy equipment then simply sent them careening across the room when they were finished. Tools and crates were stacked against the other wall. A battery-powered lantern flickered and hummed. He cocked his head; there was another sound. It was a nearly inaudible *tap tap tap* emanating from the far corner. Grabbing the lantern by its mangled wire handle, he moved closer to investigate. *There.* Setting the light closer, he could just make out a deviation in the surface of the wall, a sealed opening. *Tap tap tap.* There was that sound, clearly man-made. Was someone trapped? Were those faint taps the last effort of an oxygen-deprived man?

Cam walked the two steps to the tools lining the adjacent wall without further forethought and grabbed a sledgehammer.

——————— ◆ ———————

Evan was examining what appeared to be a symbol scratched into the side of the opening when *wham*. She was thrown backward as a blow from the other side of the wall crashed through the rock, a lethal sledgehammer stopping just shy of her chin. She scrambled back on her backside and the heels of her hands, her thoughts too scattered to form a plan. Through the settling dust, a face emerged, distinctive golden eyes scanning the confined space. Familiar golden eyes. This was the bully who had chased her from the beach—the gorgeous bully who had chased her from the beach. She sorted through the mosaic of emotions forming in her mind: outrage, apprehension, unease. She settled on anger.

"What the hell do you think you're doing?" Evan looked at the man who had so frightened her earlier. He looked... dangerous.

"I could ask you the same thing, chica. This is private property." The man spoke with a heavy accent, his callous persona apparent. His astonishing eyes traveled a path down her body and settled on the spot where her pant leg had slid up above her boot, revealing her bandaged injury. She pushed the fabric down to cover it.

"I'm an archaeologist. You're disturbing a dig site." She protested.

"You're a trespasser. You're in the March Copper Mine," he growled.

"This is part of the mine?" Evan questioned.

"March Copper Mine," he repeated.

"I see. Well, um, I better not mess with it, then." She dusted off her pants and turned to leave.

"You mean you will come back when no one is around," he challenged.

Evan spun to face him. "These caves are public land. Where does the mine start?"

The man gestured over his shoulder, then did another tour of her body as she stood. "What are you doing down here, *ratoncita*?"

She blanched at the insult, *little mouse*. "As I said before, I'm an archaeologist, here with a team. I'm due to meet them very soon."

"This team? They are in the next cave? Or waiting for you on the beach? Or did the little mouse smell a treat and go off on her own? Because that would be a big mistake."

"I'm not afraid of you," she said.

"Then you have made two mistakes," he said.

Evan took a moment to assess his threat, his words so at odds with his face. He looked boyish and handsome, poking his head through the hole he had made. A leering smile revealed straight, white teeth, a curl of dark hair artfully flopped on his forehead.

And those eyes. They were the color of wheat.

She silently cautioned herself to look away before she got lost in their mesmerizing depths. She chided herself for getting drawn in by his looks. Satan was once God's most beautiful angel.

When it was clear she wasn't going to respond, the man goaded her further. "What did you find, chica? Buried gold? A mummy's tomb? Was there a treasure map etched on the wall?"

"I won't really know since you took a wrecking ball to it." She gestured to the debris below his head.

"Hold that thought." He backed out of the aperture, and a moment later, the sledgehammer was back, obliterating the entire sealed-off entrance.

He shouldered through the rocks and debris and stood to his full height, a head above Evan's five-six. When he met her gaze, Evan had the strangest sensation. Maybe it was his oddly guarded expression; perhaps it was his marigold eyes. Whatever it was, she sensed a strange duality in this man. He loomed above her, yet the action seemed more protective than threatening. Something about him confused her.

As if sensing her assessment, he stepped back. And just like that, the warmth she had felt was gone, not from the distance but from a cold aura that suddenly seemed to blanket him. She reflexively glanced over her shoulder.

"We are alone, puta."

Whore. The word hit her like a slap.

"Don't call me that." Her gaze was steady, her tone implacable.

He didn't acknowledge her, but his sudden interest in the cave wall told her that her message had been received.

"The cave on the other side of that wall where you came from. I'd like to look at it," Evan explained.

"What's it worth to you, chica?" he asked.

"I don't have any money." Evan fisted her trembling hands and stood her ground

"I don't need money," he said.

"What then?" Her eyes widened as he adjusted his crotch. "I won't do that either."

"You sure? I'll show you a good time. I promise." He leered at her.

"I'm sure. Very sure. Just… I'm going to go. Let's just forget this ever happened." She backed away.

"I don't know, little mouse. You're very memorable."

"Yeah, well, try."

"This little mouse hunt is a secret, yes?" He kicked the small marker at his feet.

"Don't do that!" she scolded.

He kicked it again. "Why not?"

The usual caution that would have tempered her words was absent as she pulled him away from the rocks by his forearm. "I'm not sure what I've found. It certainly wasn't what I was looking for."

"This little stack of rocks points the way to your fortune?" he asked.

She knelt by the small formation. "No. It doesn't, but I estimate these little stacks were created over five hundred years ago. And I doubt they were just put here for decoration."

He gave a low whistle. "How do you figure? Did you do some fancy doctor test?"

"I did some fancy sixth-grade math. Stalagmites grow at a rate of about one-half millimeter per year. That little stack had a one-foot formation on top of it." She extended her hand in a simple-as-that gesture.

"Did I knock it off with the sledgehammer?" he asked.

Evan suddenly found the far corners of the cave fascinating. "No, uh, I did it. I fell and knocked it off when I was here the last time."

His smile lit the cave. "So, I'm not the only bull in the glass shop around here."

Her lips lifted reluctantly. "Apparently not."

"What are these rock blobs anyway?" He toed the nearest one.

"I don't know. It's a marker of some kind," she said.

"Well, I have some good news for you."

"Oh, yeah?" Evan replied, curious.

He just stared, his gaze piercing as though he could see all her secrets. She looked away, shuttering the damn metaphorical windows to her soul. When she looked up again, Evan was met with an unexpected sight. The mystery man was smiling.

"There's another," he declared. "In the storage area." He thumbed over his shoulder toward the cave from which he had come.

"Another marker?" she clarified.

"Sí."

Evan weighed her options. It wasn't as though looking in the next room would make them any more alone. "Can you show me?"

He nodded once.

"I'm Evan, by the way. Evan Cole." She had read somewhere that telling your captor your name was important; it humanized you. Not that this guy was a serial killer or anything, but better safe than sorry and all that.

When he didn't reply, she prompted, "And you are?"

"Nadie."

"Nadie?" she repeated.

"It means nobody. I'm nobody." He turned to the small opening,

"Well, that's not true. If anything, you're two people," she grumbled.

He spun around and faced her then, his eyes two yellow flames.

Cam quickly schooled his expression, but his rage still burned. Rage directed at himself. His undercover abilities were exceptional; his facility for crawling into the skin of another persona was nothing less than extraordinary. This woman, with her throwaway comment, had shaken his confidence.

Why had he even volunteered to show her the stack of stones in the first place? He pushed everything he was feeling out of his mind and slammed the door.

He gestured to the opening.

Seeing her wary expression, Cam took a step toward her, his Miguel Ramirez persona fully engaged. "Chica, if I wanted to force you, I could do it right here just as easily."

She paled at the remark and retreated. Unaffected by her distress, he tapped the face of his watch. "Come on. Let's go. El perro que no camina, no encuentra el hueso. The dog who doesn't walk doesn't find the bone."

Evan seemed to gather herself. She moved toward the opening. "That's very folksy."

"My abuela." He paused for a moment, remembering his grandmother swatting him off the couch when she would visit. "It's an old Chilean proverb."

She met his gaze with determination in her eyes. Then she dropped to her knees next to the hole he had bulldozed.

"You first," she commanded.

Cam stepped in front of her kneeling form, then he turned and ducked his head through the opening, the image of her sinking down before him stilting his movements.

Cam scolded himself for injecting part of Cam's reality—his grandmother's adage—into Miguel's legend, but he shook it off. He scanned the storage cave and found the little stack of rocks he had noted and dismissed earlier just as a cinnamon-colored ponytail popped through the ingress. When he rescued her from the stingray, he hadn't been able to discern her hair or eye color. The fogged mask hid her face, and when she finally ripped off the cap, her hair was wet and matted. On the beach, he was more concerned with impressing Atlas March than inspecting this woman. Today he noted her hair was a warm russet, her eyes, a soft, light brown that nearly matched her hair. It suited her. Despite her clumsiness and their inauspicious encounters to date, something about this woman was centered. She was comfortable in her own skin, something Cam hadn't felt in years.

She stood dusting off her cargo pants and T-shirt, and Cam was momentarily caught up in the way her hands moved across her body. It was a practical, practiced motion, yet Cam found the action of her palms traveling over the hills of her breasts and around the cinch of her waist oddly erotic. The sexiest thing about this woman was her complete lack of awareness of her innate sensuality. He fisted his palms. Miguel would invade her personal space, hit on her, give an unwelcome squeeze to her ass. He took half a step toward her, and, for the first time in the three years he had assumed the identity of Miguel Ramirez, he couldn't do it. *Cam* couldn't do it.

He was jarred from further introspection by the clap of her hands.

"Well?" She tapped the face of her watch, mimicking his action from a moment ago. Cam's gaze moved to Evan's hands. They were small, the nails unpolished. She wore no jewelry. Like the rest of her body, her hands were beautiful unadorned.

"Well?" he repeated.

"The marker?" She blew a lock of hair upwards off of her face, exasperated.

"Oh, right. Over here." He moved to the right of the opening he had created with the sledgehammer. There, in the corner, was another pile of rocks. Like the others, they were fused by the eroding limestone.

"I'm surprised you even noticed this," she commented.

"I notice everything." He scanned her body, observed her blush. She rubbed down the goosebumps on her arms. Cam wanted to raise them again. He wanted to lick the nook of her neck, leave a mark of possession.

"Do the mines and caves interconnect throughout?" she asked.

"I've only just started exploring the mines. My job is new. From what I've seen, yes. I imagine the miners use the caves as natural tunnels. As the mine shafts move higher into the mountains, there are probably fewer caves," he noted.

She assessed him, a bit of suspicion in her cocoa eyes. "You know a lot about geology for a miner."

Cam met her gaze. "I know a lot about a lot. And I'm not a miner."

"Then what are you doing down here?" she questioned.

"Security," he replied.

She blanched.

"Don't worry. You can look for your treasure. My job does not include chasing mice." He smirked.

She was apparently so relieved at his declaration, she ignored the insult. "Thank you."

"What's so interesting about piles of rock?"

She waved for him to follow her to the marker in the corner. Evan knelt beside the pile. Using a small tool, she separated two stones, revealing a bit of metal embedded in the center.

"What is that?" he asked.

"I'm not sure. Some kind of links from a chain. All the formations have two of these pieces set between the second and third rock in the stack." She removed the pieces and held them in her open palm.

Cam sat on his haunches beside her and ran his index finger over the two connected, rectangular links. "Looks like gold."

Cam's finger strayed to her skin. Evan closed her fist, but Cam didn't miss her shiver at his touch.

She cleared her throat and stood. "I agree, but I'll need to test them. Thank you for showing me. I'll check with the mine executives if my team thinks this warrants further investigation."

She was adorable. Did she really think he was buying that load of crap? She wasn't going to get permission from the March Mining higher-ups; she was trying to get rid of him. Cam forced his face to neutral and played along. "The executives are in Palma. I'm sure you can figure out how to get in touch."

She nodded, half-listening, her mind no doubt already racing with plans for her search. He threw her a bone. "The mine is open until midnight when the last shift leaves and reopens at 6 a.m., but the executives in Palma keep regular hours."

"All right." She extended a shaky hand. "Thank you. It was nice to meet you."

When he didn't take it, she turned and scurried through the hole they had entered. Cam almost laughed. She really did look like a little mouse, and just like the shy creature, she would wait until no one was around to sniff out a prize.

He knew he shouldn't get involved, but he had four days until Gemini March returned, and he did need to map these mines. He pictured Evan's angelic face with those wide eyes the color of chestnuts, full pink lips, and her blush of innocence. Then he envisioned his alter ego, Miguel Ramirez spending hours and hours alone with her, making lewd comments and treating her like every other woman he encountered.

Cam rearranged some crates to hide the hole and returned the sledgehammer to the row of tools against the far wall. When he was satisfied the room looked relatively undisturbed, he walked to a free-standing wooden closet the men had brought in to use as a pantry, took a deep breath, and plowed his fist through the door.

CHAPTER TWENTY

Washington, DC
December 5

Harlan Musgrave stared out the front window of his Capitol Hill brownstone. A stretch limousine idled at the curb. He turned and grabbed his overcoat, muttering, "Fucking Federov. Why can't he just show up in an Escalade like a normal mobster?"

Musgrave knew better than to keep the man waiting. Aleksi Federov was soft-spoken with a kind smile, but the stories of his brutality were well-known in the criminal underworld. Federov never spoke of the Bratva, but Musgrave had met him once at his home gym and seen the star tattoos that marked his shoulders, designating him not only as a *Vor* but as the head of a family.

Lifting his collar against the biting cold, Musgrave hurried down the steps and into the limo. It pulled away from the curb as he shut the door.

Federov was in his late fifties, with thick, dark hair, a lantern jaw, and the physique of a much younger man. Under a cashmere overcoat with a fur collar, he wore a custom three-piece, pin-striped suit. A diamond clip held his purple tie in place. The man did like a bit of flash.

"Our nation's capital during the holidays, is there a more beautiful city?"

Federov always started with small talk. It was cultural. He could be planning to put a bullet in a man's brain, but he would always ask about family or the weather first.

"Your wife is well?" Federov inquired.

"She's in Florida. Our daughter just had a baby." Musgrave replied.

"Congratulations." Federov said, then repeated it in Russian, "*Pozdravleniya.*"

They drove down Constitution Avenue while Federov poured vodka into two large shot glasses and passed one to Musgrave. The Russian toasted the air and downed the shot. Musgrave followed suit.

"You need a man. I have a man," Federov said.

"It's a very delicate matter," Musgrave insisted.

"He's a specialist." The Russian poured himself another.

"In what?" Musgrave asked.

"Delicate matters."

Federov spoke in clipped Russian to his driver. The car turned onto 16th Street and pulled smoothly up to the curb in front of the Hay-Adams hotel.

Before the doorman could approach, a debonair man walked out of the lobby and across the covered portico. Musgrave noted that the driver had stepped out to open the car door, a courtesy he had not been afforded. The man slipped smoothly into the opposing seat and shook Federov's hand.

"Aleksi, it's been a while," the man said.

"Two years at least. You are well, I take it?" Federov replied.

Musgrave bit his cheek to endure the pleasantries.

"Harlan," Federov brought him into the conversation. "This is Caleb Cain. Cain, the honorable Senator Harlan Musgrave."

Federov was clearly enjoying Musgrave's discomfort. Caleb Cain, however, revealed nothing. Stifling his annoyance at the use of his name and title, Musgrave extended his hand.

"Senator. Your reputation precedes you." Cain spoke without inflection.

Musgrave chose to take the words as a compliment, though he wasn't quite sure. He cut to the chase. "There is an item I need to acquire."

"Not a problem." Cain sipped the vodka Federov handed him.

Musgrave retrieved some of his bravado. "Son, it's not snatching a necktie from Macy's."

It was Federov who replied. "Do you see this ring?" The mobster extended his hand to reveal a massive jeweled pinky ring Musgrave had never noticed before. "It traces back to the Romanovs. It was stolen from my family by the Bolsheviks over a hundred years ago. Cain reacquired it for me." He took a long swallow of his drink. "From the Hermitage."

Musgrave felt his eyes bug out. "Oh, well, all right then. Sounds like you're the fellow I need for this job."

The limo stopped again in front of a lavish Russian restaurant in Dupont Circle. "I have another meeting. I'll leave you two to hash out the details." Federov slipped out of the car.

Aleksi Federov entered the over-decorated restaurant and nodded to the hostess. He made his way to the back of the room, acknowledging a few patrons as he wound through tables covered in red brocade and topped with gold candelabra. In the far corner, he parted a burgundy velvet curtain. Federov entered a private dining area with a semicircular booth and richly upholstered chairs where Nathan Bishop sat with a colleague so big he could barely fit in the space. Federov took the remaining seat. Nathan pulled a device from his ear, but the big man continued to listen to the conversation in the limousine.

Federov pulled the imposing ring off his pinky and tossed it on the table. "Dime store crap is turning my finger green."

"The Hermitage was a nice touch," Nathan smirked.

"My family descended from the Romanovs, *please*." Federov released a booming laugh. "I almost choked on my drink. The closest the Federovs ever came to the Winter Palace was to clean the shit in the street." Federov grew serious. "Before your father died, I owed him a favor. He may have been a *svoloch*, but he settled his debts." Federov normally wouldn't insult a father to his son, but he knew Nathan Bishop agreed that his old man was a bastard.

"Thank you," Nathan replied.

Federov waived the gratitude away. "In this circumstance, we have mutual interests. Musgrave screwed me on a piece of interstate commerce legislation. He thinks I don't know, or he thinks he's untouchable. Both presumptions are false."

Nathan stood with the Russian and extended his hand. "I don't foresee our interests aligning again."

Federov returned the gesture. "No, probably not."

Forty-five minutes later, Miles Buchanan, a.k.a. Caleb Cain, entered the alcove. Tox stood and greeted his twin brother with a hug before Miles took the seat Aleksi Federov had vacated.

Tox forked a pierogi. "Musgrave is after the journal and the flash drive. So now we know The Conductor's behind this. And that he has Cam."

"Maybe." Nathan was pensive.

"What's maybe?" Tox asked.

"The Conductor operates in the shadows, behind the scenes," Nathan said. "Nobody in law enforcement even thinks he exists."

Miles leaned forward. "You think The Conductor has manipulated someone into doing his dirty work."

Nathan looked at both men. "I think it's a distinct possibility, yes."

Tox slid his plate to the side. "The Conductor is uniquely positioned to know people who could be looking for Miguel Ramirez, for good or bad."

Nathan agreed, "Hopefully, Cam's handler can shed some light on who those people are. I think it's a safe assumption that The Conductor isn't going to draw attention or do anything to Cam until he has that journal and is free and clear from any blowback."

Miles knocked on the table. "I'll just have to take my time stealing it then."

CHAPTER TWENTY-ONE

Sa Calobra, Mallorca
December 6

The beam from the light on her helmet illuminated the small opening in the wall, and Evan crawled through. The cave used for storage by the March Mining Company was dark and silent. Before hungry predators and creepy crawlies could find their way into her imagination, she moved to the corner where Miguel had pointed out the marker. She came down beside it and pulled the small tactical flashlight from the side pocket of her cargo pants.

"La mina esta tancada." *The mine is closed.*

Evan shrieked and fell on her backside beside the stack of rocks. The flashlight flew from her hand and rolled to a stop at the toe of a very large boot. The helmet tumbled from her head and fell by her knees, the beam landing on the golden-eyed man sitting casually on a crate in the opposite corner eating sunflower seeds.

Her relief at seeing him reduced her fury from boiling, but her humiliation kept it at a simmer.

"You scared the crap out of me," she whisper-shouted.

"Miguel," he added. "You scared the crap out of me, Miguel."

She replaced her helmet and nodded, running the beam of light up and down his big body. "You don't look like a Miguel." She stood and dusted off her clothes.

"What do I look like?"

"I don't know. Something more ominous. Santiago or Carlo." She snapped her fingers. "What's Spanish for jerk?" Evan tapped her chin.

Miguel just smirked. "I had a feeling you'd be back."

"Why does this concern you?"

He cracked the small shell with two fingers, extracting the seed and dropping the remains on the ground. "I was curious." He looked up at her. "Isn't that why you do what you do? Curiosity?"

"No, well, yes. I suppose so," she replied.

"It killed the cat, you know. Curiosity. So I guess the mouse is free to roam." He grinned.

Evan shot him a quelling look.

"You're back to investigate your little rock piles, yes?" Miguel asked.

"Yes. I've mapped the markers I've found, and I want to explore these internal caves and the connected mine tunnels. See if they lead somewhere. Any markings on the actual limestone have eroded. All I have to go on is the placement."

"I'll accompany you," he stated.

She started to protest, but he raised a big hand. "No, chica. These mines are dangerous. You cannot explore them alone."

"All right, but there's one condition." She pointed upward.

He rose from the crate, stalked toward her, and bent down to retrieve her flashlight. He adjusted the helmet on her head, then ran the back of his index finger down the line of her cheekbone.

To her surprise, Evan didn't flinch or recoil. Miguel's hand on her face felt... nice.

"The little mouse is making demands?" he murmured.

"Yes. And stop calling me that. I'm not a mouse." Evan lifted her chin and stood her ground.

"Don't insult the mice, chica. Mice are clever. They are persistent. They are experts at avoiding predators." His finger continued its path down the front of her shirt between her breasts, stopping at the button of her pants. "Maybe you're not a mouse after all. You're not so good at escaping me." His flaxen eyes sparkled with mischief.

She stepped back and gestured to the doorway to the room that led out into the mines. "Shall we?"

Evan knew she should be fearful of this haunting man, but something deep within her told her she could trust Miguel. *Like your instincts have been so reliable in the past.* She shook off her apprehension. She didn't have much choice.

"There is one condition," she repeated.

"And what's that?" he asked.

"Don't touch anything. And definitely don't take anything," Evan insisted.

Miguel just stared at her. After a good ten seconds, he simply said, "We will see."

For three hours, they wandered. Cam was enthralled by her focus and patience. They had only spoken briefly. Evan explained features of the caves and dropped factoids of interest. Cam was surprised to discover they were interesting. Or maybe it was just the woman pointing them out. She was stunning. Her hair and eyes were the identical pale brown, and when she was concentrating, her pink tongue peeked out and rested between bee-stung lips. The way her hands roved the bumps and valleys of the cave walls had him half hard—the way she held her neck and arched her back to ease the stiffness finished the job. She was thankfully oblivious to his arousal, speaking academically and pointing out various nocturnal threats they might encounter. Cam had bitten back a laugh. No beetle or snake could compare to the *nocturnal threats* he had faced in his career.

Cam had steered Evan away from the chained-off mine tunnel he had spotted when he toured the mines with Atlas and Joseph. Something told him a different kind of nocturnal threat lurked. An hour before dawn, they returned to the storage room where they had started. They hadn't found any other markers, but Evan had made note of a cluster of caves she wanted to explore the following night. As they entered, Cam noticed her slight limp had become more pronounced.

"You're injured?" he asked.

She looked down at her calf. "It's nothing. Stingray got me."

"That's not nothing. They can kill," Cam replied.

She brushed it off. "I was lucky, I guess. A good Samaritan helped me, and I was treated right away. No long-term damage. It's just a little sore."

He couldn't resist. "A good Samaritan?"

"Yes. Just a man who helped. Thank God it wasn't you on that beach. You would have watched me drown." Evan began organizing her pack.

Cam came up behind her. "I don't know, mouse. It depends on how you would have thanked me."

Evan stilled. "Let's just focus on the search."

Cam spotted a case of water in the corner of the room and grabbed two bottles. He handed Evan one and downed the other in one go.

"It was a waste of time," he said.

"No! It wasn't. Miguel, these caves guard their secrets. Have you ever done a jigsaw puzzle?"

"Sure." He shrugged.

"I mean a really challenging one. Like a thousand pieces?" she asked.

Cam's face was blank, but on the inside, he was bursting. He wanted to tell her how every Christmas Eve, his family in Miami would eat a big dinner then break out a new puzzle. His sisters competed throughout the year to see who could find the most difficult one, and the family would try to assemble the edge before bedtime. A sudden longing possessed him, an unbidden image flashing in his mind.

Evan in his family home, sitting next to him at the big puzzle table, his arm around the back of her chair distracting her while she searched for pieces.

"Well, anyway, it's super hard at the beginning. You look at this giant stack of pieces and think it will never be a picture. But slowly, you start to assemble it, and all of a sudden, everything makes sense. That's what this search is like—all these caves, all these puzzle pieces. There are markers and gold links and tunnels and tides. We've already clicked some pieces into place. We just need to keep at it."

"Tomorrow, bring food," he replied.

She laughed then. It was a great sound, hoarse and melodic. Cam wanted to hear it when he threw her onto a bed, and her naked body bounced on the mattress. Then he would wrap her legs around his waist and replace the laughter with shouts of pleasure. Shoving his hands in his pockets, he abruptly turned toward the door that led back to the mine. Evan would leave through the hole and out through the caves to the beach.

"See you tomorrow." He lifted a hand with his back to her and disappeared around the corner.

———————— ◆ ————————

Evan secured the Zodiac at the base of the dock. The beach was deserted as she crossed the dark sand and made her way up the grassy path to the finca. It was a bit of a hike, but Evan needed the quiet and the cool air to process her thoughts. No, she corrected. Process her *feelings*.

She was twenty-seven and in the fifth year of her Ph.D. program. She was a well-adjusted, healthy, heterosexual woman... who had not allowed a man to touch her sexually in nine years. It wasn't by conscious choice. After the incident in high school, any time a man... *argh*! She kicked a clump of high grass in frustration. Panic attacks had barred her from intimacy. Until Miguel.

What was it about this man? He was a thug, a pervert, an opportunist, and those were the flattering things about him. He could be a drug addict or a criminal. But when his hand ran down her cheek, or he touched the small of her back to guide her through a narrow passage, she seemed to melt into his touch.

She huffed. It wasn't as if he was reaching between her legs, and yet more than once, as they knelt to examine a cave wall or investigate a rock outcropping, she had fantasized about just that. An hour into their adventure, her thong was wet.

When she imagined a man with golden eyes, she pictured a predator, an evil beast. But Miguel's eyes were warm and inviting, like sunshine. When he looked at her, she wanted to thrust her fingers into that thick auburn hair and kiss the life out of him.

Her laughter split the silent morning. Evan rubbed her arms over her jacket. She knew she should scold herself for indulging her reverie, but she wouldn't. She had never *ever* had these feelings of desire, and she wanted to bathe in the sensation without question or rebuke.

When she arrived at the finca, she climbed the creaky staircase to her room. Quickly rinsing the dirt of the mines from her body, she donned an old T-shirt and crawled into bed. She found sleep just as the sun was peeking up over the horizon.

CHAPTER TWENTY-TWO

Sa Calobra, Mallorca
December 7

At just after one in the morning the next night, Cam entered the storeroom to a picnic. A smile broke over his face. Evan had spread a small hand towel on the ground and set out granola bars, dates, a wedge of local sheep's milk cheese, and…

"Almond Joy?" he grinned.

"It's my favorite candy bar. They actually sell them here. Plus," she tore open the wrapper and slid out the chocolate, "it's two little bars inside, so we can each have one."

Cam dropped to a catcher's stance and swiped his half. It was his favorite candy bar as well. He savored the chocolate and coconut, trying to remember when he had last had one.

"It's not a candlelit dinner in a dark restaurant, but it looks like you're trying to seduce me, mouse."

Evan scoffed. "Hardly."

Her mouth said the words, but her eyes said something else. Miguel Ramirez would have taken her without hesitation. Cam wanted to take her without hesitation. Yet, he hesitated. Why? The answer was so fucked up, he almost couldn't admit it to himself. He didn't want Miguel Ramirez to touch her. Miguel wasn't good enough for her. Good God, he was jealous of himself. Before he gave himself an aneurysm, he snatched a granola bar and pushed to his feet.

"Pity," he winked. "Let's get going."

She wrapped up the rest of the food and stowed it in her pack for later. When she was ready, Cam gestured to the hole that led to the caves, and they set out.

"So," Evan started while scanning the flashlight around, "what do you do when you're not working security in the mine?"

"Treasure hunt with beautiful women."

He sensed her pleasure in the dark. "Besides that."

Something about the darkness and the woman and this screwed-up adventure had him speaking the truth.

"Anything and everything in the water," he said.

"Do you surf?"

"Yes."

"Do you SCUBA dive?" she continued.

"Yes."

"Getting information out of you is like pulling teeth."

"Yes."

She laughed then.

"When I was a kid, my hobby was magic," she offered.

"Magic?"

"I was super shy and had trouble making friends. My dad bought me a magic kit to bring me out of my shell."

Cam noticed the flashlight bob, making it clear she was air quoting the last part.

"Did it work?" He ducked down to avoid a rock formation and covered Evan's head to do the same.

"Not really, but I learned some cool magic tricks," she said.

"But you can't reveal your secrets, correct? The magicians' code?" Cam asked.

"I don't think I rank among official magicians, but yes. Even the instruction book in my little child's kit said never to tell how a trick is done."

"Smoke and mirrors." Cam checked around an outcropping.

"Well, yes, actually. A huge part of magic is distraction. You get the audience to focus over here." She danced the beam of the flashlight across the cave wall. "While you do magic over here." She held up his watch.

Cam grabbed her wrist. "That's not magic; it's pickpocketing. *That* I know how to do." He held up his other hand, her small card wallet between two fingers.

"You distracted me." She glanced at his strong hand gently circling her wrist, then met his gaze. "Did I reveal my secret?"

Cam spoke softly. "Don't worry. It's safe with me."

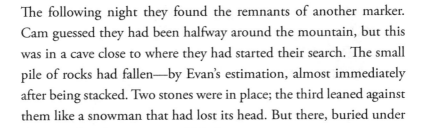

The following night they found the remnants of another marker. Cam guessed they had been halfway around the mountain, but this was in a cave close to where they had started their search. The small pile of rocks had fallen—by Evan's estimation, almost immediately after being stacked. Two stones were in place; the third leaned against them like a snowman that had lost its head. But there, buried under the second rock, were two gold links.

Evan looked up to him with unbridled enthusiasm. "Isn't this exciting?"

Cam shrugged. "It's a rock blob, and less gold than my abuela has in her teeth."

Evan sighed. "My mentor, Doctor Emberton, was on a dig in Syria where the team found a clay pot. That's it. Just a modestly decorated pot. It was cracked, and a shard had broken off."

"Does the story end with the pot being filled with diamonds?" he asked.

Evan frowned. "No."

Cam stuck a little flag in the marker as she had shown him. "Not interested."

"Miguel, that pot proved the existence of an entire tribe of people we knew nothing about. It's in the Natural History Museum in London. Isn't that fascinating?"

Cam *was* fascinated. Giving a name and a history to an entire civilization was... noble. He scanned the area around the marker, impassive.

"Treasure is fascinating," he replied.

"I agree. We just have different definitions of treasure."

"Maybe it's a language barrier." Cam grinned.

She shook her head, fighting a smile. "Come on. Let's get back. I'll add this little marker to my notes."

Cam led her back through the maze, shielding her from sharp rocks and protecting her head from low ceilings. He fought a laugh as she stumbled, then did a little hop to cover her clumsiness. Everything about her pulled him. She was like this beautiful human tractor beam.

Yes, they did have different definitions of treasure.

Cam walked home along the path through the high grass. Low mountains loomed behind him, the calm sea in the distance. It was still dark, but the clouded moonlight provided a gentle glow. He already felt her absence. He didn't know what it was about Evan, but he craved her the way one craves a missing piece of their soul.

Poets and songwriters describe this feeling like weightlessness, like floating. For Cam, it was the opposite. Evan made him feel grounded, like his feet were finally planted on the ground after years adrift. She felt like his gravity.

He didn't feel that zing his father talked about, but how could he with this lie between them. Evan didn't know the thoughtful, diligent sailor, Camilo Canto. She knew the greedy, sketchy security guard, Miguel Ramirez. Miguel could never feel a zing or a jolt or a fizzle or a pop because he was numb. Cam felt something, though.

And it terrified and exhilarated him in equal measure.

CHAPTER TWENTY-THREE

Sa Calobra, Mallorca
December 8

On the following night, Cam was waiting for her.

"Miguel, you're early."

"I think I have solved your puzzle," he said.

"What do you mean?" she asked.

"I was in this room today eating lunch, and I was thinking about our search." He withdrew a sheet of paper with a rudimentary map sketched out. "You found the first marker here." He pointed to the X that represented the cave where he first found her. "I found another marker in this room." He pointed with his chin to the corner. "We found a third in this cave." He touched the paper again. "What do you notice?"

She looked at him wide-eyed. "The markers all surround this blank space on your map."

"Exactly. So I looked at the three surrounding areas more closely, and…"

He walked to the far side of the room and stood in front of a lightweight steel storage cabinet. With a heave, he pulled it away from the wall. There, on the ground, was another marker. Next to it was another opening that had been sealed off with the same man-made clay. Silt and water had masked the outline; it was nearly impossible to see unless someone was looking for it.

He barely had time to brace for impact. Evan let out an audible squeal and threw herself into his arms. Her cinnamon eyes went to his then traveled to his lips. In that moment, Cam wanted to kiss her more than he wanted to breathe.

He couldn't break cover for any reason. Up until now, that hadn't been a problem. Cam could withstand torture, commit crimes, fuck women and never compromise the persona of Miguel Ramirez. But he knew like he knew how to break down and reassemble his Sig, if he kissed Evan, he would break.

He set her on her feet and ran a finger down her cheek. "Ready to find your treasure?"

He saw her swallow her disappointment at his rejection as she nodded. Cam stifled the pang of guilt. The last thing he ever wanted to do was cause her pain. He withdrew his hand before he did something stupid and grabbed the sledgehammer from the row of tools on the opposite wall.

Then they heard voices.

Cam held a finger to his lips, and they both stood stock still. The voices faded. Cam crossed the room and stood in front of her. "No one should be in these mines at this hour. I need to see what they're up to. If I'm not back here in ten minutes, leave through the caves. I'll meet you back here tomorrow."

"Can I help?" she asked.

Every word from her mouth burrowed into his heart. "You're helping me if I'm not worried about you. You're helping me by doing what I ask."

"Okay." She moved to a stool by the tools and sat. Then she examined the row, extracted a standard hammer, and held it.

Cam nodded his approval. "Be right back."

Cam peeked out of the storage room and, finding the tunnel empty, turned in the direction of the voices. Silent as snowfall, he navigated the mine until he found the danger sign he had noticed on his first day. The chain barring entry to the tunnel was still rocking back and forth after being disturbed. Following the path the men took, Cam ducked under the chain and crept down the tunnel until he again heard voices.

He moved forward on silent feet and peered around the corner. Three men passing a joint stood to the side of a heavy fire door propped open with a cinderblock. Beyond was a large room, and inside was a sight sadly familiar to Cam: a heroin lab. This was no two-bit operation. The equipment was new and expensive. Workers in headcovers and surgical masks stood working at long stainless steel tables. Others were piling vacuum sealed bricks into crates stamped with the familiar double M of the March Mining logo.

Cam pulled back and leaned against the tunnel wall. Copper wasn't the only product coming out of this mine.

Cam wandered through the labyrinth to get back to Evan. He had to admit, the men behind the drug lab had devised a brilliant operation. Mallorca was First World. It was nearly unthinkable to suspect it could be the source of heroin production. Fields of pristine poppies blanketed the meadows above the mines, carefully tended by farmers and monitored by officials. In the spring, their red blossoms would be a beacon boldly declaring innocent beauty. Cam suspected they were the perfect bright red herring, that the men didn't use the opium in the poppies for their drug manufacture. The cheap, easily-obtained chemical ingredients were far less conspicuous and far more potent. On the surface, the area emanated innocence and beauty; it was a different story in these dark depths.

The tunnels were also an impressive component, Cam grudgingly admitted. Safety inspectors could never explore every inch of this underground maze, and tunnels not in use were sealed off. The heroin operation was not only hidden but also remote. There was no odor, no noise, no conspicuous byproduct, and the drugs could be transported with the copper ore and offloaded at any point in the journey.

Cam headed back to the storeroom. When he entered the room, Evan stood, still holding the hammer. Her look of relief launched his soul. This time he didn't hesitate to return her embrace.

She looked up at him with concerned eyes.

He spoke with his lips to her forehead. "We need to get out of here."

"What's going on?" she asked.

"Nothing good. The less you know, the better."

She brushed back an errant lock of his hair. "Our treasure has been there for six hundred years. I guess a few more hours or days won't matter."

As if unwilling to risk another rejection, she backed away and crawled through the hole that led to the caves. This time Cam followed, making sure she made it safely to her boat. He knew she only had a short way to go, and the water was calm. When the Zodiac disappeared into the darkness, he took the steep path he had come down the day he had chased her from the beach.

The cool night and the brisk walk would clear his head.

———— ◆ ————

Cam entered the villa through the bedroom's french doors he had left ajar. He needed sleep, but first, he needed food. He changed quickly into lounge pants and a T-shirt and wandered barefoot into the central kitchen, surprised to find Atlas March in a tracksuit and trainers sipping orange juice.

"Miguel, you're up bright and early."

"I was hoping to speak with you, señor." Cam stood at attention in the doorway.

"I'm just off on my run," Atlas replied.

"Your men in the lab are sloppy," Cam said.

Atlas set the glass of orange juice on the counter.

"And you would know that how?" Atlas remarked absently.

"I saw them in the mine last night. They leave the door to the lab propped open so they don't have to enter the code every time they leave to smoke or take a break. At least one of them is using product. Also, you shouldn't stamp the March logo on the crates until they are ready to be offloaded with the copper ore. Gives you some deniability if the shipment is seized in transit."

Atlas nodded.

Cam continued, "I assume that's why you acquired a shipping company so that you can transport the heroin with the copper ore. Smart." He didn't mention that Atlas was also playing a dangerous game bypassing the services of The Conductor.

Atlas tapped a finger on his lips. "Miguel, I think you're about to get a promotion."

Cam stood taller. "I could be of use."

"Excellent. Come to my home office before you leave for the mine." Atlas bumped his fist on the kitchen island and strode out the back door.

Cam grabbed a pastry from the tray set out for Atlas and ate it in two bites. Then he headed back to his room for a blessed hour of sleep.

CHAPTER TWENTY-FOUR

Valldemossa, Mallorca
December 9

Evan trudged up the low hill, just east of Valldemossa. Sleep had been elusive, thoughts of Miguel invading her mind every time she closed her eyes. After two hours of kicking the sheets, Evan got dressed and went to work. The primary dig site was against a large hillside. It was marked off with low stakes and twine and covered with canvas tarps. Tools and equipment were scattered about. The crew had yet to arrive. Evan stepped into her coveralls hanging in the crew tent and set to work.

The day passed uneventfully as Evan lost herself in unearthing an artifact, a small narrow-necked pot. The task has successfully distracted her from fixating on her late-night excursions, but as the crew finished, she approached her mentor to update him.

Dr. Omar Emberton sat in a canvas chair, jotting notes by hand into a spiral journal. Thankfully, Evan had been promoted above the position of transcribing his notes to the digital log. She had tried for months to get him to upgrade to a tablet, but he had been intractable. *I can't keep my thoughts straight while I'm trying to stab at that damned machine,* he would gripe.

"Evan," Dr. Emberton greeted her. "What's on your mind?"

"Doctor E., I've run across something interesting in that cave system," she said.

"Ah yes, your Moorish treasure hunt." He clipped his pen into the notebook's spiral spine and set it on the folding table to his right.

"There are small stacks of stones placed intermittently throughout the caves. Encased between two of the three rocks in each stack are these." Evan reached into her pocket beneath the coveralls and extracted a small bag containing two of the links.

Emberton slid the gold pieces into his palm. "Fascinating." He set them on the table and grabbed a small magnifier. "They appear to be links in some sort of chain. Definitely gold." He looked up, his eyes bright with the thrill of discovery. "You really are onto something, aren't you?"

"I think so."

"One of our hosts this evening is particularly interested in artifacts from this era." Emberton stood and grabbed his jacket from the back of the chair. He handed her back the gold links. "I hope you're a quick-change artist. We are invited for seven."

Evan had completely forgotten about the dinner at the home of the sponsors of the excavation. Government grants only went so far, so archaeologists routinely relied on private donations. This evening their benefactors, Atlas March and Joseph Nabeel, were hosting a gathering for the team.

Emberton continued while ushering her down the hill toward the finca. "Joseph Nabeel is quite the buff when it comes to Moorish history. Be sure to mention your discovery."

Evan hurried along beside her mentor. It was a blessing in disguise that the event had slipped her mind; she dreaded these sorts of gatherings. Bracing herself for the requisite kowtowing and fake interest in the pastimes of the leisure class, she steeled her spine. If it meant she could continue doing what she loved, she would endure another boring dinner.

CHAPTER TWENTY-FIVE

Washington, DC
December 9

Nathan and Steady walked into Clancy's just off M Street and waited at the hostess stand. When the young woman in a Georgetown sweatshirt and jeans told them to sit anywhere, Nathan explained they were meeting someone. Steady, with ingrained practice, scanned the dark pub noting the patrons, workers, and entrances and exits. In the back corner sat a man in a dark suit scanning the laminated menu and nursing a draft beer. Nathan cocked his head in that direction, and the two joined the suited man in the booth.

Holding out his hand, the man lifted himself slightly from the vinyl seat. "Bill Turner."

"Nathan Bishop." Nathan completed the handshake and hung his cashmere overcoat on the hook next to the booth. "My colleague, Jonah Lockhart."

"Pleasure." Bill Turner reached behind the napkin holder to grab two additional menus and handed one to each of them.

Bill Turner was a lifer and looked the part. He was attractive but not handsome, well-dressed but not bespoke, tall but not towering. In short, he was exceptionally unexceptional. Nathan had shared his file on the flight up, and Steady had been impressed. Turner came from a politically connected family, but he had paid his dues. After graduating West Point, attending Ranger School, and serving for eight years, Turner had gone straight to the CIA, working in nearly every area of Intelligence. That was thirty years ago. His outward calm discussing this troubling situation with Cam spoke of a man who had seen it all. Steady ordered burgers for both of them while Nathan spoke to the handler.

Bill Turner dove straight in. "Deputy Director Sorenson filled me in. I have to admit, this is a first. Miguel Ramirez was a valued employee at his former job." Turner spoke in vague terms. "As you've probably discussed, no matter how capable, it's extremely doubtful anyone in that field of work would seek out a specific employee unless it was an independent contractor." Turner was referring to assassins, which Cam was not.

"We agree. Our first thought was some sort of revenge scenario, but that could have been accomplished without changing locations." The perps had plenty of opportunities to take Cam out in Harlem.

Turner returned his menu to the slot against the wall and sat back as the waitress set down a chicken pot pie. "I ordered when I got here. Best damn pot pie in D.C."

Steady eyed the golden pastry as Turner cracked the surface with his fork. "That would have been information worth having," he grumbled.

Turner blew on a chunk of dripping chicken. "Burgers are excellent too."

A moment later, Steady had forgotten his pique as he squeezed a puddle of ketchup onto his plate.

Nathan sent a text before setting his phone aside and returning his attention to the table. "Sorry about that. My wife is pregnant, so I'm on call."

The older man sympathized. "I have five kids. I was only there for the birth of two of them. This work we do…"

Steady nodded. There were a million ways to finish that sentence—satisfying, demanding, soul-crushing, necessary, all-consuming—he agreed with most of them.

Turner set down his fork. "These are the facts." He withdrew a tablet and spun it to face the men. "A security camera captured three men taking an unconscious Miguel Ramirez out of the bar in Harlem and putting him in a black van." He hit the play arrow on the screen, and the footage ran. "We picked up the van again on the George Washington Bridge heading to New Jersey. From there, could be anything. He could have been transported to a safe house, taken to an airport. The van hasn't turned up, but the Harlem contact, Luis Flores?" Turner opened another image. "He was found shot to death in an abandoned strip mall on the outskirts of Newark. Body was discovered by a patrolman doing a routine drive-by just after midnight. Flores took two in the chest. Looks like a thirty-eight, but ballistics hasn't even started working on it. He had his wallet and watch lifted but was identified at the scene by a medical alert bracelet."

"This gets weirder by the minute," Steady commented around his burger.

Turner resumed eating. "Welcome to *Intelligence*." Turner said the word like the contronym it was.

"Tell us about The Conductor," Nathan challenged.

The fork stopped halfway to Turner's mouth. "Cam told you about The Conductor?" He pinched his eyes closed. Steady suspected he was scolding himself for using Cam's real name.

"He did," Nathan confirmed. "And you know our clearance."

Turner resumed eating and spoke as if he were chatting about the weather. "The Conductor is a theory, a suspicion that there is a force that controls all illegal global shipping in the world. Everything.

Exotic animals, conflict diamonds, chemical weapons, you name it."
He mopped up the sauce on his plate with a dinner roll.

"And The Agency thinks it's one man?" Nathan asked.

"The Agency thinks it's a myth. An all-powerful man with a contraband toll booth who neither steals nor manufactures, doesn't buy or sell. He simply ensures safe passage. It's quite the niche career. If The Conductor did exist, he'd be busier than a moth in a mitten. We're talking hundreds of billions of dollars of contraband annually."

Steady gave a low whistle. "Damn."

"Makes the biggest online retailers in the world look like mom and pop stores." Turner sighed. "Look, there have been rumors about this for years: some Russian oligarch or Italian underworld don. Nothing has ever produced any concrete evidence. Why Miguel Ramirez latched onto this conspiracy theory…" He shook his head. "Waste of time."

Nathan slid his plate to the side and rested his forearms on the table. "Got any theories? Who was looking for Miguel Ramirez?"

Steady noted that Nathan, for whatever reason, had not shared the information about Cam's journal or Harlan Musgrave's interest in acquiring it.

Turner tapped the flat of his fork on the table. "That's the sixty-four thousand dollar question. We monitored chatter about Miguel; that's protocol. Nothing set off alarm bells. After Dario Sava was killed—congratulate your sniper for me by the way, one less scumbag in the world—a few of his soldiers were sniffing around. Most likely recruiting Sava's men, trying to snatch up the remnants of his empire. As expected, some people Miguel encountered ran background checks on him. Oh, and there's the woman."

"Who?" Steady asked.

Turner opened the briefcase on the seat beside him and withdrew a file. "As I said, over the past year, there have been numerous inquiries about Miguel Ramirez." He chuckled. "I'm sorry, I know this isn't a laughing matter, but a woman who made no attempt to disguise her actions has also been looking for him. I don't know what the hell our boy does in the bedroom, but it seems he makes a lasting impression." He slid the file to Nathan. "All relevant chatter is detailed and without redaction."

Nathan tapped the file. "Mind if I borrow this?"

"It's all yours," Turner complied. "Makes for some fascinating reading."

"Thanks." Nathan slipped the file into his briefcase.

Turner stood and threw some cash on the table. "This situation has spawned one hare-brained theory after the next. If you come up with a dog that will hunt, let me know." With that, the CIA handler shook both men's hands, gave a small salute, and left.

"You really think some whacko broad kidnapped our boy?" Steady asked.

"I don't know what to think, but I have a feeling there's more going on here than meets the eye." Nathan added some money to Turner's contribution and stood. "Let's head back to the plane and take a closer look at this file."

"Copy that." Together the two men walked out into the cold Washington day.

CHAPTER TWENTY-SIX

Miramar, Mallorca
December 9

Gemini had returned. Cam sighed as he slicked back his hair. He straightened the collar of the charcoal-gray dress shirt, adjusted the cream jacket of the suit, and assessed himself in the full-length mirror. He looked tired. His little late-night excursions were taking their toll, but it was a price he happily paid. He couldn't explain why, but his treasure hunt with Evan made him feel more alive and purpose-driven than he had in years. To what purpose, he had no idea, but every time they met in those mysterious dark caves, he had the unshakable feeling everything was leading up to *something*.

Laughter from the front of the villa pulled Cam from his room. He followed the voices. The grand living room was aglow with candlelight. French doors opened onto the cloistered walkways that ringed the home. To balance the cool breeze, a fire crackled in the elaborate mosaic hearth.

He stopped in the arched entrance at the top of the two wide marble steps that descended into the room. Gemini turned from the group and took the spotlight, as was her nature, standing before him in the center of the room. She was wearing a Mediterranean blue sheath that perfectly matched her eyes; her pleasure at his choice of attire evident.

"Miguel," she purred. "Come join our little party."

Gemini March seemed to emit a glow that obscured everything and everyone else. Nevertheless, as Cam took the first step into the room, his eyes found *her*. Standing behind Gemini and speaking with Joseph and two other young people was Evan. *His Evan.* She was wearing cropped black trousers, loafers, and a lightweight black turtleneck. Her cinnamon hair—the same shade as her eyes—was pulled into a low ponytail. Her makeup was minimal, just pale-pink lip gloss and mascara. She was unobtrusive and demure, and she had his full attention. So much so that Gemini March glanced over her shoulder to see who had dared to usurp her stage.

Cam quickly corrected his error. Making a beeline for Gemini, he kissed first one cheek, then the other, and whispered, "The only place I can imagine that dress looking better is on my floor." Irritation forgotten, she placed a hand on his chest. "Come meet our guests."

Gemini pulled him to the fireplace, where Atlas was speaking with a distinguished man in his mid-fifties. Dressed to impress, or more likely, fundraise, the man wore a natty suit with a perfectly tied pale-blue bowtie at his neck. A pair of round-rimmed glasses with tortoise-shell frames sat perched on his aquiline nose. The man spared Cam a glance, his eyes briefly widening upon inspection of the new arrival. He quickly schooled his expression and returned his attention to their host.

Atlas was, as always, impeccably dressed in gray trousers and a double-breasted navy blazer. He extended his hand to Cam with a welcoming greeting.

"Miguel! Glad you're joining us. Omar, this is Miguel Ramirez, Gemini's…" He paused for a moment, stymied by word choice. "…

date. And you know Gemini." The man, Omar, extended his hand. "Pleasure."

Cam reciprocated. "Likewise."

"Dr. Omar Emberton is heading up the archaeological expedition in Valldemossa. They've made some fascinating discoveries."

Emberton gave a respectful nod. "Thanks in large part to our benefactor."

Atlas waved him off. "Thank Joseph. He's the history buff. More importantly, he decides how March Mining allots its charitable donations."

Joseph, Evan, and the other two guests Cam assumed were also graduate students joined the circle. Joseph chimed in. "Our small island holds untold riches. Thousands of years before the birth of Christ, people were inhabiting Mallorca."

Atlas held out his arms. "Wouldn't *you* choose to live here?"

Evan smiled at the quip.

"And this young lady," Atlas continued, "Is Omar's most trusted Gal Friday."

Cam correctly guessed Atlas had used the moniker because he had forgotten her name. Evan extended a hand to him, looking so conspicuously nonchalant, it made him want to laugh.

"Evan." She spoke without inflection.

"Miguel." Cam nodded. He placed a hand on the small of Gemini March's back in a gesture of possession. Gemini was no fool. If there was the slightest tension between Evan and him, Gemini would notice. As if sensing the heat between him and her rival, Gemini moved into the nook under his extended arm. Cam jarred himself from mapping the swath of freckles across Evan's nose he hadn't seen in the dim light of the cave and returned his attention to the woman at his side.

A servant appeared and announced dinner.

Cam walked into the dining room with Joseph at his side. When he reached the end of the table, he paused under the portrait of Ulysses March that hung above the fireplace.

Joseph spoke reverently. "I miss the old bastard."

"He died last year?" Cam asked.

Joseph rested a hand on the mantle. "Plane crash. It was a painful blow, especially for Gemini. She adored her father. He was a brilliant businessman. A strategist. He wanted to take Gemini under his wing, but she never seemed to show any interest. It seemed the more he pressed, the more flighty and unmotivated she became. Then she discovered modeling, and the glamour and attention snared her. Ulysses always used to say, 'Gemini is the star of the show.'"

"It is the truth," Cam agreed.

"She doesn't like to be ignored, Miguel. You'd be wise to remember that." Joseph patted him on the shoulder as he moved to the table.

Ten minutes later, they were all seated, and the first course served. The conversation returned to archaeological finds and current events.

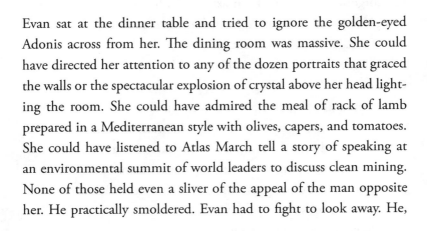

Evan sat at the dinner table and tried to ignore the golden-eyed Adonis across from her. The dining room was massive. She could have directed her attention to any of the dozen portraits that graced the walls or the spectacular explosion of crystal above her head lighting the room. She could have admired the meal of rack of lamb prepared in a Mediterranean style with olives, capers, and tomatoes. She could have listened to Atlas March tell a story of speaking at an environmental summit of world leaders to discuss clean mining. None of those held even a sliver of the appeal of the man opposite her. He practically smoldered. Evan had to fight to look away. He, on the other hand, was enduring no such hardship, captivated by the seductress all but sitting in his lap.

And yet, as Evan examined him, she saw something else in that golden gaze, a distance, a deadness. It was the same look he had the day he scared her off the beach. The man across from her was not the kind, gruff, funny Miguel from the caves. He was robotic and intimidating. Evan almost laughed at the idle thought that perhaps he was a gigolo. She shook herself from her irrational justifications. Miguel was on a date, and he was enjoying it.

Gemini March fed Miguel a bite of her lamb, uncaring that the man had the identical meal on the plate in front of him. Miguel's lips closed around the fork and pulled the morsel into his mouth. He wiped the juice from the corner of his lips with his thumb then watched while Gemini sucked the pad. Every bite, every lick, every swallow was like some erotic dance.

Thankfully, Evan's mentor didn't seem to mind interrupting the show.

"Gemini is an unusual name, Miss March. Is there a story behind it?" Dr. Emberton inquired.

Clearly annoyed at being torn from her lover, Gemini turned to Omar Emberton and explained. "I ate my twin."

Emberton sputtered, "What?"

"In the womb. My mother was pregnant with twins, but the other baby died, and I absorbed her. Dad used to say that's why I'm a lot to handle. There are two people inside me." She cupped Miguel's face and returned to her seduction.

Evan hid a smile. Emberton had never looked so sorry to have asked a question.

Jamal, her friend and fellow doctoral candidate, leaned his head next to Evan's and whispered conspiratorially, "I'd say get a room, but it's too fucking hot. My friends are never going to believe I'm having dinner with Gemini March."

"Eat your dinner and stop trying to take her picture. It's so freaking obvious," she scolded.

Jamal scoffed. "Gemini doesn't care. All she does is get her picture taken. Besides, she's too busy letting that guy grope her to notice."

Jamal leaned in and placed his hand on the back of Evan's chair. Movement across the table had her glancing up. Miguel had snapped the stem of his wine glass, and Gemini was sitting on his lap, dabbing the stain on his shirt. He held Gemini's hand as she blotted the wine, but his honey-colored eyes were on Evan. She averted her gaze.

Evan's own aggravating issues with intimacy smacked her in the face, and she gripped her fork like a vice as she chased a pea around her plate. She had never felt jealousy, never even felt arousal outside of those fleeting moments in the caves with Miguel. Yet when she returned her attention to him, watched him slowly chew his meat, a fresh glass of red wine poised at his lips, she felt her breasts grow heavy and her body heat. Shaking off the unwelcome attraction, she diverted her attention to her meal.

It was an unforgivable sin in this region to dislike olives, but Evan had always hated them. She had tried dozens of varieties to no avail. Moreover, when she left them on her plate, it was frequently an irritating topic of discussion. Employing the diversionary tactics she had learned as a young magician, she spun her wine in her glass on the table with one hand and deftly hid the olives under the parsnip puree with the other. Pleased with her subterfuge, she glanced around. Across the table, Miguel gave her a knowing glance, popped an olive into his mouth with a wink, then returned his focus to his lover.

Gemini March beamed her satisfaction. She appeared as pleased with Miguel's attention as she was with Evan's deprival of it. The model seemed to view their frottage as evidence of a battle she had won. Evan almost laughed out loud. She couldn't imagine Gemini March ever losing such a contest. Evan quickly turned to listen to her mentor discuss the excavation.

"Evan, tell Joseph about your discovery in the caves." Omar Emberton encouraged his protege.

"Oh, well, I'm not quite sure what it is I have discovered, if anything," she stalled.

"Please tell us," Joseph urged.

"Well, some boys near the dig site..." She stopped and started again. "Let me back up. At our excavation, we have discovered small stacks of stones the Talaiotic people used to indicate areas of importance: grave sites, ceremonial centers, places of worship, et cetera. A child of one of the local archaeologists told me he had seen similar markers in the caves near the shore." She had the full attention of the table as she continued. "The boy and his friends imagine themselves young treasure hunters," she laughed. "They guided me to the spot in the caves where they had seen similar markers."

"That was you!" Atlas exclaimed with dawning realization. "You were the young woman Miguel shooed off the beach last week."

Evan felt her face heat. "Yes, I am fascinated by the small stacks of stones the boys found. While they are not Talaiotic, they are of significance. Probably late fourteenth or early fifteenth century."

"Ah-ha!" Emberton pointed his fork at Joseph. "Now she has your attention."

Evan looked between the two men. Then she glanced across the table at Miguel, who was giving her his undivided attention. For a moment, she couldn't breathe. His face was so beautiful, his eyes so predatorial, yet somehow kind. It was as if there were two men inside of him.

Gemini shook her empty wine glass like a bell demanding a refill.

"Please continue," Joseph repeated.

Evan explained how she discerned the age of the markers and how many she had found. She told them about the gold links and the sealed-off entrances to various caves deep in the system. Her tale enthralled the men. Gemini March had pulled out her phone and appeared to be checking social media.

"Do keep us apprised," Joseph insisted. "Omar and I are North African. The Moors have a long, troubled history on Mallorca. I would be most interested in anything you find."

"He speaks without hyperbole, my dear," Emberton added. "The most insignificant relic of the Moors is intriguing to my old friend."

Joseph sipped his wine. "It is our history."

"Indeed." Emberton toasted his friend across the table.

———————— ◆ ————————

Cam stood in the grand front hall with Evan, Atlas, and Omar Emberton. The other graduate students had puttered off on a Vespa, Gemini had excused herself, and Joseph had retired for the evening. Atlas opened the massive front doors and led Emberton to the waiting chauffeured car. Cam guided Evan after them at a slower pace.

Dinner had been hell. He sat there while Gemini finger-fed him like a toddler and ran her bare foot up his calf. The only sensation she managed to elicit was a mild feeling of nausea. Meanwhile, Evan chased a pea around her plate with her fork, and he was hard as a lead pipe. That little trick with hiding the olives on her plate? Why was that sexy? And when that other student bent his head next to hers to share a secret, Cam had broken his wine glass trying to keep himself in check.

"Did you enjoy your meal, little mouse?"

Ignoring the endearment, she replied, "Yes, everything was lovely. Thank you for asking."

He leaned into her. "So formal," he scolded. "This is our first time breaking bread at an actual table. Above ground. Just imagine the possibilities."

"Oh, I am," she deadpanned. "Although I imagine your girl-friend might not be too happy about your exploring them."

He leaned down as they walked, their feet producing a rhythmic crunch on the gravel. "She's not my girlfriend, *querida*. She's not even my friend."

Evan stopped and turned to him. "I don't think *she's* aware of that fact." Then she cast her eyes upward, and Cam turned to follow her line of sight. Gemini March stood on a balcony wearing a black silk robe. Her arms were crossed as she observed them.

Cam looked up at the Siren, then he leaned down and placed a kiss on Evan's cheek and whispered, "See you in a few hours." She stepped back with her hand to her face.

"What about those men we heard?" she asked.

"We're far enough away to be safe. We'll meet just as the last shift is ending. I won't let anything happen to you" Cam rested a hand on her back.

"I know that," she said, the reply a simple statement of fact.

The three innocuous words fed a very hungry piece of his soul.

She turned without a word and hurried after her mentor, who was now waiting in the back of the car.

Cam shoved his hands in his pants pockets and turned back to Gemini. She had taken a step forward and now was leaning both arms onto the low wall that bordered the balcony. She looked like Juliet leaning down to her lover. Cam almost laughed. His current situation certainly had equal potential for tragedy. He looked up at her and grinned.

She smiled back. "Tell me, Miguel. Am I giving you that hard-on you're trying to hide, or did the little archaeologist turn you on?"

He made no secret of adjusting himself. "I think you know."

A look of sultry satisfaction crossed her face."You like to tease me."

He shrugged.

"Tit for tat, Miguel." She stood upright and slipped the robe off, revealing her perfect nude form. She turned to walk back into her bedroom and tossed over her shoulder, "See you in the morning, lover."

Cam masked his relief with an audible growl. Gemini turned again to close the glass-paned french doors and pull the curtains, her face smug upon discovering he was still staring up at her. Without expression, he returned to the house.

In the relative safety of his first-floor bedroom, Cam changed into jeans and a henley. He had enjoyed a delicious meal and dodged an intimate encounter with Gemini March. Well, he was almost positive she expected him to pound on her door later. And he would. He couldn't behave in any manner inconsistent with Miguel Ramirez, and Miguel Ramirez would demand entry. To her chamber and her body.

Cam shook off his trepidation. He had another, much more pleasurable task to attend to first. The night wasn't over yet.

CHAPTER TWENTY-SEVEN

Sa Calobra, Mallorca
December 9

Evan followed the now-familiar path through the caves. Anticipation eclipsed her fear. She moved with ease and ducked to avoid a low rock shelf she had passed the day before. Her heart was pounding in her chest, and bees were buzzing in her belly. She didn't even pretend to lie to herself and claim it was the thought of finding something exciting in the cave they had pinpointed. While that certainly excited her, it was the man she was meeting who fired her blood.

She huffed. Half the women on the island probably wanted Miguel Ramirez. He was beautiful and sexy and emanated a raw masculinity. And while all of those qualities certainly flipped her switch, it was something else that pulled her. Behind that facade of callous indulgence, there was something else. She saw it in his golden gaze—a battle. A war was waging within this man, some deeply troubling conflict. Whatever it was, she wanted to comfort him, ease his pain. She sighed. Before she gave herself too much credit for her selflessness, she admitted she also wanted to feel him between her legs. To touch her in a way she had been deprived of for so long. He was the only man she had ever met who doused her panic. She didn't just want Miguel. She needed him.

She climbed through the final opening into the storage room. A large, calloused hand appeared before her face, and she instinctively took it. Her eyes followed the enticing path from powerful forearm to rounded bicep to broad shoulder and finally to that arrogant, charming face. With his help, she pulled herself to standing.

"I'd never accuse you of being a gentleman, but thank you," she said.

He grunted in response.

She stared at their clasped hands, her fingers nestled in the crook of his thumb, his long thick one wrapped around her palm. Why did the simplest thing seem to have so much *meaning?* Before she could study it further, he released her from his grasp.

"Ready?" he asked.

She nodded, mute.

Miguel brought the steel cabinet away from the wall, revealing the sealed-off entrance and the marker he had discovered. Evan knelt and extracted the gold links, bagging them and making a note of the location.

Miguel grabbed a sledgehammer from the row of tools with the ease of a baseball player selecting a bat, and in one, two, three swings, there was a hole resembling the one she had crawled through earlier.

"As much as I want to watch that little ass, I better go first." He turned to the opening and began clearing away rocks by hand. Evan watched him work. There was something off about this man. The words out of his mouth were disgusting and offensive, yet his actions were... thoughtful.

She had dated a man in grad school, well, tried to date anyway. After knee surgery, she had been on crutches; he never once held a door for her or helped her down the stairs. That was a person who supposedly liked her, who wanted more with her. Yet here was this—she used his own descriptor—*predator*, a man that if he had any feelings toward her, they strayed toward the dislike end of the spectrum, clearing away rocks to ease her passage. Then, once again, he blanketed his kind gesture with harsh words.

"Let's go. You look good on your knees, but I want to find treasure."

Evan ignored the remark and followed him through the opening; she was the one who would be doing the ass-staring.

Once inside the small chamber, Cam stood and bumped his head on the low ceiling. He could hear her stifled chuckle in the dark. She came up beside him, turned on the flashlight, and scanned the space. There, in the corner, were two large, unremarkable mounds. Evan hurried to them with an excitement that belied their appearance.

"That doesn't look like treasure to me," Cam grumbled.

"Just wait." She walked around the formations but didn't touch them. "These may have been crates centuries ago. As the wood decayed, silt and limestone deposits formed around them."

Cam took a step forward, his boot landing in a deep puddle. "This cave takes on water, chica." His voice echoed in the darkness.

"We're near the shore. This cave may have even opened to the bay at one point," Evan replied.

He heard rustling and clanking from her corner, and moments later, two battery-operated LED lanterns illuminated the space. Cam watched as she unfurled a set of tools and rubbed her hands together with undisguised glee.

He couldn't resist goading her. "I'll get the hammer."

"No!" she shrieked. Then, "No," in a calmer tone.

"This time, we do the tap, tap, tap," she continued. "You're about to be promoted to junior archaeologist, Miguel."

Working together, they removed a good section of the sediment and rock that had formed over their find. Evan switched out her tools and began sifting through the top layer of earth and rocky sand.

"What is that?" he asked.

"Fifteenth-Century packing peanuts. I think whoever filled the crate used sand and rock to protect the contents, or maybe weigh it down," she replied without diverting her attention.

Cam watched, fascinated as she continued the next stage in the process. With a tool that resembled a small gardening fork, Evan dug into the mound. Minutes later, she struck gold, or most likely, bronze. A stream of small coins came spilling from the opening. She grabbed a small tray from her kit and quickly collected the items. Cam rushed to help.

"Dios mio. Treasure, *Ratoncita*. You found treasure."

With great effort, Evan controlled her excitement. "It appears that way, yes. And please stop calling me mouse."

"Never. Just like a little mouse, you dug your hole in the dirt and found a treat."

"Everything needs to be separated and cataloged. We should have been recording this. Here." She dug into her bag and removed a GoPro. "Be my cameraman."

"With pleasure." He took the device and peered through the eyehole.

"Record the dig, Miguel. I don't want to watch that later and see footage of my ass or my bra strap."

"Ah, but the ass and the bra are much more fun to watch." He pointed the camera to her face.

"Just focus on the find." She shook her head, exasperated.

Cam obliged and began documenting her work. Where had this camaraderie come from? This ease of exchange? He had maintained his Miguel Ramirez legend without fail, and yet she treated him...

She treated him like Cam.

Miguel Ramirez had beaten and killed men. He fucked and discarded women. He got high, and he drank to excess. Cam had had many sleepless nights early on coming to terms with the fact that, on paper, Miguel Ramirez and Camilo Canto were not that different. Cam had done most of those things too. Ultimately, he resolved his angst with the knowledge that what Cam did, he did for the right reasons. He did it to make the world safer. Miguel was a means to an end, a price he was willing to pay.

Somehow, someway, Evan seemed to see beneath his heretofore impenetrable facade.

Her sharp intake of breath jarred him from his thoughts, and he looked down to see Evan had revealed the corner of a metal box.

"What is it?" He peered closer.

"I'm not sure yet. Hook the camera on my helmet and come help me," she replied.

Slowly, Evan brushed away the earth surrounding the box.

"It's not rusted," he observed.

"It's gold," Evan explained. Gold is one of the least reactive metals. It's not affected by oxygen or even saltwater. That's why treasure hunters are always searching for shipwrecks. Gold can survive on the bottom of the ocean indefinitely."

Cam grunted his understanding while Evan extracted the box from the mound. It was indeed a hinged gold box, lighter than she expected and about half the size of a shoebox. Caked with dirt and mud, the detail was difficult to make out, but it was clear the case was filigreed and ornately decorated.

"Let's take it over there." Cam gestured with his head to an empty corner. When Evan nodded her assent, he helped her up and guided her to the spot.

"Clean it off first or open it?" Cam asked.

"I may be a scientist, but come on." She elbowed him in the ribs as he sat down beside her.

She worked her way around the edge of the box with a small tool, dislodging silt and debris. Then she slid the lock mechanism to the side and released the latch. Slowly, slowly she opened the box. When the lid was open about an inch, she stopped, turned her head, and looked at Cam with the excitement of a child.

"Well?" Cam urged.

Evan lifted the lid, her eyes cataloging the contents. In the center was a sizable nondescript rock about the size of a baseball. A nest of coins surrounded it, and on one side sat a large necklace. A section of the chain was missing, and the links matched those on the markers they had found. She carefully lifted the item and held it before them. A large medallion in the shape of an animal head, a cougar or a lioness perhaps, hung from the end.

"*Fijate*. That's amazing."

"It is. It's amazing." She stared at her find.

Cam reached into the box and withdrew the big rock. "This must be to weigh it down. These people..."

"Moors. These items are Moorish, late Fourteenth Century."

"*Perdón*. The *Moors* must have known the tide washed into this cave when they hid this stuff." He tossed the rock over his shoulder, and it vanished into the darkness. A plop of water signaled it had rolled into a puddle.

"Don't do that. Everything is significant. I have to catalog everything we find," Evan scolded.

He shrugged and grasped the medallion in his hand.

"For a king, yes?" Cam asked.

"Yes. Or a tribal chief. See here? This indentation?" She placed her hand over his without touching and ran her thumb over the large, shallow indentation in the face. "A jewel would go here." She drew in a deep breath. "Miguel, this is a significant find."

She turned her face to his, and they froze. Inches apart, excitement coursing through their veins. She moved her face closer.

Cam stalled her with a finger to her lips. "Shh."

Noises from outside their cave had them both jerking their heads to the storeroom. Cam moved like a cat, and in a second, was halfway out the opening pulling the steel storage cabinet back to conceal the hole, lifting it slightly to avoid the screech. He darted over to the lanterns and extinguished them, then returned to the passthrough and listened intently. He silently bounded back to his seat beside her.

"Who's there?" she whispered, her breath touching his cheek.

"The men from the last shift of the mining operation. I've seen food and trash in that room. They come in there to eat and, you know, relax. I guess they decided to hang out after their shift," he explained.

Moments later, the distinct smell of marijuana wafted through the opening. Evan turned to face him. "Miners are getting high? That can't be safe."

Cam ran a hand through his dark hair. He didn't want her to know these men weren't miners. "They're off duty."

"So, what now?" she asked.

"I don't want anyone finding you back here." Cam could only imagine the suspicions raised if the men reported to Atlas—and Gemini—that Miguel Ramirez was skulking around the closed mine with a woman.

"So we just sit here? In the dark?" she asked in a throaty voice.

"Tell me more about yourself, little mouse."

———————— ◆ ————————

Three hours later, the adjacent storeroom had turned into party central, music blared and laughter and pot smoke filtered in through the opening. Evan had told Miguel her life story. Well, that had only taken about fifteen minutes. She grew up in California wine country. Her parents had married right out of college and divorced when she was three. Her childhood had been happy but lonely. Had that taken fifteen minutes? Probably closer to fifteen seconds.

Evan wasn't one to talk about herself. She was shy, at times painfully so. Maybe it was the darkness, maybe it was the fact that this perplexing man seemed receptive, or maybe they simply needed to pass the time. Whatever the reason, Evan had opened like a blossom in their confinement.

She hadn't learned much about Miguel except that he was secretive. He had grown up on the streets of a village near Bogota and spent most of his life there until he was hired by a man in Suriname to work as a handyman. She assumed it was a handyman; the job description of "fixer" was most likely a translation error.

It was clear he'd led a hard life, different in every way from her idyllic, if isolated, life on the family vineyard. It was also clear he didn't want to talk about himself. That was fine. She was enjoying just being in his company. Whatever his life outside this cave, in this little cubbyhole, Miguel Ramirez was a kind, attentive, *magnetic* man. She didn't want facts to shatter her image of him. So she filled the silence with her own stories.

"My dad was obsessive about the grapes, tending them, protecting them. A bad harvest could ruin us. I'd tag along, and I'd just dig in the dirt. My dad would joke that I looked like a potato he'd just pulled from the ground."

Evan could see Miguel's teeth as he smiled, feel his fingers as he brushed her hair from her face.

"And the love for digging stuck," he surmised.

She held up a finger, indicating that she was getting to the good part. "One day, I was out in the vineyard, and my hand ran across something sharp. I dug it out and showed it to my dad."

"What was it?" he asked.

"A tooth."

"That's it?" She could see Miguel touch his own incisor in the dark.

Evan took his hands in hers and held the palms several inches apart. "A *tooth*."

She continued the story. "My dad knew enough to know we should take it to the natural history museum and have someone examine it. Turned out it was the tooth from a Cenozoic-era amphimachairodus."

Her declaration was met with silence.

"A saber-toothed tiger. Well, not a tiger as we know it, but a saber-toothed cat," she clarified.

He didn't speak, but she could see the whites of his eyes.

"I know, right? My dad started researching colleges with the best archaeology programs that afternoon."

"Your father, he is a good man?" Miguel asked.

"The best," Evan beamed. "The divorce was hard on him, and we had a very unconventional life, but he's a great dad."

"What do you mean unconventional?"

"Um, well, I've never had turkey for one thing. I mean, I've had turkey sandwiches and stuff but never..." She backed up a bit to clarify. "In the U.S., at Thanksgiving and Christmas, people have roast turkey. When I think of those holidays, I picture a table filled with people and a big meal taking up every inch of space."

"Yes," he confirmed. "I have relatives in Florida. I know of the holiday."

"It's such a small thing, a big family meal. I guess we always want what we can't have."

Cam was bursting. She was describing *his family's* holiday celebrations.

She continued her musings. "I think of a big touch football game in the yard and sneaking into the kitchen late at night for an extra slice of pie."

Cam bit his cheek. He wanted to tell her about the Thanksgiving where his oldest nephew rode his tricycle through the house and hit the leg of the supplemental card table holding all the pies. He wanted to explain the crazy rules of the annual family soccer game—*real fútbol*, his grandfather would say—and the battle for the coveted trophy, the "Canto Cup." He wanted to bring her into his mother's kitchen and show her how he would lift the lids of each pot and pan to smell the magic simmering beneath, how his abuela would smack his hand as he snatched a treat.

But Miguel Ramirez didn't celebrate Thanksgiving, didn't have a family, didn't care. So he listened without comment.

"My dad and I had our own tradition. Thanksgiving tacos and a double feature from the AFI top one hundred films list." She scratched her cheek with her shoulder. "I love our tradition, but a part of me wonders, you know? I've always been a bit of a loner. Never lonely, but alone." He heard more than saw her pick up a pebble and toss it into a puddle with a plunk. "Do you know the actual definition of an introvert?" She didn't wait for his response. "It's from the Latin, vertere, to turn and intro, inward. It's a person who derives their energy from being alone, contemplating rather than expressing their thoughts. For good or bad, that's me."

Cam didn't speak for fear of what might spill out. The truth was he might have loved her in that moment. It took everything in him to bridle his desire to share. Every comment she made brought a recollection to his lips. God, when she talked about being alone. He only then realized that was a big part—maybe the most significant part—of the agony of living as Miguel Ramirez. He was *never* alone. Even when he was by himself, there was always a camera or a recording device to fear, always someone listening. What had she said? Never lonely, but alone? Miguel Ramirez was never alone but always lonely.

He wanted to cup Evan's soft cheeks in his hands and confess his truth. Tell her that he understood her words to a depth he had never explored. But he couldn't. He could only connect with her the way Miguel Ramirez would connect with a woman. On some level, Cam wanted that physical connection too. *Cam* wanted to touch her. This time he didn't stop to analyze the implications of the desire he shared with his alter ego; he reached out in the darkness and ran a hand down her thigh.

"Wha, what are you doing?" she asked.

He searched out her cinnamon gaze as his hand repeated the movement. "Passing the time."

His night vision was exceptional, and he could just make out the two faint lines that formed between her eyebrows as she spoke. "That... that feels nice."

He paused for a moment at the wonder in her voice. "You sound surprised." Cam's hand traveled up her thigh, and he squeezed her hip.

"I... I don't like to be touched," she spoke on a breath.

"You sure about that, little mouse?"

His large hand spanned her ribcage, and she murmured into the pitch, "I've never had consensual sex."

The declaration had him pulling his hand back. The implication had him fighting fury.

"Explain, please," he demanded.

"It means I've never—"

"I know what the word means. Tell me what *you* mean." Cam clenched his jaw.

Evan sighed, the sound echoing off the walls of their ersatz confessional.

"Don't stop. Please," she begged.

Cam returned his hand to her body, placing it gently on her calf as she prepared to share her pain.

"It's a long story," she continued.

"Where can we go?" he whispered.

As if on cue, a bottle broke, and the sounds of fighting filtered in through the opening.

"I want to roll my eyes at the triteness of it all—my high school prom after-party. I'd had a bit to drink but not too much. The boy I was seeing…" She spoke to her lap, shame leeching off her like a scent. "I didn't say no, but I didn't say yes. I wasn't ready."

Cam wanted the guy's name. He wanted to *ruin* him. All Miguel Ramirez could do was continue to stroke her leg with a gentle touch and say, "I'm sorry."

"The worst part? Afterward, I said I wanted to leave. He wanted to stay and party, so I called a taxi. When I was walking to the car, he came up to me and handed me fifty dollars and said, 'thanks for the fun night.'"

No wonder she had reacted so fiercely to his insult. *Puta.* On Miguel Ramirez's long list of crimes, it was a misdemeanor, but somehow in this intimate cocoon, calling her a whore felt like a capital offense. He didn't know how she would interpret his silence, but Cam knew if he spoke, it wouldn't be Miguel Ramirez's voice coming out of his mouth. So, instead, he continued to touch her leg gently.

"Ever since then, when men touch me with intention, I sort of panic. Maybe a bit more than panic. I doused a date with pepper spray in college when he grabbed me from behind to hug me. I spent the evening in the hospital waiting room explaining to campus security that the entire thing was a misunderstanding." Evan laughed and shook her head. "I guess it wasn't such a long story after all."

Then, in a move that had his eyes flying to hers, she took his hand and moved it up her leg. "Do you, um, know what you're doing?" she asked.

Cam squeezed her thigh.

"Could you...?" She swallowed.

"Could I what, *querida*?" He didn't want to push her, but after what she just confessed, she needed to take the lead.

Just when he thought this little mouse couldn't surprise him, she crossed her arms at her waist and pulled the T-shirt over her head. "Could you touch me more?"

"Is that what you want?" he asked.

"Yes, it is," she replied, her words sure.

As he circled each breast over her bra and ran his fingers lazily across her torso, Cam felt her body heat and arousal spread through her like an incoming tide. Her nipples were pebbled, her breaths shallow. He could imagine her toes curling inside her boots.

"If it's too much, just tell me to stop," he breathed near the shell of her ear.

"I said yes, Miguel. Don't treat me like damaged goods."

Quick as a cat, Cam loomed above her. "Maybe the little mouse wants to be taken?"

He felt Evan arch into his body; then, she scraped her teeth over his chin.

"See, angel? When you offer your body, it can be very..." He sank his teeth into the soft flesh between her neck and shoulder as he unbuttoned her pants. He whispered into her skin, "Satisfying."

Evan circled his wrist and pushed his arm past the barricade of her waistband. Cam dipped his hand beneath her cotton underpants, pleased with the rush of arousal that met his fingers.

"Quick or slow, Evan?"

"I want..." she panted. "You choose."

A wicked grin spread across his face.

"Let's give this body what it's been wanting." He opened her pants.

With the expertise of an accomplished lover, Cam plunged two fingers inside her, eliciting a gasp. He had earned his reputation with women but not for the reasons his SEAL teammates assumed. He was good because he paid attention. Every squeeze of her fingers, every arch of her back, every quick inhale, every shudder. It mattered. For Cam, bringing his partner pleasure was as satisfying as achieving his own—a fact that was never more true than it was right now. Cam would stop the earth from turning if it meant pleasing Evan. He withdrew his fingers, held her clit, all the while watching the silhouette of her beautiful face, flushed with rapture and awe. Cam unleashed his fantasies, imagined himself pushing into her. His erection was a steel pipe threatening to burst the teeth of his fly as he pictured taking her completely, Evan giving herself completely, for the first time. He released the bud and circled it, alternating firm then gentle strokes. Evan trembled and gripped his biceps, her short nails digging into his flesh. Cam continued his ministrations, moving closer to her body, needing to feel her beneath him. Evan lifted her face to his chest, and, with a muffled shriek, she exploded.

Cam moved beside her, slipped an arm behind her head, and cradled her as she came down from the high. She opened her caramel-colored eyes and said one word.

"Wow."

Then she rolled into the shelter of his body and fell asleep.

Cam didn't bother analyzing which of his personas had delivered this woman's first orgasm from a man. He knew the answer. What's more, he didn't care. He didn't think about the implications, didn't worry about the consequences. He didn't do anything but watch over the angel in his arms, entranced.

Forty minutes later, Evan stirred, burrowing her face into Miguel's broad chest. She knew immediately where she was, who she was with, what had occurred. She also knew she needed to pull away. This man was dangerous, an enigma, a stranger. And yet, she prolonged her departure from the shelter of his embrace.

She couldn't quite wrap her brain around it, or more accurately, she didn't want to wrap her brain around it. She had let him touch her, *begged* him to touch her. *God.* Date after date, man after man had her retreating like a tortoise sensing danger. Nice boys, clean-cut, intelligent, successful professionals and academics. Never had she felt the *desire* she felt with this man.

The situation had been so wrong—a dank, dark cave, air tinged with pot smoke, a menacing man, and yet something about it had been so right. A clandestine encounter with a stranger she would never see again, to whom she could confess her deepest shame. A man who could provide unimagined pleasure. An Adonis she hadn't even kissed before she urged his hand between her legs. If Evan felt any regret at all, it wasn't over their tryst but rather their inevitable parting.

He must have sensed her wake because Miguel lifted her chin. "The men are gone. You can make your escape."

She fought the urge to nuzzle his hand. "What time is it?"

"The sun will be up soon." He reached out and illuminated one of the lanterns he had brought over to their side of the space.

Reluctantly, she climbed to her feet, snagged her T-shirt, and pulled it over her head. "I need to get to the dig site and show Dr. Emberton what we found." She gathered up the gold box and a sampling of the coins and slipped them into her canvas shoulder bag.

Miguel grabbed her messy ponytail and turned her head gently toward him. "What *you* found, *querida*. I was never here."

She didn't know why Miguel wouldn't want anyone to know he had been with her at the find; most men in his position would see dollar signs. Clearly, this man had secrets, and Evan didn't want to know them, so she nodded and stood. When they crawled through into the storage room, Evan cleared her throat. "So, um…"

Miguel spared her the awkward moment when he leaned down, took her face in his rough hands, and kissed her forehead. It was the only time his lips had touched her. "Be safe, Evan."

He disappeared into the mine, leaving Evan to retrace her steps through the cave system to the little cove where the Zodiac was hidden in an outcropping along the cliffs.

Evan emerged into the cool morning air, stood on the tea-colored beach, and watched the sky slowly pink. She stretched her arms toward the heavens and felt a corresponding ache between her legs. After taking a moment to bask in the memory, she patted the canvas bag at her hip and marched over to the boat. It was time to get down to business. Nevertheless, she couldn't help the secret smile that danced on her lips.

Best night of her life.

——————— ◇ ———————

Cam leaned against the rock wall of the tunnel outside the empty storage room and fought to corral his emotions. Why, *why* had he allowed Miguel Ramirez to touch her. He tugged on his too-long auburn hair fighting the true realization that came. In that moment, touching that angel, he had been both men, the concerned protector and the salacious deviant. The line between the two had blurred, melding Camilo Canto and Miguel Ramirez into one man and threatening to fracture his psyche. Could he reconcile the idea that Miguel was a part of him, that this impulsive, selfish man was a side of Cam?

He suddenly felt as if he had been standing on a fault line for the past three years, and this beguiling, beautiful woman was causing the earth to shake.

His thoughts turned to Evan. He bathed in the vision. There, in the dark, he saw her. She had seized her pleasure with a boldness that tapped his most primal urges. He wanted to roar when she shattered, pound his chest, and dive between her legs, extending the euphoria for minutes, hours, days… *forever*.

If a genie had emerged from a bottle and granted him his perfect woman, that woman would have paled in comparison to Evan. He hadn't even thought a woman like that could exist. She was perfect in her imperfection, a wonderful amalgam of timidity and bravery, reserve and fire. The way she passionately pursued what mattered to her it was… she was… captivating.

He didn't feel that zing his dad had talked about. What he felt was a tether, an invisible lasso pulling him toward her. And he willingly went. Even now, her absence had left him with a hollow ache, as if she were somehow essential.

Giving himself a mental slap, Cam came back to earth. Evan was spending time with Miguel Ramirez, not Camilo Canto. She didn't know Cam. What's more, Cam knew he couldn't be with any woman who wanted a man like Miguel. He'd have to take that night for what it was and move on.

Cam made his way through the labyrinth of tunnels to the mine's front exit. He looked over his shoulder one last time and allowed the memory to wash over him.

Best night of his life.

CHAPTER TWENTY-EIGHT

Miramar, Mallorca
December 10

As he had done for the past three nights, Cam bypassed the front gates and entered the March villa through the olive grove that bordered the south end of the property. Moving like a wraith, he cut through the trees and across the lawn, slipped around the pool, and climbed the broad stone steps that stopped at the retractable wall to the shower and sauna. The windows in the wall were wired to the alarm system, but the wall itself was not as it was impossible to open from the outside. Anticipating his need for a shower after these excursions, Cam had left it open just enough to slide his hand through and hit the button. The wall retracted silently, and Cam slipped inside. After sealing the room shut, he rinsed the mud and sand from his body, stepped from the shower, and stilled with the towel in his hands.

Miguel Ramirez needed to visit Gemini. Miguel Ramirez should creep into her room and wake her with his head between her legs. Without thought to the consequences, Camilo Canto crawled into bed.

He rolled to his side and watched the sun slowly illuminate the dormant olive trees. His thoughts drifted to Evan. In this vortex of turmoil, he calmed. Taking a moment to mourn what could have been, Cam resigned himself to his fate, comforted by the memory of their one and only night together. He recalled her courage as she peeled the shirt from her breasts, her innocence as he showed her what her body could do, her trust as she gave a virtual stranger her most precious gift. Maybe it was the pot smoke drifting into the room or the imminent threat of the men who drank and fought just a few yards away, but he didn't think so.

He squeezed his eyes shut. God, he had wanted to strip them both naked and plunge bare into her depths. But he couldn't. He could never let Miguel defile her, and he could never let Cam reveal himself to make love to her. So he had simply pleasured her, giving her what he could without robbing her of her dignity, without tainting the act. There was something there, between them, a bond that went beyond words, beyond circumstance. In that moment, he, *Cam*, had felt their connection. Had she felt it with Miguel Ramirez? Or had she somehow seen past his impenetrable facade?

He succumbed to sleep with the silk of her skin on his fingers and the blossoms of her scent in his nose. He drifted, listening to the melody of their encounter—half conscious, half in love.

CHAPTER TWENTY-NINE

Valldemossa, Mallorca
December 10

The alarm on the phone trilled, pulling Evan from a short but rejuvenating sleep. Her eyes opened. Instead of the timber ceiling, she pictured the image of Miguel hovering above her. Still amazed by her unhampered trust—her unhampered *lust*—she replayed their encounter, every quixotic minute.

Something about that magnificent cocktail of danger and darkness had allowed her to free her inner desires. More than that, though, it was the man. Whether he knew it or not, Miguel was a protector, a giver. Deep in his soul, beneath the callous, selfish thug, was a generous, caring man. She wanted that man. Was there any hope for them?

Her thoughts strayed to the dinner party and Miguel and the famous beauty on his lap for half the night. He had said they weren't involved. So what then? Was he simply feigning interest, or was it the more obvious explanation that he was lying?

She knew there was no future for her with Miguel, but she also knew she wanted to solve this irritating puzzle. Resolved to crack

Miguel Ramirez's code somehow, she threw off the covers and got to her day. She had an archaeological discovery to announce.

———————— ◆ ————————

Evan stepped out of the shower, wrapped herself in a towel, and scampered down the hall back to her room. The golden box sat on her bed, and she eyed it while she crossed the room as if it might float away. She was so distracted she nearly tumbled over her tiny desk. As it was, she kicked the plastic drawstring bag she had set on the floor a week ago—the bag from the hospital. Sitting in the ladderback chair, she lifted it and pulled it open. There, stuck to the swim cap, was the slip of paper with the phone number.

She rubbed her fully-healed calf. The whole incident felt like a distant dream. Nevertheless, she owed this man a phone call. Propelled by her ingrained politeness and sincere gratitude, she grabbed her cell phone from the desk and entered the number.

She didn't mask her relief when the call went straight to voicemail. "Um, hi." She crinkled the paper as she held it up. "This is... well, this is the woman you helped earlier this week. The stingray? Anyway, the medics gave me your number, and I wanted to, um, thank you... for helping me. So... thanks... you're, um, you're a good man."

She set the phone back down before she purposely knocked herself in the head with it. *You're a good man?* The guy could be a serial killer for all she knew. *Whatever.* She checked the "thank you" off of her to-do list and recalled the next several items. First and foremost, she needed to show Dr. Emberton her discovery and discuss how to proceed.

It was all she could do to bottle her excitement over presenting the gold box to her mentor. With renewed vigor, Evan moved to the closet to dress.

She pulled on a T-shirt. When her head emerged through the neck hole, her mind again drifted back to the cave. She wasn't impulsive by nature, but when she realized that brief encounter might be her only chance to experience the touch of a man, she hadn't hesitated. She recalled Miguel's massive form taking charge of her body. She wanted to reciprocate, to vent eight years' worth of bottled-up libidinous curiosity. Where was he ticklish? What made him groan or sigh or shudder? What would that thick erection feel like in her hands, her mouth, her body? *God.* She had gone from frigid to wanton in the course of one night.

She finished dressing and sent up a silent prayer that her panic attacks had ebbed, that her fear of erotic touch was fading. Could she meet a nice man and start dating? Take it to the next level? For some reason, the thought left her cold. She quickly packed away thoughts of Miguel. Hopefully, one day, she could redirect these feelings of attraction and lust. She needed to stop thinking about her dark, complicated, golden-eyed man because she knew she probably wouldn't see Miguel Ramirez again.

But she wanted to.

CHAPTER THIRTY

The call for all hands on deck came via text. Steady and Tox, sweaty from the gym, met Herc and Ren coming off the gun range, and the foursome took the stairs to the second-floor war room. Nathan was sitting at the head of the rectangular conference table flanked by Twitch and Chat, who both had laptops open.

The men moved into the room as a unit, and each grabbed a seat.

Nathan held up a hand, stalling Ren's downward motion into the chair next to Twitch. "Move down one."

Before Ren could ask, movement at the door caught his eye, and he looked up to see Sofria Kirk, laptop under her arm, striding into the room. Ren didn't mask his pleasure. She had changed so much since he first met her two years ago. She had grown confident, and she had clearly found a friend judging by the way her amber eyes warmed when she saw Twitch. Ren pretended not to notice as Sofria slipped something into Twitch's pocket. As was their habit, in an effort to hone Sofria's "spy skills," Twitch and Sofria had taken to passing jokes and amusing clips secretly via flash drive. While there were undoubtedly less cumbersome ways to share tech, flash drives were still prevalent in the world of espionage, where digital transmissions were easily captured. As a result, terrorists and criminals used devices without networks.

Nathan commenced introductions. "Some of you already know Sofria Kirk. She is an analyst at Langley and has been cleared by Cam's handler and the DDO to share pertinent information."

Sofria gave a hesitant wave to the intimidating cadre. When her eyes met Ren's, recognition lit her face.

"Professor Jameson." She smiled.

Leo "Ren" Jameson shot to his feet, knocking his phone into Steady's lap in the process.

"Hey, Sofria. It's just Ren these days. Or Leo. Ren's a nickname," he clarified.

"So is Leo, I imagine. Short for Leonard or Leonardo," she replied.

"Correct, but not short for those."

"Leopold? Leon?" Sofria rattled off names.

Ren just winked.

"Uh, guys?" Tox clapped his hands. "Missing buddy? Ask her to fucking prom later."

Ren cleared his throat and sat.

Twitch patted the table in the space next to her, beckoning her friend. Once Sofria was settled with her computer open, Nathan spoke.

"Sofria has information."

A figure appeared in the doorway, and Nathan looked up to the dispassionate, scarred face of his friend. The men nodded, and Tox stood with arms outstretched.

Nathan continued, "Sofria, this is Finn McIntrye." Nathan gestured to the brooding CIA officer and deadpanned, "He's in sales."

Finn took a seat and gave Sofria his full attention.

"A call came in on Miguel Ramirez's cell phone. The caller left a voicemail. I think it's the lead we've been hoping for." She entered a command on her keyboard, and a female voice filled the room.

This is... well, this is the woman you helped earlier. The stingray? Anyway, the medics gave me your number, and I wanted to, um, thank you... for helping me. So... thanks... you're, um, you're a good man.

Questions bubbled to the surface, but Ren started with the most important: "Where did this call come from?"

"Mallorca," Sofria answered.

"Sounds like he rescued her after a stingray attack? I mean, assuming she's talking about the fish and not the torpedo," Tox offered.

"Or it's not some criminal underworld nickname," Steady added.

"I think those are both safe assumptions," Nathan replied without inflection.

Chat added, "On a sanctioned op, he would have a prearranged means to contact his handler. This was a straight-up abduction. He needed a way to contact us without raising suspicions."

"Giving this woman the phone number was a secure way to signal for help," Steady added.

"So he's in Mallorca?" Herc asked.

Twitch took the ball. "Apparently. Operating on that information, I checked flight data from the day Cam went missing. A privately owned 737 took off from Teterboro airport in Jersey three hours after Cam's Harlem meetup. Destination: Barcelona. From there, the plane went on to Aeropuerto Palma de Mallorca."

"Ding ding ding, and we have a winner," Steady chimed in.

Twitch held up a hand. "It gets better. The plane was not a lease. It's a privately-owned craft, property of The March Conglomerate. They have a mining operation on Mallorca."

Nathan added, "The mining operation is run by Atlas March, who took over the company after Ulysses March died last year."

"What's his reputation?" Ren asked.

"Sketchy," Finn spoke. "His name has come up a time or two. He was dipping his toe into the heroin trade when he ran March Mining's Colombia operation. Now that he's in Spain, there are some rumblings in the European cartels."

"Could be a connection there," Ren said. "Cam worked in South America. His cover identity, Miguel Ramirez, is from Colombia."

"There's something else." Nathan hesitated. "Sofria?"

"Atlas March's cousin is the model Gemini March."

"No way." Herc's jaw dropped.

"The files Cam's handler gave me indicate that Cam had an *encounter* with Ms. March last year on Ibiza," Nathan added. "And that she has been trying to locate him ever since."

Ren turned his attention to the table. "Tell me this is not about some girl."

"Dude, not *some girl*, Gemini March," Herc insisted.

"Herc," Nathan scolded.

"Sorry, boss."

Nathan stood leaning his palms on the table. "This is not the time to speculate. These are the facts. Cam was taken against his will to Mallorca. One or more members of the March family or employees of The March Conglomerate are involved. Cam's abductors know him by his CIA legend, Miguel Ramirez. He gave an unknown woman his phone number. Is there anything else?"

Tox stood, six and a half feet of determination. "We only needed to know the first one. Let's go get our boy."

"Hooyah." Steady joined Tox on his feet. The other men soon followed.

Nathan gave the order, "Pack your bags. Twitch and Chat handle tech and comms. Tox, you're on weapons. Wheels up oh-six hundred tomorrow."

Tox looked at Nathan. "You're coming?"

"Not this time. Emily is too close to her due date. Plus, I want to help Miles put that sewer rat of a senator where he belongs."

"Copy that." Tox turned and headed to the armory.

"Uh, boss?" Herc scratched his head. "Do we have a plan?"

Nathan clapped him on the back on the way out of the room. "One Naval Intelligence officer, one Marine sniper, and four Navy SEALs. I'm sure we can come up with something."

CHAPTER THIRTY-ONE

South Island, South Carolina
December 11

Steady toed open the lockless, knobless front door of the beach house, a case of Coors Light under each arm and a plastic grocery bag filled with chips in his teeth. Ren and Chat followed him in with a whiteboard and a box of office supplies swiped from Bishop Security. Herc was next in line with folding chairs and a card table he had borrowed from Maggie and Charlie Bishop's garage, knowing his grandmother wouldn't mind. Tox was picking up pizza. Twitch was on her way. Nathan had opted to go home to his family. Despite his evident concern, his wife's looming due date was an unavoidable distraction.

Steady had initially invited the guys over to strip the floors and do some demo, but with the op a go, the rehab project became a plan and brainstorm project. Steady figured the odds were pretty good one or more of them would punch a hole in the drywall by the end of the night, so the demo would get started.

Tox came through the door holding eight large pizza boxes. He set the food on the kitchen counter, snagged two slices, and joined the group. Ren and Chat entered through the open front door and moved to help Steady pull the plywood from what was once a series of sliding glass doors. The missing fourth wall opened the living area to what was left of the deck and the ocean beyond.

Tox was already grabbing another couple of slices at the counter. "Hey, Steady, why don't you just leave it like that? It'd be sort of like camping on the beach every night."

"Because *camping* has such fond memories for me," Steady countered.

Tox laughed around his pizza, immediately recalling a disastrous subzero night perched on a narrow cliff in the Hindu Kush. "You got me there."

"I was kicking around the idea of attaching the nose cone of a Hornet to the opening. How cool would that be? Watch the sunrise from the cockpit?"

Steady had the extremely rare distinction of being both a naval aviator and a SEAL. He had grown up flying small aircraft and had trained in Pensacola for two years, flying multiple missions before switching over to the SEALs as an officer. Like the SEAL acronym: Sea, Air, Land, if it moved, Steady could fly it, fix it, or drive it.

Tox nearly jumped for joy. "Dude, you have to do it. I call shotgun."

Steady laughed, "My dad already had a heart attack. I can't give my mom one too."

Chat and Steady were sitting at the rickety card table organizing the additional, heavily redacted files Sofria had provided when Steady looked over his shoulder to the front of the house.

Twitch knocked on the open door and stepped into the house.

"What took so long?" Steady asked, handing her a can of soda.

"I was next door," Twitch explained.

"What were you doing next door?" Steady asked, a little too interested.

"Visiting Very. We went to college together."

"Very?"

Twitch confirmed. "Very. Her real name is Verity, but everyone calls her Very. It suits her. She is very, *very*."

Steady concentrated on listening to Twitch and trying to control the blood flow in his body. God, why was the notion of this Very woman such a turn-on? All he knew about her at this point was that she went to college with Twitch, had bright pink hair, and liked The Ramones—all big pluses but still, not much to go on.

Twitch continued, "She just moved here to work for a lab in Ridgefield. She's a chemist."

"What lab in Ridgefield?" Ren cocked his head.

"Exactly." Twitch winked.

Behind her, Finn McIntyre appeared in the doorway. The mood in the room shifted. Dressed in faded jeans, a hoodie, and trainers, darkness loomed around him like an additional garment. The hood of his sweatshirt shadowed the scars on the right side of his face, but even the casual observer would have sensed they were there. It was as if the injury had subsumed his entire aura. Finn had grown comfortable in his cocoon of grief and rage, a state of being that unfortunately aided his "legend" when he was on assignment. Like Cam, Finn was a NOC officer with the CIA. Unlike Cam, he seemed to have lost his center. Nevertheless, his team was his family; when they needed him, he showed up.

Finn walked to the pizza boxes. Tox, the man who had rescued him from that cave three years ago, slapped him on the back. Then he left his big hand on Finn's shoulder as if he too sensed the shift in his best friend. Finn shrugged it off.

"Have we learned anything new?" Finn asked.

"Just diving in." Ren held up a stack of files. "Your employer is not the most forthcoming when it comes to information sharing."

"Former employer," Finn corrected.

The announcement had Ren's eyebrows hitting his hairline.

"What happened?" There was concern in the question, but Tox didn't even try to hide his happiness at the announcement. Even Chat, who in the most stressful situations was inscrutable, looked pleased.

"I accidentally killed a trafficker they were trying to turn." Finn flipped his palms up in a *what was I supposed to do?* Gesture.

"How'd you accidentally kill him?" Herc asked, grabbing a fresh beer from the cooler.

Finn gave an evil grin. "Shot him in the face."

"Well, that would certainly do it." Steady crossed the room to hug his friend.

"And I may or may not have punched the Assistant Deputy Director of Operations. Also in the face."

"Whoa." Tox ran a hand across his five o'clock shadow. "That's a lot of fucking up faces." He instantly regretted the comment seeing Finn's own scarred profile, but it was Finn's reply that silenced the room.

"Yeah, well, when Gabriel Lorca, the most vicious cartel leader in Eastern Europe is patting you on the back for killing an informant—a guy who makes a living selling children—and the CIA is hauling you in for disciplinary measures, it kind of skews your reality." He poured straight bourbon into a red cup and took an unhealthy swig.

"You were embedded with Gabriel Lorca?" Ren asked.

"Classified." Finn finished his drink and poured another.

"The CIA put Lorca in power fifteen years ago. He kills his rivals and blows up their operations with enough C4 to put a crater in the ground. Then he went rogue. Now he's their biggest problem," Ren said.

Finn clapped both hands together. "So, what's on the agenda tonight, boys. I need to get laid."

Five dumbfounded faces stared back at him.

Chat stood. "We find our brother. We don't rest until we do."

Finn laughed awkwardly. "Oh, come on. There's nothing to do. Nothing in those files will shed any light."

Chat stepped away from the table and stood toe-to-toe with his friend. "It doesn't matter. We work with what we have. We dig. Cam isn't resting, so we don't rest. That's how this works." He grabbed Finn's forearm. "Every time."

Finn closed his eyes against the memory. Chat continued, undeterred, "We didn't sleep for three days straight looking for you. Ren made the connection between the insurgents and a local man. Tox held a knife to his wife's throat until he gave up the location of the cave."

Tox's face was expressionless, but his gaze was unashamed. Steady, nicknamed for his composure, released a rare burst of temper. "What did you think, Finn? That we hit the town and waited for Nathan and OpNav to get us intel? It was combat naps and MREs until we found you."

Finn set the bottle of booze on the kitchen counter. Shame, rage, sadness simmered beneath his skin. With an anguished cry, he grabbed the bottle and threw it against the far wall, whiskey and glass bleeding down the wallpaper. Grabbing his hair in both fists, he stormed past the men out onto the deck, where he stomped onto the decayed boards...

And promptly fell through the wood onto the sand ten feet below.

A tormented "Fuuuuuck!" rose up.

Tox lifted both hands to stop his brothers and turned to the deck. He gingerly worked his way around the rotted boards and fresh hole to the stairs and descended. He found Finn sitting under the deck, head in his hands, weeping.

Tox took a seat beside him and waited. A minute passed, then another. Finally, Finn looked up, making no effort to hide the tear tracks that ran through the sand on his face.

"Something's got to change, Miller." The fact that Finn had called him by his name spoke volumes.

"Yes," Tox agreed, "it does."

"What the fuck do I do? You think I want to be this way? Last month I put a guy in the hospital because he called me Two-Face. Before that, I smacked a woman. I was in the middle of fucking her. I don't even remember what she said." He rested his forehead on the heels of his palms. "I used to be a good guy."

Tox rested a hand on his back. "You still are a good guy, Finn, but you're not invincible. There's no shame in asking for help. Shit, *I* get therapy to work through what happened to you."

That had Finn looking up. "Get? Still?"

"Yeah, still. Look around you, brother. Look at the Spec Ops guys who struggle. You faked your way through mandatory psych evals, and those demons don't just die," Tox said.

"I thought I was fine." Finn half-laughed.

"You're not fine," Tox replied.

Finn picked up a fistful of sand and let it run through his palm. "I didn't realize..." He looked above him.

"Every minute you were in that cave, we were looking for you. How could you not know that?" Tox rested a hand on his best friend's shoulder.

"I'm pretty fucked up, huh?" Finn spoke to the sand.

"You just need help," Tox said.

"We need to find Cam," Finn insisted.

Tox stood and offered a hand to help Finn.

"You're missing too, Finn. Everybody understands. Let's get you some help."

Finn clasped Tox's outstretched hand and rose, dusting the sand from his jeans. "Yeah, okay. I need to do something first. I'll be in touch." He didn't miss Tox's concerned expression. "Don't worry. I've had a muzzle to my chin a hundred times and haven't pulled the trigger yet."

The half-joke didn't help.

"Relax. I just need to see someone. I'll be in touch."

Tox just nodded and unconsciously rubbed his stomach to ease the pit forming. Finn slapped him on the arm. "Calm down, Sasquatch. We'll continue the hair braiding and pillow fights tomorrow."

Tox chuffed, "Sounds good. I'll talk to you tomorrow."

Finn started to walk off, then turned back to his best friend. "I love you, you know."

"Oh, fuck you, asshole. Now I'm worried all over again."

He could hear Finn's laughter even after his silhouette had disappeared into the darkness.

CHAPTER THIRTY-TWO

Beaufort, South Carolina
December 11

Twitch was usually a sound sleeper—the sleep of the innocent—but the blustery December night had tree branches demanding entry at her window. More than that, though, the air stirred, a silent disruption in the quiet.

She sat up in bed. She should have screamed. Pulled the gun from the nightstand. Hit the security panic button. She didn't. And she knew why.

The silhouette moved closer and, as it passed the window, the intermittent moon lit his scars.

"Finn?" She spoke softly. "What's going on?"

He sat at the foot of the bed and looked at the floor. "I'm sorry."

She hugged her knees to her chest and let him find the words.

"I'm going away for a while," he said.

"How long?"

She observed his unmarred left profile as he lifted his head and stared out the window.

"I have to get right. I don't know if I can, but I have to try."

She nodded in the darkness. "I'm glad."

"I don't want you to hold out hope for me. Even if I manage some kind of normalcy, I'll never be…" He tugged on his sandy hair. "I can't be responsible for your happiness when I can't even find my own. You have to take that burden off my shoulders."

She didn't wipe her tears. Didn't pause to ponder his choice of word, *burden*. She simply nodded again. "It's okay, Finn."

"Is it?" he asked.

"No." She laugh-cried. "But it will be. I do have hope for that. I've always believed in you. That won't ever change."

Finn shook his head slowly as if she had spoken in another language. He gently slapped both thighs and stood. Twitch lifted her face to him as he moved to the head of the bed and bent down. Then, ever so gently, he placed a kiss on her forehead. "You need to give all that love to someone who knows what to do with it."

She turned her head away. *Too late.*

He squeezed her delicate hand, stood to his full height, and turned to leave. Twitch held on and quietly said one word. It was the last word spoken in her room that night.

It was a word that said, *I have faith.*

It was a word that said, *I forgive you.*

It was a word that said, *Goodbye.*

"Stay."

It was still dark as Finn McIntyre repacked his gear in the cheap oceanside motel room. He didn't think. He didn't feel. He just did.

Clothes, Dopp kit, weapons, gear: everything went neatly into its place in the unmarked duffle.

His cell buzzed on the end table.

He read the text reply, tapped out another, and shut off his phone, hoping he hadn't just made a colossal mistake.

CHAPTER THIRTY-THREE

Bishop Security Jet
December 12

"I accessed hospital records. Evangeline Cole was treated for a stingray sting and released." Twitch's fingers flew across the keyboard. "She's a doctoral candidate in anthropology at Stanford, on Mallorca on an archaeological dig."

"I thought Mallorca was all beach hopping celebrities and royals on private jets," Herc commented.

"Look around you. You're not exactly slumming." Steady tossed a balled-up napkin at Herc's head.

"And the women are topless," Herc plowed on. "Beaches just filled with topless women."

"There were topless women on our beach, fool," Steady chided. "Between that and the stash of porn you probably have on some old MacBook under your childhood bed at Gramma Maggie's, you should be set."

Herc flushed beet red and turned his attention to the travel brochure he was holding.

The Bishop Security jet certainly rivaled any luxury craft in the sky. Tox and his wife, Calliope, sat side-by-side at the oval conference table. Steady, Ren, Herc, and Chat sprawled on cream leather couches and recliners. Twitch was perched at the head of the table, surrounded by tech, piecing together the last several days of Cam's life.

"Actually," Ren explained, "Mallorca is rich in ancient history. A civilization known as the Talaiotic people thrived in the region from about two thousand B.C."

"Exactly," Twitch agreed. "A dig in 2013 unearthed some nifty Talaiotic stuff. Archaeologists have been flocking to the area ever since. Evangeline Cole is there with a team headed by Dr. Omar Emberton of Stanford and the University of Cairo." Twitch activated the plasma screen on the wall and started a slide show of the excavation from the university's website.

"I'd love to speak with Doctor Emberton. What a fascinating project," Ren mused.

"Whoa." Herc elbowed Steady when the next slide appeared. They both sat up in their reclined seats.

"That's Evangeline Cole?" Herc asked.

It was a promotional photo used to accompany journal articles and for faculty listings on Stanford's website. In it, Evan stood before a vast desert holding a small artifact, the dirt and sand on her face failing to obscure her evident pride at her discovery.

Chat peered at the picture. "I can see why this woman threw him off his game."

"You've got to be kidding me!" Herc practically shouted. "Gemini March is on that island. Gemini-freaking-March. She was *Miss March*, and I don't mean her name."

Tox begrudgingly agreed, "The kid has a point. The Cam we knew would go for the centerfold."

"I don't know." Chat moved his head side-to-side like a metronome. "The Cam we *knew* is not the Cam we *know*."

"I don't know how he does it," Herc remarked. "Goes undercover. I can't even lie to my grandmother."

"None of us can lie to Maggie. She'd have our asses." Steady's comment was met with general agreement.

"Still," Herc continued, "to pretend to be another person? I sure as shit couldn't do it."

Ren leaned forward in his seat, resting his forearms on his thighs. "It's actually a fascinating psychological study. CIA NOC officers and other deep-cover operators, the good ones anyway, actually create a full persona, an alter ego, if you will. It can take an operator months, sometimes years, to shed their legend after they resurface. Those men and women make a huge sacrifice doing what they do. They don't give their lives, but they sacrifice who they are."

There was a moment of respectful silence before Tox, in true SEAL fashion, broke through the quiet with humor. "Well, maybe the undercover gods are smiling on our friend, and *Miguel Ramirez* is knee-deep in hot women and sandy beaches." He gestured to the image on the screen.

Calliope guided her husband's face from the picture of the woman to her. He kissed her with a smile.

"What's the plan, fellas?" she asked, still staring at Tox.

Tox leaned back in his seat and crossed his long legs at the ankle. "The March villa is located about ten clicks outside of Palma. We'll set up surveillance and go from there."

A photo of the sprawling Mediterranean estate appeared, the sparkling water of the bay in the distance. "Twitch, get us a boat. Chat, you and Ren up for a little sport fishing?"

"Always," Chat said. They wouldn't catch anything, but the cover would provide an unobstructed view of the entire back of the property.

"Got the boat," Twitch confirmed. At Tox's surprised glance, she shrugged. "They're easy to book. Now, convincing the captain to take the day off is your problem."

"Not a problem." Ren didn't look up from the archaeological journal he had pulled up on his laptop.

"Well, whadda ya know?" Twitch typed furiously as she spoke.

"What's up, Twitch?" Tox asked.

"As I was looking at the satellite imagery for the closest marina, I noticed a Zodiac that might prove useful."

Tox sat up. "Perfect, can you talk to the harbormaster or whoever's running the place about procurement?"

"I don't think we'll need to. The owner may be willing to let us borrow it, seeing as she owes Cam a favor."

"She?"

"I already contacted the harbormaster. The Zodiac belongs to Evangeline Cole. I'll see if I can track her down," Twitch said.

"Hot damn," Steady exclaimed. "Most spooks have a network of embassy informants and back alley lowlifes; Cam has a little black book. He doesn't love 'em and leave 'em; he Pied Pipers that shit."

Twitch ignored the remark. "I'm also getting you a van. And Herc? You up for a scenic bike ride?"

"Hell, yes." Herc rubbed his palms together.

"I figured a motorcycle would give you the most flexibility if you, you know, need to climb a tree or find a perch somewhere," Twitch added.

Tox agreed, "Good thought. So, I estimate seventy-two hours of surveillance. Let's see if we can spot our boy."

"Or…" Twitch typed out something and finished with a flourish. "We could take advantage of Calliope's skillset." She turned the laptop so Tox and Calliope could see the email she had just written.

Tox slapped the flat of his hand on the conference table. "Twitch, you're a genius." He turned to his wife. "What do you think, Cal?"

Calliope gave the group a Cheshire Cat smile. "I think I'd like to show you boys how it's done."

CHAPTER THIRTY-FOUR

Valldemossa, Mallorca
December 12

Evan knocked softly on Omar Emberton's door. He opened it dressed in his usual work attire: khaki pants, a button-up shirt, and worn boots. He had his canvas jacket draped over his arm.

"Evan," he greeted her. "I was just headed to the site. What brings you by?"

She beamed at him. "May I come in?"

"Of course, of course." Emberton seemed to sense her excitement because he didn't hesitate to pull the door wide and extend a hand to the small couch and pair of chairs in the cozy living area.

"We found something, Doctor E." Evan perched at the edge of the sofa and pulled her messenger bag onto her lap.

Emberton took a seat, looking strangely out of place in the chintz slipper chair. "We?" Emberton squinted behind his glasses.

Evan quickly covered her misspeak. "I mean 'we' the team."

Emberton nodded, pleased. "Continue."

"I mapped the markers and realized they seemed to surround a small cave that had been sealed off. When I entered, I found a deteriorated mound." She pulled the GoPro from her bag. "I recorded what I discovered."

Her mentor leaned forward on his elbows and intertwined his fingers. "And what was that?"

She withdrew the items from the cave. She set the gold box and several coins on the coffee table. Then she sat back and waited.

Omar Emberton pulled a monogrammed linen handkerchief from the back pocket of his khaki pants and methodically cleaned his glasses. He replaced them on his nose and shifted his chair slightly to face the table fully. Donning a pair of thin cotton gloves—and managing to scold Evan for not doing so with merely a look—he made a cursory examination of the coins. He quickly moved on to the box, examining the exterior, running his fingers along the engravings with care.

Evan sat still as a statue. She knew this discovery was significant, but she had never seen her mentor rendered speechless. Then, from beneath his glasses, a tear slid down his cheek.

After a time, he commented absently, "My grandfather is from this village." He indicated an inscription on the side of the box.

He opened the box and poked through the coins looking more like an old woman searching for a dime in a coin purse full of pennies than an archaeologist examining a find. He withdrew the medallion and thumbed the void. "This is wonderful, Evan. Was there anything else in the box?"

Evan was taken aback by Dr. Emberton's misdirected enthusiasm. She would have thought he would have been excited by what was in the box rather than what was not, or the box itself for that matter.

"No. Just the coins and the necklace," she replied.

He set the box on the small table and ran a hand over it reverently. He spoke to Evan with his eyes on the box. "This is one of the great joys of this work, Evangeline. Finding something from the past that takes your work in an entirely different direction." He looked at her then. "This box is Moorish, late Fifteenth Century, no doubt hidden when the Moors fled the Crusaders."

"Yes, that was my estimation as well," Evan agreed.

"You remember Joseph Nabeel from our dinner. He's not an archaeologist by trade, but he knows more about artifacts from this period than any colleague I've ever encountered. He would be very interested in examining this box and accompanying you to this secondary site. Your other work can wait." Emberton gestured vaguely in the direction of their primary dig site with a flip of his hand as if it hardly mattered.

"Of course. I'll map it out. I stumbled on it quite by accident."

Emberton laughed. "Isn't that always the way?" He leaned forward conspiratorially. "As a graduate student, I got lost driving to an excavation in Niger. I pulled to the side of the road and explained to a local woman, in the most rudimentary sign language and broken French, who I was and what I was looking for. She took me by the hand and pulled me to a field where her husband had been digging a well. He had unearthed a small statue, and they didn't know what to do with it."

"The Aterian Culture discovery?" Evan's jaw dropped.

Emberton winked. "Let's keep that our little secret." He picked up the gold box with both hands and held it out. "This goes in the vault." He gestured to the standing safe in the corner. "Let's photograph and catalog it and see that it's securely stored."

Emberton spoke his instructions without ever taking his eyes off of the box. Evan thought he might have actually stroked it. When he did look up, he was all business.

"Your next task is cartography. Create a detailed map of the path you took, document markers and focal points, anything and everything of note."

She nodded. Emberton's instructions, if overly enthusiastic, were standard for a new find.

"Would you like to take someone to assist you?" he asked.

Evan instantly thought of Miguel. How she would have loved to recruit the March Mining security guard to be by her side, but that wasn't what Omar meant, and the suggestion would be wholly inappropriate. Moreover, while Emberton did not seem overly concerned about their timeline, she knew that if the team hadn't made any significant discoveries—any significant Talaiotic discoveries—by the end of the year, their grant money would evaporate. "No, you need your people working. The mapping should be easy. It won't take me long."

"Excellent. Keep me apprised of your progress. I'll reach out to Joseph Nabeel and set up a meeting." As a dismissal, he dug his phone from a deep pocket and began scrolling his contacts.

She turned to go, but Emberton called her back. "Evangeline."

"Yes?"

"Be careful in those caves," he warned.

She assured him she would and set to work on her long list of tasks.

After the golden box had been documented and stored in the safe in Dr. Emberton's rooms, Evan returned to her quarters, gathered her gear, and prepared to set out. Map-making was a far cry from a compass, binoculars, and a spring divider. Her cartography equipment was in the form of a portable scanner and software. As she was zipping her bag, a gentle fist tapped on her door.

"Evangeline?"

She looked up and found a fairy of a girl standing in her doorway. Her copper hair hung over her shoulder in a long braid. Evan could tell they were about the same age, but with her jeans, backpack, and hoodie, the woman could have passed for a middle-schooler.

"Can I help you?" Evan asked.

"God, I hope so." The woman bounced into the room and sat at the desk chair, balancing the backpack on her lap. She blew out an exasperated breath. Evan liked her immediately.

Rocking forward on the chair and pushing up on the balls of her lime-green Converse, the woman asked, "Do you happen to remember a guy saving you from a stingray?"

After thirty minutes and phrases including *the behest of the United States government* and *decorated US Navy SEAL*, Evan gave Twitch permission to use her Zodiac; apparently, this woman's colleague, a man named Cam, needed it for a critical mission. After they exchanged contact information, Twitch thanked her and said she'd be in touch.

With her equipment packed and ready, Evan headed out on her mapping expedition.

CHAPTER THIRTY-FIVE

Miramar, Mallorca
December 13

In an ice-blue suit that matched her eyes, nude peep-toe stilettos, and her dark hair in a neat chignon, Calliope Buchanan was every bit the polished entertainment reporter she claimed to be. She sat in the back of the Mercedes and tapped a short pale-pink nail on her iPad screen. Steady pulled up to the guardhouse of the March villa and announced her. Sensing her disquiet, he spoke over his shoulder as he pulled through the gates. "You doin' okay back there?"

"I don't know why I'm so nervous," Calliope confessed.

"It always means more when it's one of our own. Just stay mission-focused," Steady instructed.

"What does that mean?"

"It means, do the interview. You probably did a dozen when you actually worked at *The Harlem Sentry*. This is just one more. You're a reporter getting a fashion story from a supermodel. Ask the questions you prepared. If you happen to notice our boy or anything else interesting, you know what to do." Steady kept his head forward, navigating the winding drive with ease.

If Cam was within earshot, Calliope would mention the beach-front restaurant, La Sirena.

Calliope steeled herself with a deep breath. "I got this."

Steady kept his head straight as he pulled up to the imposing estate. "Yeah, you do."

———— ◈ ————

A camera-ready Gemini March crossed one mile-long leg over the other and blew on her tea in a move that was both practiced and seductive. Calliope sat dutifully at Gemini's elbow at the small, glass table in the solarium and hung on the model's every word.

Gemini set the teacup in the saucer without taking a sip and finished answering the question on a laugh. "And the buckles! I mean, the man is a genius, but getting into some of the garments can take hours."

The man in question was New York designer Marcus Arroyo. Gemini March had plucked him from obscurity by wearing his gowns on red carpets two years ago. She and Arroyo had both made tabloid headlines when she arrived at the Grammy Awards in an Arroyo original made entirely from fig leaves. Since then, the de-signer had experienced a meteoric rise as an avant-garde formal wear designer.

"I've walked his shows in Milan, Istanbul, Bangkok, Paris—there's always some 'incident' with those damn buckles," Gemini continued.

Calliope giggled along with her host. "He has repeatedly called you his Muse."

Gemini's smile bloomed. "Marcus is like that best friend girls have in middle school. We're joined at the hip. We're always texting and FaceTiming. We travel together. He's deathly afraid of flying, so

I send a March jet for him in New York. He picks me up in Palma, and off we fly. That way, I can hold his hand—and get him good and drunk." She winked.

"Is there a romance brewing?" Calliope held up her tablet, making a show of preparing to jot down Gemini's juicy response.

"Oh, God, no. He's like a baby brother to me. He's happily sowing his wild oats. I don't see him settling down for a while. I prefer a man with a little more..." She spun her teacup in the saucer. "Maturity."

Calliope grabbed the opening. "Looks to me like you're talking about someone in particular. I'm sure our readers want to know what's new in your love life."

With calculated restraint, Gemini reached for the small silver tongs and pinched a sugar cube. "Well, I do have some news on that front." She summoned the maid. "Renata?"

The unobtrusive woman stepped forward. "Yes, miss?"

"Is Miguel on the property?" Gemini inquired.

Calliope masked her excitement by returning her gaze to her tablet and tapping out some notes.

"Yes, miss. He's in the gym," the maid replied.

"Perfect." Gemini's lips parted.

Calliope could practically see the salacious thoughts flash through the model's mind as she imagined him working out—back on the bench, bar above his glistening chest.

"Tell him his presence is requested. No need to shower or change."

The maid hastened from the room, and Gemini returned her attention to Calliope.

"Miguel?" Calliope probed.

"It's new." Gemini applied coy like a layer of makeup. "Well, not *new* exactly. We met last year, shared one explosive night, but life took us in different directions. We reunited recently, and things are going…" She looked at her lap with a girlish sigh. "Really well."

"Sounds like things are progressing quickly," Calliope encouraged.

"I'm at the point in my life where I know what I want," Gemini replied.

Calliope hummed her understanding, but her next question was halted by a knock on the open door and a thickly accented, "You wanted to see me?"

Calliope turned in her chair and took in her friend. His face registered no recognition as he stood leaning against the jamb in a sweaty gray T-shirt with a towel draped around his neck. She concealed her elation with less prowess than the trained NOC officer, but she managed.

"Miguel, say hello to Calliope Buchanan. She's a reporter with *The Harlem Sentry*. We were just talking about you," Gemini beckoned.

Without sparing Calliope a glance, Cam sauntered into the room and tipped Gemini's chin up with two fingers. "And what were you saying, camaleón?"

He called her *chameleon*. Calliope registered the odd… endearment? It made sense, she guessed. Gemini March was in the business of changing her appearance as the occasion required. Nevertheless, chameleons also blended with their environment to inconspicuously lure their prey. Cam was telling Calliope in as subtle a way as possible that Gemini March had a hand in his disappearance. If Gemini took offense, she didn't show it; her face glowed, serene.

Calliope smoothly interjected, "Gemini was just telling me about your romance."

"Was she?" Cam gazed at Gemini, still holding her chin.

"And what did she say?" he asked.

"Just that it was new. And promising," Calliope answered.

"I think she is right about that. This beauty has captured me," Cam said, never taking his eyes off of Gemini.

Gemini removed his hand from her face and kissed his fingertips. "You mean captivated, darling. Not captured."

Cam turned to the door. "I need a shower." He nodded to Calliope. "Enjoy your visit."

"We were just finishing up," Gemini said.

Calliope seized the opening. Gathering her things, she directed her comment to Gemini as Cam headed out the door. "Oh, that reminds me. My assistant mentioned a restaurant on the water outside of town, La Sirena? Do you recommend it?"

Gemini followed the bow and flex of Cam's backside as he walked from the room then returned her attention to Calliope. "La Sirena? I don't think I know it, but you can't go wrong with most beachfront bistros. They catch the fish right there. Try the caldereta. It's a local seafood stew. You won't be disappointed."

Calliope passed Gemini a business card and stood. "Be sure to keep me updated—on the fashion and the romance." Calliope leaned closer. "From the look he just gave you, I'm betting there will be more to the story."

Gemini did not mask her pleasure at the observation as Calliope continued, "And best of luck with the runway show in Jakarta."

"I'm thrilled to be doing it. Marcus is showing his line all over the world in the coming months. Indonesia is our first stop, then on to Tokyo, Beijing, and Kuala Lumpur. The days of fashion hubs being limited to New York, Paris, and Milan are over. The top new designers are coming onto the scene in places like Budapest and Stockholm. It's an exciting time to be in fashion."

Calliope made note of Gemini March's Asian itinerary. "I'm sure his new designs will be amazing. New Yorkers will be waiting for his return with bated breath."

Gemini escorted Calliope to the villa's main entrance. They exchanged air kisses and pleasant goodbyes as the sedan pulled up.

Calm and composed, Calliope waited until the car was out on the main road before she squealed.

———— ◈ ————

Cam entered the bathroom and stripped off his sweaty clothes. With perfunctory efficiency, he started the shower and stepped in. For a long time he stood, face in the stream, soap in his hand. Then he laughed out loud.

They had found him.

Cam was used to being on his own. If his cover were blown or he were taken, he would simply vanish. If he were killed on an op, his family would receive word that he died in a car accident or a plane crash, and that would be that. A new NOC officer would be put in place; the silent war would wage on.

This new reality brought him back to his SEAL days, a squad of brothers—all of them willing to lay down their lives for their country or their teammates. Cam had forgotten what that felt like until he stood in the doorway of that room and saw Calliope.

There had been times in his work for the CIA when Cam had nearly broken cover—an informant had been outed, or a woman was being assaulted. However, he had remained stoic, repeating the mantra that kept him sane: *the greater good*.

His work went beyond the emotional toll of merely living as someone else; it rattled the foundation of what made him moral. It hollowed out his soul. It had isolated him in a way far beyond simply being alone. And now here he stood, naked in a shower, secure in the knowledge that Calliope was right now reporting her findings to

Steady, Tox, and the team. Cam had to pull his lips into his mouth to stifle the *Hooyah!* that wanted to burst from within him.

He lathered the bar with renewed vigor and formulated a plan. He didn't need to be rescued; Atlas had repeatedly said Cam could leave any time. Although, he wasn't convinced Gemini echoed that sentiment. What he needed was support, and the men and women of Bishop Security had come to provide it. Cam imagined this feeling was something like when a bully corners a kid in the schoolyard and threatens to kick his ass, and out of nowhere, the kid's friends appear behind him and say, "We'd like to see you try." The Conductor was orchestrating some dark scheme that involved Cam. He knew it like he knew the sun would rise in the morning. Well, now he had his team at his back. *We'd like to see you try.*

As he ran his hands over tired muscles, his thoughts strayed to Evan. Evan and her little golden box—he almost laughed at the double entendre. She was so perfect in her flaws, so sexy in her naivete, so beautiful in her passion for her search. Cam hadn't felt that fire for his work in years. He swallowed the regret that threatened to choke him. Evan would never know Cam; she knew Miguel, a man without conscience and incapable of redemption. Cam might have loved Evan, but Miguel knew only apathy. Miguel had excavated compassion from his hollow soul.

Soap trickled into his eye, jarring Cam into the now. Rinsing quickly and drying off, he made his way into the bedroom to change. He needed to go another round with Gemini March, a task that was proving more exhausting by the hour. More importantly, he needed to find a way to get to the restaurant Calliope had mentioned, La Sirena, and explain to the team what was happening.

CHAPTER THIRTY-SIX

Beaufort, South Carolina
December 13

Dressed in worn jeans and a fisherman's sweater, Miles Buchanan stood before Nathan and Emily Bishop's refurbished Victorian home and took in the scene. On the front lawn, there was a child's toy that popped balls under a plastic dome when pushed by its long red handle. A small sneaker sat beside it. Dormant peonies lined a path that led to a wraparound porch. A coffee mug sat on a small end table next to a porch swing. This was a home.

Miles loped up the front steps, but before he could knock, the door swung open. Nathan Bishop greeted him wearing lounge pants and a henley. He whispered, "Everyone is napping. Let's head around back."

Miles hiked the strap of the leather messenger bag over his shoulder and followed Nathan around the porch to a patio bathed in the afternoon sunlight. Nathan took a seat at the teak dining table, and Miles joined him opposite. Uncomfortable with personal small talk, Miles ventured, "Family good?"

If Nathan noticed Miles's awkwardness, he ignored it. Nathan Bishop had a way of putting those around him at ease regardless of the situation. "Charlie climbed the shelves of the refrigerator earlier. Pulled down a dozen eggs and a pint of blueberries." He shook his head with a laugh. "That kid."

Miles laughed too. "That was me. Miller was the lookout. He was always way more concerned with right and wrong when we were kids. The idea of getting into trouble terrified him. Meanwhile, all I did was get us into trouble."

Nathan chuckled. "That sounds about right."

"Especially considering how we turned out." Miles shook his head in amusement.

Despite the ease and flow of the conversation, Miles was eager to share his ideas. He reached into the bag and withdrew a leather-bound book. "How does that look?"

Nathan nodded. "Nearly identical to the actual journal."

Miles pushed the book across the table. "I had a bit of fun filling it in. If Musgrave bothers to read the thing, he'll never know it's fake, but the contents are gibberish. Fake names, dates, I threw some Nirvana lyrics in there when I got bored."

Nathan flipped through the pages. "This is a fucking work of art."

"Thanks."

Nathan fished a flash drive out of his pocket and handed it over. "Here's the copy. I'm not sure what The Conductor thinks is on this footage. It's just the arms dealer Cam was tracking, two security men, and a couple of party guests and topless women sunbathing on the deck. Other than the name of the ship, *The Maestro*, there doesn't appear to be anything incriminating in this video."

"Maybe just the name of the yacht is enough." Miles took the drive and tucked it into the spine of the lookalike journal.

"All right then," Nathan clapped once. "Let's sting a senator."

The top half of the Dutch door opened, and Emily Bishop leaned her forearms on the ledge. "I was going to make some tea. Can I get you anything?"

Nathan leapt up as if an alarm had gone off. Miles failed to see the emergency until his host pushed open the door's bottom section to reveal his wife's pregnant belly.

"You sit, Emily, love. I'll make the tea. Are the boys still asleep?"

Emily yawned. "One of them." She jerked her head to indicate the unnoticed toddler holding two of her fingers and going to town on a pacifier.

Nathan swept Jack up into his arms. "Come here, buddy." He turned back to Miles. "Something to drink?"

His first instinct was to decline and be on his merry way, but something had him smiling up at the little family and saying, "Sure."

CHAPTER THIRTY-SEVEN

Cam volunteered to pick up a romantic dinner for two to enjoy with Gemini.

La Sirena was a small but bustling seaside restaurant. The bar crowd gathered inside and out, and diners sat at tile-topped tables with postcard views. Even at this time of year, the place still drew a crowd, and the mild day allowed for the french doors that skirted the building to be kept open. Cam stood next to the Mercedes he had taken from the March garages and eyed the establishment from a distance, walking casually like any other traveler exploring a beachfront restaurant. A deep happiness swelled within him.

Enticing aromas wafted on the bay breeze. Patrons ate and talked. Ren and Chat sat at a high-top table on the porch. Seagulls trolled the beach for scraps. Steady and Herc were chatting up two women waiting for a table. A waitress stopped at a group of laughing women to take an order. Twitch nursed a martini at the bar. A group of kids threw a ball and chased each other on the beach. The team had woven themselves seamlessly into the tapestry of the scene.

Cam entered La Sirena and snaked through the crowd to find an empty, wicker-backed bar stool. He took a seat and ordered a beer in Catalan. *"Una cervesa, si us plau."*

The bartender set a bottle of Estrella and a frosted glass in front of him. Cam handed him some Euros, glanced at the chalkboard menu on the wall, and ordered two of the sea bass specials to go. The man nodded, took the cash, and moved on.

To his knowledge, Twitch had never done any sort of undercover work, but she was playing her part well, sitting in a floral-print dress, scanning a sightseeing pamphlet, and eyeing him as a likely prospect for a vacation fling. He tilted the glass and poured the beer, shooting her a receptive smile. Martini in one hand, brochure in the other, she slid off the high seat and slinked over to him—sort of slinked. Twitch clearly wasn't used to walking in high heels and stumbled, sloshing vodka over the rim of her glass. She composed herself quickly, though, and finished the short journey, setting the drink down next to his.

"English?" she asked.

"Of course," Cam replied.

"Are you a local?" Twitch continued.

"No. It's a beautiful island, but I'm hoping to get home to my family," Cam said.

"My family is here with me," she commented. "I thought I'd explore the nightlife."

"I haven't seen much. It's the off-season," Cam countered.

"Oh, there's plenty going on. The beach at Ca'n Pastilla is wild at night. We're staying on a boat, The Orion. It's pretty cool. I'm a Pisces, so I guess I'm drawn to boats. Are you into the Zodiac?"

Cam lifted his beer to his lips, committing her coded words to memory. "Not really."

"Yeah, I guess it's just superstition." She mimicked him and sipped her drink. "Anyway, we're going to try fishing tomorrow."

"Good luck," Cam said.

"I was just reading more about deep sea fishing in this brochure. My brothers are really into it. They pull the craziest stuff out of the water. It gets really active an hour or so before sunset. You should check it out." She forced a fairly convincing giggle.

She slid the brochure in front of him. He picked it up and examined the front photo: a group of men on a beach, each holding their catch.

"Maybe." He slipped the brochure into his back pocket. "Thanks."

The bartender placed the two dinners Cam had ordered wrapped to go on the bar.

"So, can I give you my number? Maybe we can set up a fishing date," Twitch flirted.

Cam held up a hand, broadcasting his rejection to anyone who may be watching. "Sorry, I'm spoken for."

Twitch nodded. "Okay, well, if you change your mind, just look for the bright pink umbrella. Nice talking to you."

"You too. Enjoy the rest of your evening." Cam grabbed the bag of food and worked his way around tables and patrons to the exit. As he passed the table where Ren and Chat were perched, Chat gave his dinner companion a discreet nod. A moment later, Ren hopped off his seat and bumped right into Cam.

"*Perdón, señor*," Ren slurred.

"*No hay problema*," Cam replied, then skirted his friend without acknowledgment and left. Back in the car with the food in the passenger seat, Cam felt in his exterior pocket and touched the GPS locator Ren had slipped in when they collided. He reviewed his conversation with Twitch and noted the relevant information. The team was anchored off the coast near Ca'n Pastilla. There would be a Zodiac beached near a pink umbrella. The meet-up was an hour before sunset.

Atlas March had told Cam at their first meeting that he could leave at any time. Gemini might disagree. Plus, there were too many strange happenings for Cam to take what was going on at face value.

As the questions piled up, he had one answer that he knew with certainty: he needed his team.

After a few more minutes, and a few more beers, the Bishop Security team filtered out of the restaurant and piled into the rented SUV.

"Twitch, you're a pro." Steady bumped her fist with his.

She beamed at the compliment. "I was so nervous; vodka kept sloshing out of my martini glass."

"From where we were sitting, you looked like a regular spook," Steady continued.

"I don't know how those guys do undercover work. I'd constantly worry I was saying the wrong thing," she said.

"That part's easy." Herc buckled his seatbelt. "Any time someone asks you a question you don't know how to answer, you just…" He held up a finger and scrunched his nose as he looked at the ceiling. "Pretend you have to sneeze. Then you change the subject. Watch. Steady, ask me a question I don't want to answer."

"Okay, on the beach last week, that woman who walked up and slapped you, what was that about?"

Herc repeated the action, holding up his index finger and scrunching his face. After several seconds he addressed the car. "Ren, did you clock the guy who was watching Cam?"

Behind them, Ren cleaned his glasses with the tail of his shirt. "Yeah, he left after Cam. Got into a blue Renault and followed… Hey! That actually worked."

"Well, I'll be damned." Steady laughed. "Maybe this covert ops shit is easier than we think."

From the front passenger seat, Tox scolded, "Yes, it's a walk in the park. Cam's just one fake sneeze away from bringing down an entire global trafficking organization. Twitch, everything set for tomorrow?"

"Almost. Just confirming the timing to commandeer the Zodiac." She tapped out a text to Evan and immediately received a thumbs-up emoji.

"Is the locator working?" Steady asked.

"Got a beautiful little red dot on my screen moving toward the March villa," Twitch confirmed.

A maid was waiting when Cam entered the villa. She took the bags containing the meals and instructed, "Dinner will be served on the terrace off of your bedroom." He acknowledged her comment and headed that way. As he entered the bedroom, a soft, salty breeze wafted by, and the sheer curtains billowed. Through the open french doors, he spied Gemini March on the terrace. She was dressed in a blood-red peignoir and matching silk robe. The evening chill appeared to have no effect as she casually sipped champagne from her flute. Cam noticed the first micro-expression to cross her face when she spotted him was anger which almost instantly morphed into a seductive gleam.

He crossed to the open doors and stood on the threshold.

"Men don't keep me waiting," she said, her smile masking her irritation.

Cam took the seat across the small wrought iron table and examined the label on the beer bottle at the top of the place setting. "They have to prepare the food."

"And the woman who kept you company while you waited?" She set her glass down and ran her finger along the rim.

Ah, now Cam understood her anger. He stood and circled the table. When his hips were in front of her eager face, he bent down and caught her earlobe between his teeth. "What woman?"

She released a husky laugh. "Very smooth, Miguel."

The same maid who had met Cam at the door silently approached and set down their plated fish. Once she had retreated, and Cam was back in his chair, Gemini continued.

"Between women in bars and archaeologists in caves, I'm beginning to feel neglected." She pouted prettily and poked at her food.

Cam chewed with methodical bites as he stared at her. His outward appearance gave no indication of his fury at the mention of Evan. Where had Gemini watched them? How much had she seen? Her affected jealousy implied that she was probably only aware of their encounters outside the caves: the stingray rescue and the dinner party. Had she known the way Cam had touched Evan, he had a feeling her temper would flare with a bit more intensity.

Rather than defend innocuous actions, Cam smirked. "It's hard to imagine you feeling insecure, *hermosa*."

"I didn't say insecure. I said neglected," she pouted prettily.

Cam set his fork down, wiped his mouth, and met her gaze. "Come here."

Gemini March was not one to take orders, but at his imperious command, she stood and came around the table. Cam grabbed her by the waist and guided her onto his lap. He then snagged her champagne and fed her a sip. "Are you feeling neglected now, *mi belleza*?"

The endearment felt thick on his tongue, but Miguel Ramirez played his part.

She grabbed his wrist and returned the glass to her pouting lips. "Less so."

Cam ran a hand up her thigh, pulling the silk from the negligee across her skin. She tipped her head back and rested it on his shoulder, the move lifting her breasts like an offering on a platter. He ran the backs of his fingers over the swell and down her side. "We can't have the princesa feeling neglected."

"No, we cannot. Let's go inside. I'd like you to not neglect me all night." She ground her hips into his lap.

On the surface, Miguel Ramirez was inflamed. Lust sparked in his golden eyes as his conquest ground against him. His powerful body stood with Gemini in his arms, skimming every inch of her body as he set her on her feet.

Inside, there was nothing. Cam wasn't there. He had trained himself to switch off during moments of profound discomfort: beatings, executions, and, yes, sex. In rare times of reflection, Cam thought these situations mirrored a porn movie—two attractive people performing a sex act for a purpose other than attraction or pleasure. His actions would be proficient, even passionate, but there would be no emotion at all.

Miguel fisted her hair and exposed her neck. He licked a path to her ear lobe then took it in his teeth. She reached for his fly, palming the outline of his erection. He removed her hand and used it to pull her toward the bedroom.

The sound of a throat clearing had him looking up. Joseph stood in the open doorway. "Forgive me for intruding. Gemini, I need a word."

"Now?" she all but shouted.

"I'm afraid so. It's a rather pressing matter," Joseph insisted.

Gemini turned to Cam. "Don't move."

He kissed her cheek and spoke into her ear. "I'll be right here."

She swept from the room with Joseph in tow.

Cam was tempted to follow, then rethought. What qualified as an emergency in Gemini March's world hardly mattered. He sat on the bed and turned on the television, grateful for the reprieve.

CHAPTER THIRTY-EIGHT

Palma, Mallorca
December 14

The following evening, after a calming walk on the beach, Evan tucked into an early dinner at a quaint pub near the marina. She knew she shouldn't be here, but she couldn't help her natural curiosity. The text from the girl named Twitch, confirming her people would be borrowing her Zodiac, had Evan's instincts aflutter. She wanted to watch this secret spy mission and see that man, Cam, take her Zodiac and escape. What harm could it do? She was just a patron at a local bar enjoying a quiet dinner. No one would be the wiser. Moreover, she justified, the man had rescued her after the stingray attack, possibly saving her life. It was natural to want to make sure he made it to safety.

Who was she kidding? She wanted to spy on the spies. See the good guys win.

Her thoughts wandered to another man, a man who most definitely was not a good guy. She hadn't given herself time to process the events in the cave—neither the discovery nor the self-discovery. She had experienced pleasure at the hands of a man. What's more, she had wanted to take it further. She almost couldn't admit to herself her uninhibited desire to push Miguel Ramirez onto his back and fuck his brains out.

It was crass. It was primal. It was dirty. And it was a massive breakthrough for her. Evan had downplayed the impact of her first sexual encounter. She was shy as it was, the date rape driving her further into her shell. She forced herself to be social, even date, but when all was said and done, Evan always seemed to breathe a sigh of relief when she entered her quiet bedroom at the end of the day. In that cave, however, the sigh of relief came when Miguel touched her, not when he stopped.

The memory flowed through her like warm whiskey. She shuddered. God. Of all the men in the world, why him? He was dark and threatening and most certainly some sort of criminal. And yet, as she recounted the event in her mind, Evan felt neither shame nor recrimination. He had been a study in duality: kind yet fierce, considerate but passionate, protective yet threatening. The combination was... intoxicating.

She glanced up from her food, and through the window, she saw a man prowling toward the dock: his build and gait familiar. It was not, however, the man who was supposed to be there.

It was Miguel Ramirez. Heading straight for her Zodiac.

Evan jumped from her seat and tossed all the Euros in her wallet on the table without bothering to count. She burst out the doors of the restaurant.

Moving like a jungle cat, Cam loped across the wet sand and climbed up onto the wide wooden dock. There. Just as Twitch had said, the Zodiac bobbed in the water a safe distance from the larger boats, a pink beach umbrella poking from the sand on the nearby shore. He started to move again when quick footsteps coming up behind him had him spinning, his hand reflexively reaching for his holstered Sig that was not there.

Evan. Suddenly it became clear. This was her boat. She must have been watching from a distance and assumed Miguel Ramirez was up to no good. His suspicions were confirmed when she stage-whispered, "What the hell do you think you're doing? You need to get out of here right now. There are, er, officials in the area who won't like you poking around down here. If they find you here, you'll be in big trouble."

He started to approach her, to deliver a threat and scare her off when suddenly his eyes locked with her steely gaze, and he realized something. She wasn't reprimanding him. She was warning him. Yes, she wanted him gone, but it was as much for his safety as the integrity of the op. He grinned.

"What are you doing?" She whisper-yelled again

Cam knew what he had to do. Despite being utter anathema in his world, he felt the impulse with the certainty of a sunrise. For the first time in all his time with the CIA, he did it.

He broke cover.

"Relax, Evan. I'm Cam. You're the one who needs to skedaddle." He spoke in his ordinary, American voice.

Cam leaned forward, and, with a gentle finger to her chin, he closed her mouth.

"But...but...oh."

"I don't have time to explain," he continued, "but thank you. For the boat."

"Oh, ah, okay." Evan stared at him in a daze, processing the ramifications of his admission.

Without thought or hesitation, he leaned forward and pressed a chaste kiss to her lips. It lasted only a second, but Cam felt it to his toes. It was as if someone had struck a tuning fork, and whatever note his body emitted matched perfectly with her note. He pulled away, his lips clinging to hers, and breathed her in. Then he turned and made his way to the Zodiac. Only once he had released the boat from the cleat and silently paddled away from the dock did he turn back to Evan.

There she was, still as a statue, a torrent of emotions on her beautiful face.

There he was, in uncharted waters, watching her as the small boat drifted.

There it was.

Zing.

At the edge of the beach, standing in the mist next to the man who had been following Miguel Ramirez since he arrived, Gemini March stood in a trench coat and fedora, looking like a World War II spy.

She was displeased.

CHAPTER THIRTY-NINE

One nautical mile off the coast of Palma, Mallorca
December 14

Cam navigated the boat out into the Mediterranean. Minutes later, he spotted the cabin cruiser.

Thirty minutes later, he was standing on the deck, being greeted by his impromptu family. Cam took a minute to bask in the sanctuary of friendship, then he turned to Tox.

"Got a place we can talk."

Tox circled a finger in the air to corral the group, grabbed Calliope by the hand, and said, "Follow me."

In an interior room of the vessel, Steady rested his booted feet on the empty chair next to him. "This may be the first mission in history that started with a psycho model stalking an operator."

"Who she thinks is an arms dealer," Ren added.

"Yeah, Gemini had me brought to her." Cam sighed. "She's not used to being blown off, and I guess she wanted to explore the possibilities."

"Dude, what do you do to these women? You need to write a book," Steady mused.

"There's more going on here, fellas. Her cousin Atlas took over the company a year ago." He leaned forward and rested his forearms on the table. "He's running a heroin operation out of the mine."

The group nodded.

"How could you possibly know that?" Cam asked.

Tox and Ren spoke at the same time. "Finn." Ren continued, "He's heard chatter about Atlas March's extracurricular activities."

Cam confirmed, "Yeah, he was on The Agency's radar when he was working in Colombia."

"Is it possible someone was pulling Gemini's strings? I mean, you're a strapping man and all, but that's a bit extreme for anyone." Tox rubbed the back of his neck.

Cam shook his head. "I don't think anyone pulls Gemini March's strings. She's used to getting what she wants."

Tox rested his hand on his wife's back. "Well, psycho supermodels aside, there is definitely more going on here than meets the eye." He leaned forward. "Cam, The Conductor is somehow involved in all of this."

Cam shot to his feet. "How do you know about The Conductor?"

Ren answered, his face serious. "Nathan filled us in."

"Good, because I think I know why The Conductor is interested," Cam said. "Atlas March is not only manufacturing heroin; he acquired a shipping company and plans on moving the product himself. The Conductor doesn't take too kindly to traffickers trying to circumvent him."

"There's another reason," Tox added.

Cam heard the trepidation in his friend's voice. "What?"

"When you were with The Company, did you cross paths with an officer by the name of Raymond Greene?" Tox asked.

"Yeah, why?" Cam replied warily.

"His body was discovered washed up on a beach in Crimea two weeks ago. According to the local authorities, the water had done its worst, but it was pretty clear he had been tortured before being shot. That ship you documented in your notes? *The Maestro*? It was docked at a marina in Sevastopol four days before Greene went missing." Tox explained.

"I got a call on my agency phone three or four weeks ago. It didn't connect, but the call originated in Crimea, where Greene was stationed. I wondered if it was Greene. Maybe he was trying to warn me." Cam hung his head. "Greene wouldn't have broken. He was solid."

Tox spoke quietly. "He also had a daughter. If The Conductor knew…"

Cam understood instantly. "Greene would be vulnerable. Shit. For about a year, I kept a log of notes on The Conductor—anything that pointed to a commonality in different smuggling or trafficking operations. Greene knew about it," Cam explained.

Tox took over. "Then, a year ago in Rabat, you tracked an arms dealer and recorded his activity on *The Maestro*. We have to assume someone saw you taking the video, and you landed on The Conductor's radar."

"I left the CIA shortly after that and came to work here."

"If The Conductor broke Raymond Greene, that means you're blown, and you have to get out," Tox said.

"Not yet," Cam insisted. "I don't think any of the immediate players know that Miguel Ramirez is a cover. Certainly not Atlas March, who is bringing me into his heroin operation. As long as I know, I can be prepared."

"Tread very carefully, my friend," Ren cautioned. "The Conductor may want to bring down Atlas March, but he wants to bring you down, too. The gauntlet's been thrown."

Cam gave a wicked grin. "Challenge accepted."

"What do we have on the yacht, *The Maestro*?" Tox asked.

Twitch looked up over the screen of her laptop. "It's owned by a retired Russian oil executive who keeps it docked in Odessa. According to his people, he leases it out and loans it to friends but rarely uses it himself."

"Let me guess," Tox interjected. "He keeps no paperwork, and these quote-unquote leases and loans are handshake deals."

"The good news for us is because *The Maestro* is a legitimate purchase, so it has GPS tracking. It's in the area, currently docked in Ibiza." Twitch said.

"The Conductor's keeping watch." Tox drummed his fingers on the table.

"And there's nothing suspicious on that video?" Ren asked.

"Not that I saw," Cam replied.

"What happened after you recorded it?" Tox urged.

Cam recounted the events. "I received intel that the arms dealer I was after had another meeting with The Conductor on Ibiza. I needed to head south, but I was getting fixated on catching him, and I was practically in the Mediterranean. I should have thought it through. The Conductor would never be that careless."

"What happened?" Herc asked.

"I went to the nightclub and knew almost immediately I'd been played. The arms dealer I was tracking did business in warehouses and hotel rooms, and The Conductor has never shown his fucking face. I sat at a table with my thumb up my ass for three hours. Around midnight, Gemini March showed up with an entourage from a pho-toshoot." Cam rolled his hands as if to say, *you know the rest.*

"I once saw Betty White at an airport." Herc gestured with a tortilla chip. "That's the closest I've come to seeing a famous chick."

"Moving on." Steady sat up.

Chat leaned forward. "I think The Conductor knew exactly what went down between you and Gemini March. I think The Conductor did show up that night, and you were being watched."

Ren took over. "The working theory is that The Conductor is taking advantage of Gemini March's obsession with you in order to secure the evidence you've compiled."

Cam nodded in understanding. "And once he has the evidence, I meet with an unfortunate accident on my romantic getaway."

"As an added bonus, Atlas March goes down for trying to ship heroin without paying the piper," Ren added.

"And The Conductor is nowhere in sight." Cam finished the thought.

"He doesn't have the evidence yet, but he will shortly." Tox clapped the table.

"What does that mean?" Cam questioned.

Tox gave Cam's shoulder a reassuring squeeze. "Let's just say my brother, Miles, and Nathan are approaching this from another angle. They think you, with a little help from the team, can bring this whole house of cards crashing down."

Cam checked the time. "I better get back."

Twitch peeked over her laptop. "We'll keep an eye on you."

CHAPTER FORTY

Washington, DC
December 14

Harlan Musgrave stepped out of the shower and smelled coffee. That was odd. He had spoken to his wife the night before; she was still in Florida, and he was usually out the door before the housekeeping staff arrived. *Perhaps Maria has set the timer on the machine.* Donning a tan suit and red tie, Musgrave trotted down the central staircase and walked back to the kitchen.

A man Musgrave had never seen was sitting at the granite island sipping coffee from a travel mug and scanning a paper copy of The Washington Post. A momentary thought flashed through Musgrave's head that he was in the wrong house. Sanity quickly returned.

"What the hell do you think you're doing?" Musgrave demanded.

"Good morning, Senator." The man set the newspaper aside.

There was a security panic button on the wall within reach, but Musgrave waited.

"Do I need to repeat myself?" he demanded.

"I have a message for you from The Conductor. The progress you have made retrieving the items is unacceptable."

Musgrave tried valiantly to look like he wasn't terrified. "It's being handled."

The man finished the coffee, refilled the mug, and returned his attention to Musgrave. "You have seventy-two hours, or The Conductor will be forced to explore alternative avenues." He folded the newspaper, tucked it under his arm, and, coffee in hand, walked out the back door.

Musgrave checked through the window to make sure the man was gone, then he slid down the wall onto the kitchen floor and cried.

Senator Musgrave sat behind his old, storied desk in the coveted corner suite in the Russell Senate Office Building. He was uncharacteristically short-tempered.

Rather than use the intercom, Musgrave simply shouted toward the door. "Arlo, where the hell is that slick bastard?"

The heavy door opened wide enough for a face, and Arlo poked his head into the room. "Security just alerted me that he's in the building. He should be here any minute."

"Send him straight through. I don't have time for this shit," Musgrave barked.

"Of course, sir." Arlo frowned at his boss's unusual tone and retracted his head.

A moment later, the distinguished man, carrying a leather briefcase and dressed in yet another impeccable suit, stood in the doorway. He entered and took the seat opposite Musgrave's desk without being prompted.

"About time," Musgrave snapped.

In a blatant show of disrespect, Caleb Cain crossed his legs and pulled his phone out of his breast pocket to check his texts.

"I was in D.C. on another matter," he tossed out. "You're lucky I could come as quickly as I did." He made a show of checking the time on the Breitling that circled his wrist.

"The timeline has shortened. I need Canto's journal and flash drive yesterday."

At the look of surprise on Caleb Cain's face, Musgrave huffed, "What? You think I shouldn't discuss *business* in my office? Trust me; this is by far the safest place. The Feds can bug my townhouse; they can listen in at a table in a restaurant or capture a conversation in a park. But here? Do you know how hard it is to surveil the office of a United States Senator? Shit, I could plan to assassinate that asshole up the street," he jerked his head in the direction of The White House, "and nobody would ever know."

The senator withdrew a bottle of bourbon from the bottom drawer of his desk and doctored his coffee. "Snort?" He pointed the bottle at Cain.

"No."

"Where are you with this?"

Without missing a beat, Caleb Cain pulled the briefcase onto his lap and, touching his thumbs to the biometric locks, opened it. He placed the worn leather book on the desk.

Musgrave flipped through the diary pages; it was quite obviously the evidence The Conductor was eager to destroy.

"The flash drive is in the spine," Cain explained.

Musgrave felt along the binding and withdrew the device. "Have you watched it?"

Caleb Cain nodded. "To confirm the contents."

"Outstanding." Musgrave opened his own briefcase and placed the items inside. Then, he turned and withdrew a small laptop from the wall safe behind him. "You prefer Bitcoin, as I recall from our conversation."

The fixer handed him a slip of paper. "Here are the transfer instructions."

Musgrave pecked away on the keyboard while Cain rechecked his messages.

"There's talk about the ship in that video. *The Maestro.*" Cain threw out.

"You don't strike me as a man who trades in idle gossip." Musgrave kept his attention on the laptop.

"So, The Conductor is a myth?" Cain pressed.

"A fiction. You'd be wise to remember that," Musgrave warned.

"There have been a lot of rumblings over the years."

The senator stopped typing and looked up. "There's an expression on the farm. Don't piss upstream of the herd. Protect your revenue sources, Cain. Speculation like that doesn't do anybody any good."

Effectively chastised, Cain returned to his phone. Three minutes later, their business was concluded.

At the door, Musgrave placed a hand on Caleb's shoulder. "You've done very well. I'm sure I'll be in touch."

"Actually," Cain commented, his arrogant demeanor returning, "I'm retiring."

Musgrave scanned the man's face. "That's a shame. It's hard to find reliable help these days."

Cain was impassive. "There are plenty of others who do what I do."

Musgrave snorted. The fixer had cast his rod fishing for a compliment. Musgrave wasn't biting. "True enough. Take care of yourself, Cain."

Closing the door, Musgrave returned to his desk. He had calls to make.

Constitution Avenue was bustling as Miles Buchanan made his way out of The Russell Senate Office Building, slowly shedding the persona of Caleb Cain as he walked. He made a quick right onto Delaware Avenue and cut across the Senate Park. Twenty yards in, Nathan peeled away from a coffee kiosk and moved in next to him. Walking abreast, the men continued on their path.

"Everything go as planned?" Nathan asked.

"Better," Miles replied. "The little gadget worked like a charm."

The device to which Miles referred was the remote cloning device Twitch had fine-tuned for this meeting. Musgrave would assume it was a phone. Miles simply had to sync the tech to Musgrave's WiFi, which he did—with a bit of help from Twitch—when he first sat down, then wait for the Senator to access his hidden financial accounts. Miles had pretended to check messages while Musgrave made the bitcoin transfer. In reality, he was watching the progress bar showing the successful mirroring of the hard drive.

"Outstanding. Let's cut over to D Street. I have a car waiting." Nathan motioned to his right, and they continued.

"Where are we headed?" Miles asked.

"Our former parent company, Knightsgrove-Bishop. Their cybersecurity people rival—"

"The Pentagon?" Miles supplied.

Nathan replied, "I was going to say they rival Twitch, but yours works. Come on. Let's send that rat Musgrave back to the sewer."

CHAPTER FORTY-ONE

Valldemossa, Mallorca
December 14

Evan closed the door to her bedroom and slid to the floor. *Miguel was some sort of government agent? He was on some kind of mission? What could possibly be amiss on this Arcadian island? Miguel wasn't Miguel at all.*

While the thought chilled her, it certainly explained a lot.

A soft knock on her door had her pushing to her feet, her surprise evident when she glimpsed the man standing in the hallway.

"Mr. Nabeel?" Evan said.

"Please, call me Joseph." He smiled.

"What can I do for you?" she asked.

"Forgive the late hour. Is this a bad time?" Joseph scanned the small room, his eyes coming to rest on her open computer and the paper notes scattered on her cluttered desk.

"Not at all, please." Evan gestured to the only other seat in the room, a small tufted stool at her dressing table. Joseph sat.

"Do you remember our dinner conversation?" he asked.

"Of course. You have an interest in Moorish artifacts," Evan replied.

"*Interest* may be downplaying it a bit. I'm afraid my fascination with my culture borders on obsession," Joseph commented.

"I know a few archaeologists who suffer from the same condition," she nodded, amused.

Joseph smiled. "Yes, I'm afraid there is no cure." He tapped his fingers on the glass-topped dressing table. "Have you ever heard the story of The Panther's Eye?"

Evan furrowed her brow. "I don't believe so."

He leaned forward and interlaced his fingers between his knees. "Near the end of the Fifteenth Century, a famed Moorish King ruled in Northern Algeria. The village where I was born was the seat of his land. After defeating an invading army, the king took possession of a gem. The story goes that the gem was a massive yellow diamond."

"The Panther's Eye," she rightly guessed.

"Exactly." Joseph continued, "The king planned to cut the diamond to fit a medallion and declared the talisman would bring prosperity to his people for centuries to come."

Evan nodded, rapt.

"In 1478, the Spanish king launched Christian crusaders to the region to destroy the Moors. Knowing he could not repel the sizable and well-funded forces, the Moorish King fled, and the people of his realm scattered."

On a deep inhale, Joseph went on. "He boarded a ship with a skeleton crew in the dark of night, attempting to flee to Turkey. Perhaps he intended to hide his treasure on Mallorca, knowing the Moors in power would help him, or, more likely, the ship was blown off course in a violent storm. Either way, the oral history and a map and letters from the king and the crew all indicate The Panther's Eye was hidden on Mallorca. The king had placed The Panther's Eye in a golden box with the medallion that would one day hold the jewel."

Evan gasped.

Joseph turned to face her fully. "So you see, my dear, why I have come."

"You think at some point a diamond was in the box I discovered," she said.

"Not just a diamond," he clarified. "The Panther's Eye is estimated to be a two hundred and eighty-carat gem. When cut, the estimated size is ninety carats. It would be the largest yellow diamond ever discovered. Its worth is inestimable."

"Would you like to examine the box? Dr. Emberton has it in a safe in his room," Evan offered.

"I have seen it. It is the exact box described in our lore."

"Minus the diamond."

Joseph clenched his jaw. "Yes. I believe that my diamond is near your discovery site. It's possible it fell from the box or was removed, but I'm sure it is still hidden. Assuming you haven't found it and hidden it away."

His tone was joking, but Evan heard the suspicion in the comment.

"If someone had found it already, surely we would have heard about such a momentous discovery," Evan replied, ignoring the accusation.

"Yes, exactly. That is why I believe my diamond still may be at the location where you found the box," he stated.

Evan opened her laptop and brought up the mapping software she had used. Joseph stared over her shoulder. "It's here. Navigating the cave system is tricky, but it's also accessible through the mine. Can you believe how close it is to the March Mining tunnels?"

Joseph stared intently at the screen. "Yes, that is unexpected." Evan couldn't miss the barely leashed anger in his voice.

"I'll take you there tomorrow. Omar can assemble a team, and we can examine the mound. There is still quite a large area that I have yet to excavate."

Joseph expelled an audible breath, relieved. "That would be wonderful. Thank you."

"Of course. Archaeologists restore history. It would be my privilege to help." She pressed her palms together. "Just the idea of unearthing such a magnificent stone…"

Joseph squeezed her shoulder and turned toward the door. "Well, it won't be so glamorous. The uncut gem looks hardly more interesting than a big rock. If you didn't know what it was, one could easily cast it aside. I'll call Omar and set a time for the morning. Thank you, my dear."

"You're welcome."

Joseph turned back to her at the doorway. "You know, I have been looking for The Panther's Eye for almost thirty years. Then, out of the blue, Gemini brings a man with yellow eyes to the house. I knew it was a sign." He disappeared into the hallway before she could respond.

She closed the door and leaned against it. His words were benign enough, but something about the encounter felt threatening. Was he even aware he was referring to it as *his diamond*?

Evan walked two steps toward her small desk and stopped. *The uncut gem looks hardly more interesting than a big rock… a man with yellow eyes… cast it aside…* Suddenly she remembered the rock Miguel had pulled out and tossed on the ground, assuming it was a weight to prevent the box from washing away should the cave flood with the tides.

"Oh my God." Her knees buckled, and she sat on the bed.

Miguel had found The Panther's Eye.

And thrown it away.

Evan stepped to her balcony doors and peeked around the curtain. Joseph's car was just pulling away. She started to grab her gear when she remembered the guard patrolling the beach. If he caught her this time, Joseph would surely know she was up to something. She'd have to sneak in through the mine. With coveralls from the excavation site and her spelunking helmet, Evan could blend in with the miners and hide her face from the security cameras. With a rudimentary plan in place, all she could do now was wait.

CHAPTER FORTY-TWO

Miramar, Mallorca
December 14

The March Villa was quiet when Cam walked in the front door at half-past nine. He walked through the empty house and into his bedroom. Candlelight on the terrace caught his eye.

He stood in the doorway and spotted Gemini, sitting at the small table in a black negligee. Other than the color she wore, the setting felt like deja vu. A bottle of champagne rested in an ice bucket between two tapers, a beer next to it. Gemini refilled her flute then poured the beer into a glass.

"Welcome home, darling. Now we can pick up where we left off." Gemini gave him her most seductive smile.

Cam sauntered over and took the empty seat. He swallowed down half the beer, poured the rest, and scanned her body. "No more modeling emergencies?"

"My work is actually quite demanding. Most people dismiss it, but you'd be surprised at all the working parts: photoshoots, interviews, runway shows, social media. Never a dull moment." She sipped her drink. "I gave the chef and the staff the night off. We can raid the refrigerator later if we need sustenance."

Cam downed the rest of the beer and lost his balance, nearly tipping backward in the chair. He shook his head to clear the sudden fog. "What is this?"

"You'll see. We're going to have a little fun tonight. Let me help you to the bed before you pass out. You're too big to carry." Gemini rose from her seat.

Cam staggered to standing, swept his arm out, and knocked the beer glass to the terrace where it shattered on the flagstone.

Gemini tsked. "Save that passion for later." She came around the table and pulled him inside. Cam stumbled along and collapsed on the bed. He watched through blurred vision as Gemini hauled up one of his legs, then the other. She took a syringe from the pocket of her robe and injected something into his arm. She leaned down and whispered in his ear. "You rest while that kicks in. Tonight, I'm going to remind you just how good we are together."

After commandeering an ATV and a set of coveralls from the dig site, Evan had driven to March Mining. It was just after midnight, and the last shift of miners was filtering out. Deciding the pack would be too conspicuous, she grabbed a flashlight and shoved it into the deep side pocket. Just as she was about to walk to the front entrance, she noticed a group of miners entering the mine through a smaller side entrance.

She had thought Miguel had said the last crew finished at midnight, but they must have added a shift. Keeping back a safe distance, she followed them into the tunnel. The men all turned and ducked under a chain barricading part of the mine. Evan continued on and then stopped. From thirty feet away, she could hear talking and laughter from the storeroom. *Damnit.* She hoped the men weren't planning another all-night party. Voices at the entrance to the storeroom had her retracing her steps and ducking under the security chain. She peered around the corner and assessed her options. Suddenly, a large hand covered her mouth; another encircled her waist and lifted her off the ground. The man carried her down a series of tunnels, through a steel fire door, and into a room that looked like some kind of lab. *What is this place?* Before she could look around, she was thrown to the ground, her forehead hitting the concrete.

Evan rolled onto her back and stared up at a building of a man with long hair and a full beard. He was explaining to two others in clipped Catalan that he had caught her spying. The men spoke quickly, and she was seeing stars from her knock on the head, but one sentence was clear: "Call Señor March."

One man entered a number and put the call on speaker so the others could listen. When the calm voice of Joseph Nabeel came over the line, Evan silently cursed. She knew deep down Joseph would resort to desperate measures if he thought she knew where to find The Panther's Eye.

Evan needed to get out of there now. The men were facing one another and seemed to be arguing over how to restrain her.

Quiet as the mouse Miguel accused her of being, she inched slowly back. By the time one of the men looked up, she was only a foot from the steel door. Evan leapt to her feet acting on pure impulse, pushed open the heavy door, and took off. She heard expletives and shouts from the room, but she had already disappeared around the corner. She had been carried down these tunnels backward with a hand covering her mouth, but weeks in this underground labyrinth had honed her spatial awareness. She saw the chain ahead of her and ducked under it. She knew her destination. If no one had discovered her small treasure cave in six centuries, surely it was the perfect hiding place. She ran with familiarity, passing spots she and Miguel had noted on their adventures.

When she came to the storage room, she ducked in. Thankfully the men had cleared out. Without hesitation, she heaved the steel cabinet away from the wall and crawled into the opening. Then gripping the underside, she pulled the heavy cupboard back into place. She flopped into the little treasure room and clapped both palms over her mouth. Air puffed from her nose over the backs of her hands. She waited in the silence.

Five minutes passed, then ten. Eventually, Evan turned back to the entrance Miguel had created with the sledgehammer and began stacking rocks to cover the opening. It wouldn't bar anyone from entry, but the added layer was certainly better, and it gave her something to do.

When she had covered the hole as best she could in the darkness, she turned back to her treasure room. She mapped the small space in her mind—the mound in the far corner where she and Miguel had found the gold box, the flat rocks to her left where they had opened their magical find.

Then she remembered Miguel discarding the rock they had both assumed had been placed there to weigh the box down. *Hardly more interesting than a big rock.* It wasn't a weight. She knew it was the Panther's Eye. He had tossed the massive diamond over his shoulder. She had heard the thunk as it hit the ground and the plop as it rolled into the water.

She pulled the small tactical flashlight from her pocket and stepped out of the bulky coveralls. She knew how she would be passing the time.

CHAPTER FORTY-THREE

Palma, Mallorca
December 14

Unlike the last time he had regained consciousness in the March villa, Cam didn't allow the lure of Egyptian cotton and Siberian goose down to pull him into complacency. Especially with his arms tethered to the bedposts and Gemini March standing at the foot of the bed in a black demi bra and lace thong. She was holding an equestrian whip.

Cam squinted at her. "Well, chica, you've officially ruined this fantasy for me."

"Oh, come now, I bet when you close your eyes at night or touch yourself in the shower, this is pretty close to what you picture. That is, if my fan mail is anything to go by," she replied.

"Untie me, Gemini. I can't make your fantasies come true like this," Cam ordered.

She climbed atop his body and straddled his narrow hips. "You certainly can't make them come true treating me like some pathetic nobody and spending your time in my cousin's mines." She lifted her arm and brought the crop down full force across his chest, immediately raising a welt.

Cam cried out. "What the fuck, puta? Stop!"

She moved further up his body, her full weight on his diaphragm shortening his breaths. "But I don't want to stop. I want to keep going." She struck him on the thigh. "I asked you on our first night together at the Villa who you were really looking for on Ibiza. Do you remember what you said?"

When Cam remained silent, she held the crop in both hands, bending it in threat.

He spoke through gritted teeth. "I said I was looking for you."

She giggled. It was a girlish sound in complete antipathy to the sadistic dominatrix above him. "Yes, and you were. You just didn't know it. But you will. Tonight, I'm going to show you what you've been missing. Tonight, the Boss of Fuck will work for me."

"You're psychotic." Cam tugged on his bonds.

"You'd be surprised how appealing a little crazy can be to some men. Especially when it's wrapped in a pretty package." She bent forward and licked his chest.

"Sorry, sweetheart. You've got the wrong guy. Nothing about this turns me on." Even as he said it though, Cam felt his hard-on throbbing.

"Ah, but you see, that's what the injection was for. My cousin has access to all kinds of experimental concoctions. Sometimes I think drug smugglers have more advanced R & D than pharmaceutical companies." She reached behind her and fisted his length.

Cam fought his body's unwilling response, but it was no use. The drug she had given him was making arousal inevitable. She scooted down his body and licked the tip of his growing erection. "Mmm, what a delicious treat. No condom, I think. Wouldn't that be great fodder for the tabloids? A supermodel with a mysterious pregnancy? Imagine the wild speculation."

"Get the fuck off me." He bent his fingers toward his left wrist, unsuccessfully trying to reach the short-range distress beacon on his watch

She leaned back up. "You're a big disappointment, Miguel. All I wanted was to enjoy a week or so with you between my legs." She brought the crop down hard as she spoke. "All I wanted was that remarkable cock. I was even prepared to submit to your dominance. But instead, you run all over my island with some little piece of trash and ignore me. Well, there's no ignoring me now."

"Leave Evan out of this," he spat.

Gemini dismounted and stood next to the bed.

She wielded the whip, smacking Cam across the pelvis. Dots of blood appeared in a line. He grunted. She moved to the foot of the bed, leveling a blow to the bottoms of his feet. Cam cried out in pain, and her eyes lit. She walked forward, staring at his erection and pulled back the crop.

"Oh, trust me, Miguel. That little nobody has no place in our bedroom. Joseph tells me she's quite the daring treasure seeker. She could be buried under a rockslide in her precious caves for all I care."

With a roar, Cam pulled his body forward, ripping the entire brass headboard from the bed. Gemini stepped back in shock as small metal rods separated from the frame and fell to the floor. He stood to face her, the headboard like a cross on his back. She smiled as she slowly backed into his closet, then turned and disappeared. Cam moved to follow, but the length of the brass prevented his passing through the doorway. He gripped the buckle of one tether with his teeth, freeing one wrist then the other. He tossed the headboard aside and entered the closet. It was empty. He felt around the walls looking for a latch or hidden panel but saw nothing. He flew out of the closet across the bedroom and through the terrace doors. He stumbled on the lawn and collapsed, the drugs still heavy in his system. Naked and aroused, he activated the distress beacon on his watch.

He made his way to the edge of the lawn overlooking the bay.

A vintage wooden Chris Craft race boat came shooting out of the stone and stucco boathouse, Gemini March at the helm. She turned and scanned the bluff. He saw the moment she spotted him. Then she blew him a kiss and sped out to sea.

Cam hobbled back to the bedroom, the pain from the whipping just now registering. He fell onto the bed and stared at the ceiling. Thirty minutes later, his head had cleared just as a booted foot kicked in the bedroom door.

Tox and Chat entered in standard formation. Steady and Ren on their heels.

"It's clear. She's gone," Cam muttered.

Ren was a medic and rushed to his side.

"Where's Evan?" Cam groaned.

Ren spoke as he assessed Cam's injuries. "We don't know. She's not at the finca where she's staying or the dig site."

"I need to find her. She had to have gone back to the caves. She doesn't realize she's a hair's breadth away from a heroin lab. I need to know she's safe."

"And you will, we will, but you have to let me patch you up." Ren treated Cam's wounds with a field kit. When he came to the injury at his engorged groin, Cam explained. "She drugged me."

Ren dabbed antibiotic ointment on the bleeding welt. "I always knew you were attracted to me, but let's take it slow."

Cam laughed then hissed in pain.

"That's one crazy bitch, my friend." Ren helped Cam sit up.

"Find me some underwear, and let's get the fuck out of here." Cam was already swinging his legs off the bed.

Ren found Cam's boxers on the rug, and Cam pulled them on. Ren and Chat each took one of Cam's arms, and with Tox taking point and Steady on their six, the men exited the March villa. In the front hall, the men paused while Steady grabbed a spare set of fatigues from his pack in the rented SUV. He helped Cam into the pants, then looked his friend directly in the eye and added with feigned seriousness, "and remember, for erections lasting more than four hours, please consult a physician."

Even Chat laughed as they quickly made their exit.

They entered the mine quickly and silently in standard tactical formation. Cam took point, Steady and Ren followed with Chat and Tox on their six. The men bypassed the elevator and moved through the descending tunnels. The only thing more dangerous than a long hallway in an incursion was an elevator car. The mine was silent as death.

They came to the chained-off area where Cam had caught the men making the drugs. Voices drifted through the tunnel. *"She's here somewhere."*

Cam released a breath he hadn't realized he was holding. Somehow she had escaped. The Bishop security team moved closer and, using a small handled mirror, spotted two men around a turn speaking in hushed voices.

"The men watching the beach and the front entrance haven't reported seeing her," one of the men barked.

Steady murmured into his comm, "That's because the men at the front entrance are on break."

Herc and Calliope were currently keeping a watchful eye on the guards they had incapacitated. Cam scratched his stubbled jaw.

Evan's first instinct would be to run to the caves and exit to the beach. The men there would shoot her on sight. Then it hit him.

"Think you guys can handle these two? I know where Evan is," Cam said.

Tox huffed, "Please."

"We'll rendezvous at the side entrance," Steady said.

Before anyone could make another glib comment, Cam was off like a shot.

He ran through the maze of hallways, desperate to find Evan. Rounding a final corner, he skidded to a stop. Atlas March stood before him flanked by two men, their guns trained on Cam. He held up his hands.

"Miguel, I require a moment of your time," Atlas turned and began walking.

One of the guards stepped forward and drilled Cam in the temple with the butt of his gun.

When Cam came to, he was tied to a chair in an isolated room in some peripheral section of the mine. He'd barely cleared his vision when one of the guards delivered a blow to his jaw so forceful, his comm device flew from his ear and landed on the ground at his feet. Atlas March faced him. "I gather from the goons running roughshod through my mine, you are not who you claim to be."

Cam remained silent.

"Did The Conductor send you?" Atlas demanded.

Cam kept his gaze forward. "Why would you think that?"

Atlas threw up his hands. "Because I refuse to be extorted. I own a fucking shipping company. I'll transport my own drugs."

"The Conductor doesn't allow that." Cam played along.

"Well, let's see how he likes it when his man comes back to him in a body bag." Atlas unbuttoned his suit jacket and casually sank his hands into his trouser pockets. "But before that, I have some questions."

"I don't have any answers," Cam said.

"You will tell me what I want to know, *Mr. Ramirez.*" Atlas snapped his fingers and pointed to one of his men.

One of the guards slid spiked brass knuckles onto his fist. Cam struggled, but his bonds held. He waited for the first blow, lifting his eyes to his captor, who was staring back at him with a peculiar expression on his face. Cam noticed a small red spot appear in the middle of Atlas's white dress shirt. Slowly, it bloomed. A moment later, Atlas March dropped to his knees before collapsing dead onto the floor. Cam's gaze shot to the room's entrance, where a man in black tactical gear with a balaclava covering his face fired two more suppressed shots. The guards fell at Cam's feet.

The man entered the room, bypassed Cam, and set his pack on a table. "You Miguel Ramirez?"

Cam remained silent. The man withdrew a karambit from the duffle. The black curved blade was lethal, and Cam knew it took years to master the knife's use. "I was told I'd know you when I saw you— the eyes," the man said, tapping the tip of the weapon to his cheek.

Cam stared at the wall. "Yes."

The man stepped in front of him and, with impressive expertise, cut the ropes. "You're free to go."

"I don't understand." Cam rubbed his wrists.

"I was instructed not to kill you. I'm not killing you. The man I work for said to tell you; you can thank your scar-faced friend."

"Who do you work for?" Cam asked.

The man returned to the pack and started pulling out bricks of C4. "Someone who doesn't like competition. Go. Now. You have about twenty minutes."

Evan. Cam snapped up the comm device and inserted it as he raced out of the room. "Tox, Steady? You copy?"

"What's your status?" Tox barked.

Cam spoke as he raced through the tunnels. "Atlas March is dead, and the mine is wired to blow. Get everybody clear. I don't have an exact count, but call it T minus fifteen to be safe. Move the rendezvous point beyond the low hills to the west. That should be clear of the blast zone. I'm getting Evan, and we'll meet you there."

"Good copy. Out."

Back at the storeroom, he pulled the steel cabinet away from the wall. When he saw the rocks stacked haphazardly in the entrance to the treasure cave, he wanted to shout for joy. She was here. To abate her fear, he spoke through the small gaps.

"Evan? It's Cam. I'm coming in. Don't nail me with a rock or anything, okay?"

A tiny voice replied. "Okay."

Cam pushed away the rocks and barreled through the small hole like the hulk. It was pitch black, the lanterns from the storage room casting a sliver of light near the entrance. Cam switched on his flashlight and scanned the small space. There, sitting by a wide puddle, was Evan. She was smiling.

She scrambled over to him, and he fell back on his ass, lifting her into his lap. No words escaped before his lips found hers. The kiss was filled with passion, relief, concern, and, most of all, hope. Cam deepened the kiss, their tongues dancing. He lost himself as they melded. It wasn't a zing he felt. It was a fucking sonic boom.

He pulled her body closer, deepened the kiss further. All he could think in that moment was, *I love her.*

He broke the kiss and cradled her head into the crook of his neck. This was madness. How could he love this woman? Then she pulled back, and her cinnamon gaze met his alight with happiness. "I was really hoping you'd show up."

How could he not love her?

The words were on his lips when she said the one thing that drew his declaration to a screeching halt. "All I kept thinking this whole time was I wish Miguel were here."

Cam pulled back like he'd been stung. *Miguel.* He schooled his expression and smoothed her hair. "Come on. We gotta get out of this mine."

"But first…" Evan reached into the side pocket of her pants and withdrew a rock. Cam stared at it.

"Oh, wait, no. This is an actual rock." She held it in her fist. "I stuck it in there in case I needed, you know…" She swung the rock down through the air. "Whack any bad guys."

She replaced it in the side pocket of her cargo pants and withdrew another. "*This* is what I wanted to show you."

It was round like a geode and the size of a baseball. He saw nothing of note in the dim light.

"Evan, some psychopath is going to blow this entire mine off the side of the mountain in about…" He checked the timer on his watch. "Fourteen minutes."

"This is the rock that was in the gold box we found," she explained.

"Okaaay."

"It's not a weight." She grinned.

"Tell it walking, beautiful." Cam grabbed her free hand and pulled her toward the hole. A hole now filled by Joseph Nabeel's slim frame. His Ruger trained on Cam. He climbed through, never taking his eyes off his target.

"Go ahead, dear," Joseph said. "Tell him the story of my diamond."

Cam moved Evan behind him.

"Joseph, what are you doing?" she asked over Cam's shoulder.

"More than half my life I've been looking for that diamond. And you, you stumble upon it like a child finding a euro in the street."

Cam glanced at his watch. Eleven minutes. He couldn't call for help; the team couldn't get in and out in time.

"Joseph," Cam said calmly, "we need to get out of this mine."

"I'm not leaving without The Panther's Eye. You are not leaving at all." Joseph aimed the gun at Cam's chest.

"You want it? Go get it." Evan whipped the object in her hand over her shoulder. It flew through the air and plopped into a tidal pool.

"No!" Joseph shouted.

Taking advantage of Joseph's distraction, Cam nailed him in the chest with a sidekick. He collapsed on the ground, the gun spinning from his hand. Cam grabbed Evan by the waist and practically threw her through the hole into the storeroom. "Run, Evan! I'm right behind you."

"But…" she protested.

"No buts, Evan. Go."

He turned back to the room, then checked the time: four and a half minutes. It took at least three just to navigate the mine. They were out of time.

Joseph scrambled over to the tidal pool and plunged a hand into the water.

"Joseph, this mine is full of C4. You'll be strip mining this mountain tomorrow." Cam tried to reason with him.

"I don't care. Go ahead. I saw where it went into the water. *It's right here.*" He plunged his hand into the pool again and again. "It's so close. I'm so close."

Cam knocked the older man out cold with a well-placed punch. He backed out of the cave pulling Joseph through the hole.

Two delicate hands grabbed the older man and heaved.

"Damnit, Evan, I told you to run," Cam snapped.

"I'm not leaving you, Miguel," she calmly replied.

Cam growled his frustration, hoisted Joseph onto his shoulder in a fireman's carry, and moved to the door.

"No." Evan stood by the original hole Cam had made with the sledgehammer when he first caught her in the cave. "This way."

She was right. It would be tricky in the dark, carrying a body, but the distance to the beach was much shorter. "Go. I'm right behind you."

Together they made their way through the darkness, dragging Joseph through the tight openings, moving as quickly as the enveloping rocks would allow.

When they emerged into the large entry cave, Cam yelled, "Get to the water!"

Together they sprinted into the surf. Evan was a strong swimmer, and Cam had been trained to swim with an incapacitated teammate. Joseph regained consciousness after a few strokes, and together they maneuvered to a buoy and held on.

It started as a low rumble in the darkness, like the sound of a freight train. Then came muffled explosions, one after the next. Cam and Evan stared up as the mountain seemed to collapse into itself. Finally, a violent eruption blew from beneath the ground. They could see the flames even from sea level. Huge chunks of rock and debris flew through the air showering the beach and falling into the water. Smoke poured from every cave opening along the shore.

"You should have left me there." Joseph stared without seeing. "The Panther's Eye is truly lost."

Cam turned to Evan, and she bobbed into the circle of his arm. He kissed the top of her head. For a second before he held her, she had the strangest look on her face.

———————— ◆ ————————

After the team had located them and Joseph was taken into custody, Cam told Tox he'd catch up, and the group had fallen back to give him a moment. Cam and Evan stood on the beach, facing each other in the dim dawn. He cupped her face in his palms.

"I need to show you something." Evan reached into her pocket and withdrew the diamond.

"What the hell? How?" Cam stared at the stone in shock.

"I threw my whacking rock. I switched them when you pushed me behind you to shield me."

"Well, I'll be damned."

"Distraction and sleight of hand." She spread the fingers of her free hand and fanned them in a circle.

"My little magician."

"I need to get this to Doctor Emberton," Evan said.

"What'll happen to it?" Cam asked.

"I imagine it'll be turned over to the Spanish government. The caves are public land. I know I don't get to keep it."

"Well, you better get a finders fee or something. You earned it." He brushed her hair back from her face.

"Technically, you deserve the finders fee. You found it."

"Nah. I was never there. Remember?"

She slipped the gem back into her pocket and laced her fingers between his.

Cam looked at her. "I wish I could take a picture of you right now. This pink light…" He shook his head without finishing the thought.

A tear ran down her cheek. "I don't know why I'm crying. We're safe. The good guys won, and we made the archaeological discovery of a lifetime." She swiped at the tears.

"Lost potential, I think," he said sadly.

"Maybe we can find it again, our potential. We're good at finding things."

"Maybe we can." He cupped her face. "I know I don't want this to be the last time I see you."

"So... you'll be in touch?"

"I'll be in touch." He bent to kiss her.

"I think I love you, Miguel."

Miguel. Her words cut him like a knife. She loved Miguel. It was more than Cam could process, so he continued the motion and placed the kiss meant for her lips on her forehead.

"Bye." He stepped back.

"Bye *for now.* Right?" she clarified.

He stared into tear-filled cinnamon-colored eyes, choking on words unspoken. Of all the things bouncing around in his fucked up head, the one thing that had come out was the last thing he ever wanted to say to her. *Goodbye.*

"Right."

She smiled through her tears. "Bye."

Cam ran his fingers down her cheek in the now-familiar motion she loved, then turned and walked away.

CHAPTER FORTY-FOUR

Palma, Mallorca
December 15

Cam emerged from the shower and dried off, careful to avoid his injuries. The pain was almost a relief. It was easier to focus on his marred skin than the pain in his chest. Evan had called him Miguel. She had wanted Miguel. *Why?* He applied a fresh bandage to his hip, pressing down on the raw flesh. Miguel was a lowlife out for his own gain and nothing more. How could she be drawn to such darkness? How could she want a man who had done the things Miguel had done?

It was like a psychotic love triangle.

He shook off the lament. It didn't matter. His work with the CIA was over. He could now finally bury Miguel Ramirez. And Evan? His emotions were a knotted ball of twine that he just didn't have the energy to untangle.

He pulled on a pair of sweatpants and walked out to the bedroom only to halt when he spotted Chat sitting at the desk reading something on his phone.

"Hey, *hermano.* Everything okay?" Cam asked.

"I was going to ask you the same thing," Chat's brown eyes met his.

"Just bracing myself for the shitstorm of ribbing from the guys."

"Yeah, I can't help you there, brother. A supermodel kidnapped you. It sounds like the title of a bad porno."

"That's exactly what I said!" Cam bellowed.

When their laughter subsided, Cam pulled on a T-shirt and v-neck sweater.

"So, how did you leave things with Evan?"

Cam turned to the dresser to avoid his friends' probing gaze. "There are no things to leave."

"You sure about that?" Chat probed.

The simple question broke Cam's emotional dam. He sat on the bed and spoke to the floor. He shared how his undercover work had created this fracture in his personality, how he had taken all of his negative qualities and poured them into Miguel Ramirez. How he sometimes felt physically sick thinking about the things he'd done. Finally, he confided the worst of it. Evan had wanted Miguel. She had prayed in that cave for Miguel to help her.

Chat listened, his bald head nodding along, his chocolate eyes understanding. When Cam had finished, Chat drummed a pencil on the desk. "That's a lot to unpack."

"Yeah."

"Let me ask you, when you go under, when you take on the persona of Miguel Ramirez, you prepare, correct?"

"Yes, for weeks. I study his background, establish the legend. I have to be prepared for any situation. I have to respond as Miguel without hesitation."

"But this time, you didn't have time to do that, correct?"

"Well, the identity is already established." Cam countered.

"Yes, on paper, you know everything about Miguel Ramirez, but were you him? Had you immersed yourself in the cover?"

Cam thought about it, keeping his eyes to the ground.

Chat continued, "I ask because I think when you rescued Evan from the stingray attack, you were Cam."

Cam spoke to the floor. "She called me a seal."

"What?"

"When I was carrying her out of the water, she said, 'You're a seal.' She meant the animal, but I almost dropped her."

"That proves my point," Chat insisted.

"What is your point?"

"That regardless of what you called yourself on this op, you were Cam. Would Miguel Ramirez have reacted to a SEAL reference? Would Miguel have even gone into the water to save her? You may have used the accent, changed your walk and your demeanor, but I think you know deep down that when you were with Evan, you were Cam. Think of all the things you would have done differently with her if you had been Miguel Ramirez."

Cam's eyes shot up to his friend. "How can you possibly know that?"

"Because Miguel Ramirez is not capable of love. And you, my brother, are in love."

Cam didn't deny it. Chat stood and sent a text. Cam's replacement phone that the team had delivered buzzed in the corner. "I can spot a man in love, but you may need some help with the other stuff. I texted you the name of a doc in Beaufort. He's a veteran and a smart guy. Nobody expects you to sort this shit on your own. Frankly, you'd be a fool to try."

"I seem that fucked up, huh?"

Chat grinned. "Seriously fucked up. See you at lunch, brother."

CHAPTER FORTY-FIVE

South Island, South Carolina
December 20

The new deck smelled of cedar and varnish. Holding a mug of coffee, Steady tested the surface and, finding it dry, stepped out into a chilly morning.

The beach was framed by a rosy sky, quiet but for the swoosh of the incoming tide. Steady turned the other way. The sky was not the only pink thing enhancing the beauty of the scene. A puff of a pink ponytail bounced away from him in the distance. His neighbor, Very. Yes, he thought, she was *very*. Very intriguing, very sexy, very smart—then when she turned and headed back the way she had come, he added another descriptor to his list—very beautiful.

Her feet pounded the sand as she sprinted the final distance. Long legs in turquoise tie-dye flew. She slowed to a jog when she reached his stretch of beach. Then she stopped and faced him.

"Are you Steady? Twitch's friend?"

Delighted Twitch had mentioned him—hopefully as the handsome and handy guy next door—he nodded enthusiastically. "That's me."

She stared at him for a moment, her chest rising and falling under an orange University of Virginia hoodie. Then she shouted, "keep that telescope pointed at the sky, pervert."

And with that, she jogged off, the red neon stripes on her trainers fading like disappearing taillights.

Steady set his mug of coffee on the flat railing and stood there for a full minute with his mouth hanging open. Then he threw back his head and laughed. This girl was aptly named. She was Very.

CHAPTER FORTY-SIX

South Island, South Carolina
December 21

"Son, let me educate you on the subtleties of poker." Steady puffed on a cigar and fanned his cards on the table. "See these two ladies here? They are queens. And they beat that dumpster fire of a hand you're showing me."

Steady, Tox, Herc, Ren, Chat, and Cam were on Steady's newly repaired deck, crammed around a makeshift card table consisting of a plank resting on two sawhorses. Platters of sandwiches and bowls of snacks, courtesy of Maggie Bishop, bookended the poker game. The folding card table Herc had commandeered from Charlie Bishop's garage served as the bar.

It was a cool night, an Atlantic breeze blew in, and the full moon hung low on the horizon. It was an idyllic setting for anyone, but for these men who had camped on frigid mountain cliffs, trudged through swamps, and slept in critter-infested jungles, it was heaven.

"Whatever." Herc Reynolds shoved his pair of nines into the center of the table.

Steady grinned around his stogie and gathered the chips.

Cam tossed his cards back. "Let somebody else deal, Steady. I've had shit hands all night."

Tox shoved his shoulder. "Cam's just grumpy he has to look at our ugly mugs across the table."

Herc reached for a sandwich. "Gemini March. Jeez, I had her poster above my bunk at sniper school."

"And I bet you hit that target a few times." Steady's jibe was met with a shower of popcorn from Tox.

"Dude, spare us that image." Tox puffed out his cheeks in a fake gag.

Cam gathered his cards one at a time as they were dealt. "Who's the craziest woman you've ever met?"

That popped the lid on a can of worms.

Chat slid a hand across his bald head. "Who wants to go first? Steady? The omelet girl? Ren? The screeper?"

"Okay, elaborate." Cam urged, happy to have the attention off of him.

Steady just stared at his cards. "Suffice it to say, I was getting raw egg out of shit for *weeks*."

"What's a 'screeper'?" Herc asked around a bite of a turkey sandwich.

Ren banged his forehead on the table. "Screamer, weeper."

Tox did his best impression. "Re-hen-hen-hen, *Re-hen-hen-hen!* I didn't know if you were railing her or killing her."

Ren still had his head on the table. "She was doing that before I did either one, so, trust me, it was a tough decision."

Ren popped his head up and laughed out his question. "Remember that chick who showed up at the base claiming to be Tox's wife?"

Steady slapped Tox on the back. "And she didn't know his real name."

Herc sputtered, "Who did she say she was? Mrs. Tox?"

"Yes!" Ren laughed.

"So, take that crazy and multiply it by ten." Cam traded two cards to the dealer.

Herc smirked. "Still might be worth it."

"I don't know." Chat fanned out his cards. "Things worked out for her pretty well in the end."

"How so?" Cam asked.

"Her beloved father dies in a suspicious plane crash, and a cousin she has every reason to despise swoops in and not only takes over the company but sets up a heroin operation. Meanwhile, she just happens to be hot as hell for a guy who just happens to be an undercover CIA officer, and she just happens to put him right in the middle of her cousin's drug ring. That's a lot of happy accidents for a flighty model who just wanted to get you into bed."

Tox drained his beer and grabbed another from the cooler. "Gentlemen, let's raise a glass to Cam." The men all grabbed their beverages. "To the only motherfucker in the Navy," he glanced around as if he were checking for eavesdroppers, then stage-whispered, "or the CIA, who could land himself neck-deep in shit because some broad was obsessed with his trouser torpedo. To the undisputed Boss of Fuck."

Cam shook his head, smiling as the men clinked glasses and bottles. "That fucking nickname is gonna haunt me."

"Till the day you die." Steady spoke around the cigar as he arranged his cards.

Cam set his cards down. "She called me that."

"Who? Gemini?" Ren asked.

"Yes, Gemini," Cam confirmed. "She called me the Boss of Fuck."

"How could she have known it? It wasn't Miguel's nickname." Steady asked.

Cam stood and walked over to the railing like a zombie, images flashing in his head like a slideshow:

Gemini walking into the club in Ibiza when his informant failed to show up.

Who are you waiting for?

You.

You're right about that.

Joseph talking to him beneath the portrait of her late father.

He was a brilliant businessman. A strategist. He wanted to take Gemini under his wing, but she never seemed to show any interest...

Gemini is the star of the show.

Gemini straddling him and whipping him.

Tonight, the Boss of Fuck will work for me.

The truth hit him like a bolt of lightning crashing through his being.

Gemini March is The Conductor.

He repeated the thought aloud.

"Gemini March is The Conductor."

"You're kidding, right?" Steady said. "She's featured in *Glamour Magazine* this month discussing the pitfalls of liquid eyeliner."

Herc added, "You think the gorgeous supermodel thing is just some cover?"

"No. It's not just some cover. It's the perfect cover." Cam explained. "Her father, Ulysses, was a brilliant strategist with a global network. Joseph Nabeel told me Ulysses tried to bring Gemini into the business, but the more he tried, the more she became interested in modeling. What if her father laid the groundwork for The Conductor while she laid the groundwork for the perfect alternate identity?"

"Calliope did make a note of Gemini's travel schedule when she interviewed her. Lotta hotspots on that list," Ren noted.

Tox said, "According to her official bio, she started modeling at fourteen when she was discovered in Paris. She's been in the business a long time. She'd certainly know how to work the system to her advantage."

"Exactly. She can be in Malaysia for a runway show or Somalia for a humanitarian mission. It's fucking genius when you think about it." Cam turned to the group. "Where's Nathan?"

"At home with his family, I imagine," Ren said.

"Call him and tell him I'm coming. I need to see that video."

Cam tore through the house and out the door, hopped into his car, and took off.

Nathan was waiting on the front porch, barefoot in jeans and a T-shirt.

"What's going on?" he asked.

"You still have the flash drive?" Cam stood at the foot of the porch steps.

"It's in my office. Come on in." Nathan waved him inside.

Cam followed Nathan through the house and closed the office door behind him. Nathan booted up his laptop, donned a pair of reading glasses, and inserted the flash drive. Cam pulled a chair around, and the two men sat side by side as the video played.

"There." Cam pointed to the screen. On the upper deck, a topless blonde was sunning on a lounger, a floppy hat covering her face, a crew member standing at the ready.

"That's Gemini March. Can you zoom in?"

Nathan manipulated the trackpad, and Cam leaned closer. "She has an earbud in one ear. How much do you want to bet she's not listening to music?"

"She's away from the crowd, listening to the meeting." Nathan caught on.

"Gemini March is The Conductor."

Both men sat, stunned.

"She travels all over the world. She can be anywhere for a modeling shoot, a party, a humanitarian mission, a vacation. She has all her father's shipping and trade connections." Cam turned to his boss. "She followed me to Ibiza. She either wanted to see who I was meeting or find out what I knew. If I hadn't snuck out of that hotel room, I'd probably be dead."

Nathan stepped to the bar and poured them each a scotch.

Cam took a fortifying sip and continued, "She didn't bring me to Mallorca for a romantic getaway. She broke Raymond Greene in Crimea. She *knew* I was CIA, and she brought me so she could steal the journal and the flash drive without *The Conductor* ever getting involved."

Nathan interjected, "As an added bonus, she puts you in a position to bring down Atlas March. Gemini March wants him dead because she suspects he arranged her father's murder. The Conductor wants him dead for shipping heroin without paying the piper. She planted you in his drug operation better than any government agency ever could. Clever girl."

"Where is Gemini March?" Cam asked.

Nathan tossed the glasses on his desk. "I imagine she's on a modeling shoot on a beach somewhere. While all of this adds up," Nathan's gesture encompassed Cam and the laptop. "It's certainly not evidence of a crime. And I imagine she's well-staffed with attorneys to prevent anyone spreading baseless accusations."

"So, what? She just continues on? We do nothing?" Cam balled his fists.

"We regroup. We reassess." Nathan sat back in his chair and drummed the side of his thumb on the armrest. "Let me make a call. Sometimes these things work out in unexpected ways."

CHAPTER FORTY-SEVEN

Outside Beaufort, South Carolina
December 22

Cam sat in the passenger seat as Chat drove up the interstate to the Charleston Airport. They listened to the news story detailing the arrest of Senator Harlan Musgrave.

Cam pointed to the radio. "Musgrave is claiming there's a cadre of corrupt Senators, judges, and cabinet members who have set him up. He's asserting that he was trying to infiltrate and expose the group, and these accusations are their way of shutting him down. His conspiracy theory is getting all kinds of traction on social media."

"Of course it is." Chat shook his head.

"I'd hate to be the U.S. Attorney prosecuting this clusterfuck."

"And we thought catching the bad guys was the hard part." Chat shook his head.

"Any word from Finn?" Cam asked. "I'd like to thank him."

"Not a word. He knows how to disappear. I just hope he's getting the help he needs to get his head straight. We all remember this easygoing, positive guy. He may never be that man again, but there has to be something better than what he's become."

Cam nodded sadly. "All right."

"Another story broke this morning. An archaeological team in Mallorca discovered the world's largest yellow diamond."

"You know," Cam looked over at his friend, "when we first found it, I thought it was a weight to keep the box it was in from getting swept away by the tides. I threw it into a puddle."

Chat's eyes grew laughably large. "You tossed away the world's largest yellow diamond?"

Cam lifted his hands in a what-are-you-going-to-do gesture. "I didn't know what it was."

"Seems like you've done that more than once of late. Tossed away something of great value."

Cam didn't pretend not to understand. "I can't stop thinking about her. You're right; she is that diamond, but you know that op messed me up. I want her so much it hurts, but I need to get right. She deserves that."

Chat continued, "How'd the first therapy session go?"

"Really well. The doc you recommended is great. I get so balled up about shit; sometimes I just need someone to shake out my brain."

"I know what you mean, man. Shit, I've never gone under, but we all have a dark side. It's like that Cherokee fable," Chat said.

"Which one?" Cam asked.

Chat looked out at the road, his hand dangling casually over the wheel. "A grandfather tells his grandson that two wolves are fighting inside of us. One is evil and darkness, one is goodness and light. The grandson asks him which wolf wins the fight. The grandfather answers, whichever one you feed."

Cam blew out a heavy breath. Of course, he hadn't conjured Miguel Ramirez out of thin air. The dark desires and prurient impulses Miguel acted on were there. Inside Cam. Cam had just never been put in a situation where his two identities had come face-to-face. On

Mallorca, had he been a darker version of Cam? A better incarnation of Miguel?

Chat helped him realize something that Evan seemed to know instinctively. Evan, that gorgeous, shy, damaged woman, had understood all along that he was simply one flawed man. All the qualities that his alternate persona possessed were within him, and that was okay with her. When he ceased to play the role of Miguel Ramirez, he boxed up those darker urges, but he had to accept that all of them—violence, greed, and certainly lust—were there within Camilo Canto. He simply chose not to feed that wolf.

"You feed the right wolf, Cam," Chat said, echoing his thoughts.

Suddenly, Cam was overcome with an urgency so powerful, he opened the door before the car had come to a stop at the curb.

Chat grabbed his shoulder. "You okay, man?"

Cam turned back to his friend. "Not yet, but for the first time in a long time, I can honestly say I think I'm going to be."

Chat grinned. "Have a good flight."

Cam hopped out, grabbed his duffle from the back seat, and waved as the car pulled away. He had the strangest feeling Chat knew he wasn't heading to Miami. Not yet.

Entering the terminal, Cam went straight to the counter with his phone to his ear. Twitch answered while he stood in line.

"Yes, I can track her phone," she said without greeting.

Cam chuckled. "What can I say? I'm slow on the uptake."

"Nah, you're just a mess like the rest of us." He could hear the sound of her fingers moving across the keyboard. "She's in Palo Alto. I'll text you the address."

"Thanks, Twitch."

"Go get her, tiger."

Evan left her suitcase by the front door. Everything in it needed to go straight to the laundry.

In five days, she had been from Palma to Algiers to Cairo to Madrid and finally back to Palo Alto. The sheer madness of the diamond discovery, the travel, and the press had taken every minute of her time. Almost every minute. She would have thought the hectic schedule would have been enough to distract her from thoughts of Cam. It was not. Everywhere she looked, there was some reminder—an Almond Joy in an airport gift shop, a question from the media about the discovery, the smell of the ocean. Even now, the yellow flame of the jasmine-scented candle burning by her bed had Evan imagining Cam's hungry eyes.

On the flight from London to Cairo, she had downloaded an article on undercover operatives from a medical journal. She'd read about how immersive and taxing the process was for deep cover agents, and she'd felt awful. Calling Cam "Miguel" was an honest, understandable mistake, but she had profoundly underestimated the impact doing so would have. Evan didn't care about his name, but for him, the name mattered. Miguel Ramirez was not a role he relished; Miguel was not the man Cam was. When she had expressed her feelings, *her love*, and called him Miguel…

She passed through her cozy living area, grabbed a bottled water from the kitchen fridge, and headed straight into the bedroom.

She set the water on the end table next to the stack of classic novels she and her father had committed to reading. She ran her hand along the spines: *Jane Eyre*, *Nicholas Nickleby*, *The Scarlet Pimpernel*, her fingers stopping on her father's choice, Robert Louis Stevenson's *Dr. Jekyll and Mr. Hyde*. She winced. She didn't think of Cam's cover identity as Mr. Hyde, but she imagined that's how Cam felt.

She flopped onto the bed, her frustration welling. She wanted, no, she needed to see Cam, to explain that she had always seen the real man beneath his cover. He may not want Evan the way she wanted him—his absence was a painful ache—but she needed to tell him how she felt. Evan thought back to the night in the cave when she had explained the meaning of an introvert. She processed emotions rather than expressing them. Well, that ended today. She loved this man. Cam. She loved him. And that was too important to bury under layers of shyness and inexperience.

First, she needed sleep— weeks of non-stop work had taken their toll. Evan staggered to the shower and quickly rinsed the day of travel from her body. Slipping into a weathered Stanford T-shirt she had had since freshman year, she crawled back into bed and let sleep claim her. Tomorrow she was going after her man.

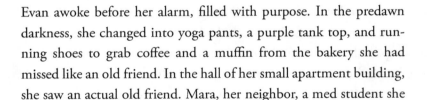

Evan awoke before her alarm, filled with purpose. In the predawn darkness, she changed into yoga pants, a purple tank top, and running shoes to grab coffee and a muffin from the bakery she had missed like an old friend. In the hall of her small apartment building, she saw an actual old friend. Mara, her neighbor, a med student she had known since junior year, was just returning from a run.

"You're back," Mara greeted with a smile.

"Finally." Evan puffed out a breath.

Mara placed her hands on the wall and stretched her calves. "And rumor has it, you're a celebrity."

"Hardly, but it was pretty awesome."

"I need the whole story. Every detail," Mara insisted.

Shooting a thumb over her shoulder, Evan said, "I'll grab your chai and a muffin and tell you all about it." She leaned closer. "There's a man involved."

"That might be bigger news than finding a diamond where you're concerned." Mara assessed her friend then checked her watch. "Shoot, I'm due at the hospital in half an hour. Come by tonight. We can get into the wine."

"Perfect. I still have a few bottles from the case of Pinot my dad sent," Evan replied.

"I knew having a friend who grew up on a vineyard would pay off. See you tonight." Mara smiled and disappeared into her apartment.

The sun was just peeking over the buildings to the east when Evan rounded the corner with her coffee and cranberry muffin set in the cup holders of the cardboard tray.

She stopped. An imposing, shadowed form sat on her stoop. A man—a man she had seen in dim light enough to recognize immediately.

Cam. He was here.

Evan halted, frozen in place. Cam scanned the street. When his eyes found her, he stood and stepped down to the sidewalk, facing her. Wearing military green pants, combat boots, and a gray T-shirt, he stood calm and ready. Evan could see those incredible irises even half a block away.

She dropped the drink carrier and ran. Cam met her halfway and crushed his mouth to hers. They were a tangle of lips and tongues and hands. He lifted her by her backside and pulled her thighs around his waist.

"Cam," she breathed out between kisses.

He kissed her cheek, his lips traveling down to her neck. "Say it again."

"Cam. *Cam.*" She shivered.

When they broke apart, he helped her stand.

Then he stood before her and said, "My name is Camilo Canto."

She grabbed his T-shirt with her fist. "Camilo Canto," she repeated. "You're here."

"I came back to find *my* diamond. Another one I should have never tossed away to begin with." He touched her cheek in the familiar way she had missed.

"Cam, I get it. I really do." Evan made a point of repeating his real name.

"No, *I* get it. I think you always did. It just took me a while to get there."

"Understandable considering the work you do," she said.

"Did," he corrected. "That part of my job is over. Just Cam from here on out. Miguel Ramirez is in there, as much as I hate to admit it, but he doesn't define me."

"I'm glad you worked through it." Evan ran her hand down his forearm and entwined their fingers.

Cam touched his forehead to hers. "I haven't completely worked through it, but enough to know I'm not letting my zing get away."

"You're zing?" Evan asked.

"I'll explain later. Let's take a walk." He pulled her to his side. "I want to do this right. Take it slow. Get to know you."

Evan met that incredible golden gaze and said, "I'd like to get naked."

She watched his expression morph from incredulity to hunger. He grabbed her hand and tugged her forward.

"Your way's good too."

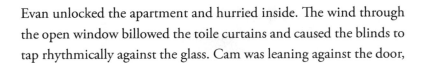

Evan unlocked the apartment and hurried inside. The wind through the open window billowed the toile curtains and caused the blinds to tap rhythmically against the glass. Cam was leaning against the door, his hands shoved in the pockets of his fatigues, drawing her eye to the outline of his sizable erection.

"Cam?"

"I don't think I can hold back," he said.

Evan closed the distance between them. Just like she had done in their cave, she pulled the tank top from her body. "Then don't." She toed off her trainers, peeled the yoga pants down her legs, and stepped out of them. In a white lace bra and matching thong, she stood before him. "Don't hold back, Cam."

Slowly, he pulled his hands from his pockets. He reached up and flicked the clasp between her breasts. Evan started to shed the garment when he stayed her movements with a quiet command.

"I'll do it."

She nodded on a deep inhale. He smelled like the ocean. He smelled like a memory. Cam's big hand occupied the space between them. Extending his index finger, he traced the inside swell of her breasts. He pushed away one lacy cup, then the other. That devilish finger snaked up and under the strap and sent the bra sliding down her arms.

He had only touched her with one finger, and Evan's skin prickled, her breasts ached. She squeezed her thighs together to ease the tension. He noticed.

Cam took a step forward, and she mirrored the action. He ran the back of his hand down her flat stomach and past the elastic of her thong. Then, still fully clothed, he followed the panties to the floor, kneeling before her. He placed a kiss at the bare apex of her thighs and slid his hand through the seam of her wet flesh.

Then, he stood and said, "Bedroom."

With a confidence born of desire, Evan turned and walked the length of the room. Cam stalked her at a distance.

At the foot of the bed, Evan faced him. She could feel the down comforter brushing her calves, the carpet under her curled toes. She watched as Cam reached behind his head and pulled the gray T-shirt from his body. From his rounded pecs to the ladder of abdominal muscles to the cradle of his hips, Cam's bare torso was battle-worn and beautiful. He knelt to unlace his boots.

"I'll do it." Repeating his words, Evan stepped in front of him and sank to her knees. Once the boots were off, she lifted a hand to his waistband.

"Can I?" she asked.

"I'm all yours."

Evan removed Cam's pants and boxer briefs in one slide, lifting her head to his impressive erection. Holding the base in her fist, she traced her tongue around the head. Evan tasted him, teased him, sensing his breath catch and his body tense. She had never done this before, but instinct guided her. That, and Cam's muttered Spanish when she took him in her mouth.

Still sensing his restraint, Evan repeated her plea, "Don't hold back." With a growl, Cam's strong hands came under her arms. He lifted Evan and threw her on the bed.

"My turn," he said.

Cam snagged a condom from his pants pocket and followed. Holding her hips, he pulled her to the edge of the bed. Evan supported herself on her elbows as he lifted one leg at a time and draped them over his shoulders. The look he gave her had her squirming. This wasn't about him or her; it was about the space between them, the short distance that seemed to vibrate with their colliding attraction. His head disappeared between her legs.

Evan stared down in amazement. The combination of skill and unadulterated pleasure was mesmerizing. More than that, though, Cam seemed to understand her desire on a molecular level—what she needed, what felt just right as if her body, her need, were his own. Sensation consumed her, and she fell back onto the bed. Her legs dangled over his shoulders, her heels digging into his back. Cam was a beast of fierce precision, working her with fingers and tongue until she exploded, her body ignited and dazed, like fireworks on a hazy night.

Cam stood at the foot of the bed, sheathed and erect. She inched back to the headboard, and Cam prowled over her, his hips spreading her thighs. She looked into his beautiful face, and he ran reassuring fingers across her cheek.

Then he drove into her. Evan gasped and shouted, gripped by the sheer intensity. Like an ocean wave, it crashed, retreated, and crashed anew. She held onto his shoulders. She could tell he was checking without asking directly. He read her face, her body. When he was satisfied with what he sensed and saw, and she tipped her hips to encourage him, he continued the onslaught. He braced himself above her with one thick arm. His other hand was everywhere, pinching her nipples, caressing her thighs, squeezing her ass. He fucked her with relentless determination, plunging into her again and again like he couldn't get close enough.

Like he wanted to fuse their souls.

The very thought of it ripped the orgasm from within her, the blast as much mental as physical—the bond they formed, all-encompassing. The dam burst again like a movie reel backing up and replaying, her cries drowned out by Cam's as ecstasy consumed them.

After an eternal minute, he lifted his head and brushed the sweat and tears from her face. Then, still buried within her, he gently kissed her lips and asked, "You okay?"

"No. I was okay when I got my muffin at the bakery." She wrapped the auburn curl that had flopped onto his forehead around her finger. "I am incredible."

"Yes, you are." He ran his nose down the length of hers.

Evan took a deep breath as he withdrew. Cam rolled to the side, bringing her with him. Words of love were on her tongue, but they didn't leave her mouth. She was still learning this man, but she knew with every fiber of her being that she loved him, loved Cam. Despite promising herself she would be bold, her shyness kept her silent.

"What are your plans for the holidays?" he asked.

"Um, well, I planned to catch up on some reading, and I'm submitting a new proposal for my dissertation."

"You're spending Christmas alone?" He traced a line down her arm.

"My dad's traveling, and my mom and stepdad are visiting his son in Texas. I don't mind."

"Baby, pack a bag."

Baby. Her whole body tingled at the endearment. The man holding her was everything.

"Okay."

Cam laughed. "Don't you want to know where we're going?"

"It doesn't matter. I trust you. Wherever you take me, I'm sure it will be an adventure."

CHAPTER FORTY-EIGHT

Coconut Grove, Florida
December 24

Cam thanked the Uber driver and climbed out of the SUV, holding Evan's hand. He paused, standing before the pink stucco home nestled among lush greenery and coconut palms. The house was decorated for the holidays. Pine roping wrapped with white lights outlined the front door, a wreath with a red bow hanging in the center. On the front lawn, a garish inflatable Santa in his sleigh disrupted the tasteful landscaping. Cam knew instantly his parents had put it out for his little nieces and nephews. Evan stood next to him, scanning the tableau with delighted eyes, almost the same way she examined a discovery in the caves.

He retrieved their luggage from the back and returned to her side. She stood close, wrapped both hands around his big arm, and smiled. "You grew up here?"

"Yeah. Fell out of that tree when I was eight and broke my arm." He pointed to a huge magnolia in the side yard. "And that trellis to the second-floor window? That's how we would sneak out."

"We?"

"Oh yes, my sisters taught me more about espionage than the CIA." He winked.

"Cam?"

"Yeah?"

"I'm so happy right now." She looked up at him, her cinnamon eyes glowing. Cam felt it to his toes. He wanted to put that expression on Evan's face every day for the rest of his life.

"Are you nervous to meet my family?" he asked.

"Nah." She waved him off. "Parents love me. I'm the nerd, remember? They assume I'm the one who's going to keep their kids from getting into trouble."

"Little did they know." He bumped her gently.

"Right?" She laughed, that husky, sexy sound that drove him wild.

"That's why you're perfect for me. You look all sweet and innocent, but I see that troublemaker inside you."

The front door opened.

Cam's mother leaned down to pick up a package. When she stood back up, she looked to where they stood, and Cam lifted his hand with a broad smile. Kate Canto dropped the box and covered her mouth with both hands. Cam could see the tears running over her cheeks and the backs of her fingers. She turned back to the house and shouted for her husband.

"Aarón! Aarón! Come here right now!" Then she hurried down the stone steps and rushed to where he stood at the end of the driveway. His mother was a tiny woman, but she crashed into him with full force, sending him back a half-step and knocking a laugh out of his mouth. She didn't say a word, just squeezed him as if reassuring herself he was actually there. Cam gave her a minute—she was always open and emotional, but he sensed she needed this—then said, "Hi, mom."

Cam returned Evan to the circle of his arm.

With a sniff and a swipe at her eyes, his mother pulled back and assessed her son and the woman by his side.

"And this must be Evan."

"Hi, Mrs. Canto. It's so nice—" His mother's embrace cut off her words.

"Welcome, Evan. Cam has told me so *little* about you." She shot Cam a mock glare. "Come on inside, and I'll get you fed."

"That's the best thing I've heard in months," Cam agreed.

As they started up the walk, his father appeared in the doorway.

"Camilo!" his father shouted as he came barreling up to them. Cam was a younger version of his father. At sixty-seven, his dad still had a thick head of chestnut hair with just a touch of distinguished gray at the temples. He had the same golden irises that were now misted. If anything, Aarón Canto was even more emotional than his wife. He lifted his son a foot off the ground, then set him down, clapped him on the back, and grabbed the duffle that had landed on the lawn. He greeted Evan like she was already a member of the family.

"Merry Christmas, Evan. Aarón Canto." He held out a hand, and she took it. "Cam picked a hell of a week to bring his first girl home. It's going to be a madhouse for the next several days."

Cam felt her pleasure at his father's words, and she leaned closer. She looked up at him as she replied. "In my experience, Cam doesn't do anything halfway."

"Ah-ha, she has your number." Aarón led them into the house, and Kate guided Evan toward the kitchen.

His father held Cam back. "Cutting it pretty close, my son."

"Sorry it took an extra day, but it was necessary."

Aarón Canto's gaze went to his wife as she disappeared down the hall. "I understand."

"Interrogation later, dad. I'm here for the food."

Through his laughter, his father said, "there's my son."

"It's good to be home."

CHAPTER FORTY-NINE

Beaufort, South Carolina
December 25

Nathan Bishop was a light sleeper. Years in the military bookended by years of disquiet had made for restless nights. At the moment, inner contentment and the beautiful body molded next to him had quite the soporific effect. As a result, he had twice swatted at the hand that shook his shoulder before registering the urgent whisper.

"Nathan? *Nathan?*"

"I'm up. I'm up. What's going on?"

"It's time."

Nathan yawned. "Nah. Can't be. It's still dark out. Go back to sleep, Emily."

Emily sat up in the bed and waited. *Five, four, three...*

"I'm up. It's time? *Time* time? I'm up."

Emily's face contorted in pain as she gripped her belly.

"Boy, they got bad fast. That was seven minutes in between."

"Seven minutes!" Nathan hollered before jumping out of the bed.

"Well, they've been twelve minutes apart for a while. Now seven. So I think it's time."

"Twelve then seven?" Nathan hopped around with one foot stuck in the leg of his jeans as he grabbed a T-shirt from the dresser. "Jesus bloody hell, how long have you been faffing about with the timing?"

"Excuse me? Did you just refer to labor as *faffing*?"

Nathan righted his clothes, took a deep breath, and sat next to his wife on the bed.

"Emily, darling. How long have you been experiencing contractions?"

"Since noon."

"*Noon*!!!—" Deep breath. "I see." He pulled her hand off her belly and held it between his own. "And why haven't you mentioned it?"

"I wanted to be one of those cool, together moms. You know, third baby, she's-got-it-all-figured-out. Plus, I didn't want to bother you with all this Cam stuff going on, but I may have waited a bit too long. I think my water just broke. I didn't account for the fact that this is my first actual labor."

Their twins had been delivered via a scheduled C-section.

"Right." Nathan sent a quick text to his Aunt Maggie; the godsend had offered to watch the twins should this very circumstance occur. He cleared his throat. "In the future, when you are forty weeks pregnant, I would like to be apprised of everything from a gas bubble to a pebble in your shoe. Understood?"

"Copy that." She saluted.

Nathan held the back of her head and took his wife in a fierce kiss. Emily whimpered in response. Then moaned as another contraction seized her. Nathan shifted seamlessly, placed a hand on her middle, and checked his watch.

"Maggie should be here straight away. I'll get your bag." He found her violet gaze as the contraction ebbed. "Let's go meet our daughter."

CHAPTER FIFTY

Coconut Grove, Florida
December 25

Cam kissed Evan's hair as she snuggled close. At three in the morning, his dark childhood bedroom looked normal enough, but he knew once the sun rose, she would see the bedroom of a teenage boy. The walls were decorated with posters of Dan Marino and the Red Hot Chili Peppers. Shelves were filled with high school soccer and baseball trophies. His dresser held framed photos of Cam with his sisters and school friends. There was a picture of him with a former Vice President at a reception after Cam had been awarded the Silver Star. Of course, there was also a picture of a six-year-old Cam in traditional Chilean garb performing a native folk dance.

He placed his hand over Evan's, where it rested on his broad, smooth chest. He was planning to slip out of bed when a thought hit him. He had extracted himself from a woman's bed so many times—easing her body away and tiptoeing around the room to grab his clothes from the floor, leaving a note on a counter or a table. This was different in every conceivable way.

It pained him to separate himself from the woman melded to his side. The moment he slipped to the edge of the bed, he felt her absence. Nevertheless, he had a tradition when he was home. He didn't know if it was superstition or hunger, probably both, but he always crept down to the kitchen in the middle of the night, snagged a plate of leftovers, and ate alone at the granite island in the quiet.

Years of training had enabled Cam to move with the silence of a shark. He descended the front hall stairs and crept into the kitchen. The bright space was yellow and white with gleaming countertops and professional appliances. He pulled the container of stew from the stainless steel fridge, poured a generous bowl, and grabbed a spoon while it warmed in the microwave. Meal in hand, he turned and came face to face with his father wearing pajamas and a smirk and holding a coffee mug.

"You never could sneak around worth a damn." Aarón jerked his head toward the living room.

Cam whispered, "I don't know why I'm sneaking around anyway. Shit, I'm thirty-five."

"Language," his mother scolded, walking through the room and heading to the walk-in pantry.

"It's three in the morning." Cam scratched his stubbled beard and accompanied his dad.

Aarón spoke as he strolled to the couch. "It's Christmas. Your mom's been cooking, and I've been wrapping. Ever tried to wrap a bicycle?"

Cam entered the vaulted living room; the ten-foot Frasier Fir was heavy with ornaments, tinsel, and white lights. Cam covered his mouth to silence the laugh; it looked like his father had simply unrolled the wrapping paper in circles around the small bike and then done the same with the tape. Strategically placed bows hid the worst of it.

His father shrugged, "Jamie won't care. The paper will be in shreds in thirty seconds."

Cam followed his dad and took a seat. The room was decorated in pale gray and white with blue and sage green accents in the art and the throw pillows. Pine roping and candles decorated the mantle, a nativity scene in the center.

Aarón crossed an ankle over the opposite knee and spread his arm across the back of the pewter linen couch. "Now. Tell me about your girl."

"My girl," Cam repeated, loving the words.

"The look on your face? I think it was the exact expression I must have had when I first laid eyes on your mother."

Kate Canto appeared at the arched entrance to the room.

Cam stood and hugged his mother. "Merry Christmas, mom."

"I love you, Camilo." Kate sat next to her husband. "Now, tell us about Evan."

Aarón squeezed her shoulder. "I think he felt the zing." He kissed his wife's temple.

She shook her head. "You and that stupid zing."

"What? It was a zing. I felt a zing when I first saw you."

"I felt no such thing," she huffed.

"Impossible." Aarón pulled her close. "What did you feel, my love? A spark? An explosion?"

They were talking to each other now. "Guys?"

Aarón and Kate turned to their son. Kate spoke. "Sorry, love. Tell us how you two met."

"I will, but I also need your help with something. Evan's never had a big family holiday meal, so I'd like to pull out all the stops."

"So business as usual then?" his father joked.

"Basically. I just want your help making it perfect."

"We'll help as soon as you admit you felt the zing," his father insisted.

"I felt it." Cam sensed his face coloring.

"I knew it!" Aaron Canto cheered.

"But not at first. The first time I met her, she threw up on me, punched me in the face, and flipped me off."

His mother laughed and pulled her legs beneath her. "Sounds like the start of an epic love story."

After telling his parents the story, leaving out some of the details so Evan could share them at dinner, he returned to his childhood bedroom. He stood in the doorway, staring at her sleeping form. Just like in the caves, he knew her in the dark. She had scooted into the space he had occupied and was lying on her side, hugging his pillow with one hand; the other was stretched across the mattress, seemingly seeking him out. He obliged.

Stripping off his T-shirt and sweatpants, Cam crawled into the bed in gray boxer briefs and pulled her close. She slipped her knee between his thighs and pressed against his side; her breasts, through the thin fabric of her camisole, rubbed against his bicep.

Who needed sleep?

Cam slid down, dragging her panties down as he went, and draped a long smooth leg over his shoulder. Evan arched her back and bent her other knee. With that subtle green light, he buried his face between her legs. God, this woman, every muffled moan, every curl of her toes against his shoulder, every clench of her fist in his hair drove him mad. She tasted like oranges dipped in honey, and he wanted to devour her. Her body was the map guiding him to her treasure. She tensed as he stroked her with his fingers and tongue pulling the orgasm from deep within her.

When he lifted his head, she was watching him through drunken eyes. She opened her arms, and he grabbed a condom from the nightstand and settled between her hips.

"Next time, I'd like to watch you do that," she whispered.

"Would you now?"

"It's just so *erotic*."

He positioned himself at her entrance and stroked her face. "Maybe I should fuck you in front of a mirror, *mi amor*? Would you like that? Would you like to see what I do to you?"

He thrust as she gasped, "*yes*."

Well, well, well, his little mouse was as adventurous in the bedroom as she was everywhere else. Interesting. Their sex was already off the charts. Cam had never been with a woman long enough to explore their sexuality together. The thought of doing it with Evan had his erection throbbing as he thrust inside of her.

"Cam," she breathed against his neck.

"Again," he commanded.

"Cam. *Cam*." Every time she said his name, a painful wound inside him healed.

Together they exploded.

When they awoke again, it was to an overcast day and voices coming from downstairs. Cam reached for his phone on the nightstand to check the time.

"It's eleven. I haven't slept this late in ten years." He yawned.

Evan snuggled close. "I'm usually up at six. I guess all the traveling took its toll."

"Nah, I think I wore you out."

They had been awake until dawn, exploring each other with a hunger that never seemed to ebb. She nuzzled his neck. "You always smell so good, like ocean air."

"You smell like sex. Like I've been at you all night. Damn, I'm hard again, but from the sound of it, at least one of my sisters is downstairs with her kids."

"Oh my God, it's Christmas." She shot up in the bed.

Cam pulled her back to his side. "Relax, baby. My sisters do Christmas at their homes. They're not due to come here until this afternoon."

"Then what are we listening to?"

"That's probably Antonia and her kids. Her oldest, Ricky, is on the autism spectrum, and holidays can overwhelm him. She brings him over early to show him the tree and let him open his presents; it's too much commotion when the rest of the family is here. Her younger two, Kara and Theo, are hell on wheels."

"How many nieces and nephews do you have?" Evan asked.

Cam listed them off. "Antonia has the three downstairs, Sylvie is Antonia's twin, and she has three girls. Maria is the oldest, she has two boys, and Lena is closest to me. She's divorced and has one daughter."

"Nine?"

Cam nodded. "Four boys and five girls."

Evan blew a lock of hair from her face. "I may need to hang out with Ricky. I can see how that could be intimidating."

Cam traced his fingertips over her bare shoulder. "You'll be fine. I've got you."

Cam's sisters and their families had arrived en masse at noon. After his sisters had covered him in teary kisses and met Evan, his nephews had mobbed him, pulling him to the ground, mixing hugs with wrestling moves. Cam had seen them intermittently throughout the years, but he was still amazed at how much the children had grown. Soon the wrapped packages in the next room stole their attention, and the children wasted no time getting to the presents. Cam sat next to his dad and watched the pandemonium. His oldest sister, Maria, tried to keep some semblance of order insisting the kids take turns and thank their grandparents after opening each gift. He saw his mother take Ricky into the kitchen, where he knew she would park him on a stool and put him to work with some small task. A moment later, he noticed Evan, who had been speaking with Lena, follow them. He slipped from the couch while his dad was helping his nephew, Jamie, sit on his new bike.

Cam peered around the doorway and saw Ricky sitting at the kitchen island peeling carrots. Evan was perched on the stool next to him, cutting celery. She focused on her assignment as she spoke. "Your job is more important than mine."

"Why?" Ricky asked.

"Because carrots are easier to see and taste. Nobody notices the celery," she said.

"The carrots are important," he repeated, continuing to peel them.

Kate looked up at her with a warm smile. "I was an only child too. They're my family, and even I get a little overwhelmed sometimes. It's normally not this crazy. Cam's really showing you the full force of the Canto family."

"I love it," Evan replied. "It's exactly how I imagined."

Over his shoulder, Cam heard a door open and close and a new commotion.

Kate said to Evan. "That will be Cam's grandparents, Aarón's mom and dad. My parents won't arrive until dinner. They're a little more sedate than the Canto crew."

"Thank you for having me, Mrs. Canto."

"Please, Evan, call me Kate."

"Kate," Evan amended. "You're so kind to include me at the last minute like this."

His mother snapped the ends off of green beans as she spoke. "What's one more? Besides, I know my son, and if you feel about him the way he feels about you, this will be your first of many family holidays in this house."

Evan lifted her head to speak just as shouts echoed from the front of the house. "Camilo! Get out here. Your grandparents want to see you with their own eyes!"

Cam backed away, but not before his mother cast a knowing glance in his direction.

He turned and nearly plowed into his sister, Lena. They were the closest in age, only ten months apart, and she and Cam shared a bond.

"Well, well, well, Teen Wolf, still spying, I see." She called him by his childhood nickname. When she teased him about spying, she wasn't referring to the CIA. He was routinely chased, screamed at, and grounded for eavesdropping on his older sisters.

"Busted," Cam confessed.

"She's it for you, yes?"

"Yes."

"If you tell me you felt dad's stupid zing, I'm going to kick your ass."

Cam pulled his lips inward.

"You're kidding?" Lena threw her hands up. "I certainly never felt a zing with Jake. Maybe that's why we're divorced." She tapped her chin. "Nah, I'm pretty sure it was the banging the secretary that did it. Maybe she felt a zing."

"I'm sorry, Leen." Cam put his arm around her, and they walked to the front of the house.

"Don't be." She waved the apology off. "My zing is out there." She thumbed over her shoulder. "And your zing is in the kitchen.

You better go grab her. You know abuela is going to search the house until she finds her."

Cam shook his head with a smile. "You're right about that. I'll get her and introduce them. Then I'm going to steal her away for a bit. I think it's a little crazier than she expected."

"What? This family?" Lena grinned. "Nah."

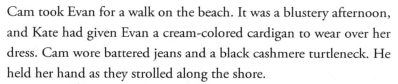

Cam took Evan for a walk on the beach. It was a blustery afternoon, and Kate had given Evan a cream-colored cardigan to wear over her dress. Cam wore battered jeans and a black cashmere turtleneck. He held her hand as they strolled along the shore.

"How long have you done that kind of work?" she asked.

"I was in the Navy for eight years, six of them as a SEAL. The CIA for four. I was a NOC, which means non-official cover officer, during that time."

"And it's over now?" she asked.

"I left The Agency last year," he explained.

"But you were undercover in Mallorca."

Cam picked up a seashell, blew the sand from its iridescent interior, then tossed it aside. "It was unfinished business from my past, but it's over now."

"And playing the role of Gemini March's lover was part of that unfinished business?" she asked.

He took her by the shoulders and turned her to face him. "Evan—"

"It's okay, Cam." She cut him off. "I understand that in that role, Miguel had to do things that Cam would never do. It would be demeaning to you to say that it was no hardship to seduce a gorgeous woman. If it's not something you have a choice in, then it's difficult no matter what."

Cam pulled her into his arms and hugged her. "Thank you."

"The guy in high school? The one I told you about who forced me?"

Cam gave a stiff nod.

"He was the best-looking guy in our class. When I tried to tell one of my few friends about what happened, she waved it away. In her mind, every other girl in my position would have said yes, so the fact that I didn't was my mistake. Like it was my fault. So yes, I understand better than most about having to be with someone you don't want to be with no matter how things appear."

Holding her close, Cam spoke into the wind. "When you told me that story… I still want that guy's name. He needs to be taught a lesson."

"He's in jail. He took the fall for an insider trading scandal at the financial firm where he worked. So justice was served, karmically at least."

She heard his noncommittal grunt as they continued forward. A subject change was in order. "What will you do now that your secret agent days are over?"

"I work for a small firm, Bishop Security, based in South Carolina."

Evan stepped out of her flip flops, lifted the hem of her honey-colored sundress, and stepped into the surf. "I've never been to South Carolina. When I was a kid, I had a map on my bedroom wall with pushpins in all the states I had visited. I've been to Alaska, even Hawaii, but never South Carolina."

"I plan to remedy that shortly." He kicked off his Nikes, rolled up his jeans, and followed her into the ankle-deep water. "I'm bringing you back with me."

Evan beamed at him. "So Cam is bossy. I think there are a few traits you share with your undercover identity."

"Yeah, I'm trying to work through that."

"And you will," she reassured him.

"Thanks."

"I think the Miguel I knew in the caves had a lot of Cam mixed in." She gathered up the hem of her dress and reached down to touch the foamy water.

"What makes you say that?"

"The first time I saw you? When you frightened me off the beach the day I came to investigate the markers? I was terrified of you. I couldn't for a second imagine getting to know that man. But in the caves, whatever the reason, I saw Cam beneath the surface. Every rude comment Miguel made, Cam was there being kind to me or protecting me. So if you think I don't know Cam, you're mistaken."

"Actually, that wasn't the first time we met." He took her hand and continued walking.

"What do you mean?" she asked.

"The stingray?"

Evan looked at his beautiful face, her eyes shifting from one golden iris to the other. "Oh my God, that was you? You rescued me?"

"I'm a SEAL, ma'am. No man, or woman, left behind."

She threw herself into his arms then almost immediately broke away, covering her face with her hands. "I barfed on you!"

"Several times."

"Ohmygodohmygodohmygod. That has to be the worst how-did-you-two-meet story of all time."

Cam picked Evan up like a bride and sank down in the sand with her in his arms. "And that's what makes it the best how-did-you-two-meet story of all time."

"Says the gorgeous man who saved the bleeding, puking girl."

"You also punched me and flipped me off." He grinned.

"Cam—"

"And I still thought you were the most beautiful woman I'd ever seen." He kissed her temple.

"I don't believe you for a minute, but I love you for saying it."

"You love me?" He asked with such an earnest innocence, Evan felt her eyes mist.

"I love you, Cam. I should have told you when you showed up in Palo Alto. I've felt it for so long, but as I told you in Mallorca, I don't express my emotions easily. The first time you touched me and I didn't flinch, I knew you were different." He winced. "No, Cam. Don't for one second think that Miguel Ramirez was the man who touched me in that cave. It was you, Camilo Canto. You can call yourself The Incredible Hulk for all I care. I see *you*."

She beamed at her beautiful, complicated man.

He tucked a loose lock of hair behind her ear. "I think I've been waiting my whole life for you. I love you, Evan."

Before she had a chance to respond, he was kissing her. She snaked her arms around his neck, getting lost in his powerful physique. She hadn't been hoping for the touch of a man, she realized. She had been hoping for the touch of *this* man.

Cam pulled back and cupped her rear. "The Incredible Hulk, huh? If we can get a minute alone, I may make you call me that."

"I'd like to scream 'Cam' a few more times if it's okay with you."

"More than okay." He took her hand and pulled her to standing. "Come on. We need to get back."

Cam paused on the stoop of his family home and kissed his woman. Evan glanced over his shoulder, and he followed her gaze to the window by the door where a curtain rustled.

"I think we have an audience," she whispered.

Cam leaned his forehead against hers. "Yeah, that happens a lot around here."

"We should go inside. I know your mom went to a lot of trouble. We shouldn't be late." She tugged on his arm.

Cam stayed where he was. "I love you."

She smiled up at him. "I love you too."

"Come on."

They entered Cam's family home, and chatter and laughter halted behind two closed double doors. Cam opened them with a flourish.

Before her was a dream come to life. Cam's entire family was crowded around the long rectangular dinner table.

Right on cue, his mother and father came in from a back hall that led to the kitchen. They were each carrying a turkey. Aarón set his tray on the sideboard and helped his wife place hers on the table.

Kate Canto wiped her hands on a dishtowel and said, "Merry Christmas, Evan. Shall we eat?"

She and Cam took the two remaining seats.

"Eat up, Evan. You'll need your strength. We've got a bear of a puzzle started in the family room. It's Van Gogh's *Starry Night*," Aarón added.

The food-laden table blurred through her teary gaze, making the setting seem even more like a fantasy. Cam leaned down and whispered in her ear. "How'd I do? Is this what you imagined, *querida*?"

"It's better." She turned her eyes to him. "You're here."

"Ready for your first big holiday meal?"

She nodded as he wiped away her tears with his thumbs. "I love you, Cam. So much. And I love experiencing *all* of these firsts with you."

Her innuendo had the desired effect, and he squeezed her thigh under the table.

"Looking forward to many more," he whispered.

Once they were seated, Cam's abuela said the blessing, and all hell broke loose. Voices increased in volume as children demanded food and changed seats, and people argued about the Dolphins and discussed the alligator living on a nearby golf course. Through it all, Cam kept his big hand on her knee. She circled his wrist and held him in check when his fingers occasionally wandered, an action which, oddly, brought a pleased tilt to his lips. She couldn't take the time to analyze it, though; she was too busy soaking up every second of this big, loving, chaotic, argumentative, wonderful family.

She leaned into Cam's body. "Merry Christmas, Cam."

He put his arm around the back of her chair and kissed the top of her head. "I can't imagine a better present for Christmas than you."

CHAPTER FIFTY-ONE

Beaufort, South Carolina
December 25

The hospital room looked like a Christmas store had exploded. An artificial tree sat in the corner with an entire stuffed zoo beneath. Twinkle lights rimmed the ceiling, plastic snowmen perched on the sill, elves sat on shelves, and candy canes hung from a string over the door, a sprig of mistletoe among them. Calliope and Twitch had gone wild. Twitch had even cast a video of a roaring fire to the television bolted to the ceiling. Emily sat upright in the bed, holding the newest addition to the Bishop family. Nathan had dozed off in the chair beside her bed.

Tox walked in, his head parting the candy canes like one of those beaded curtains in a head shop. "It looks like Santa Claus threw up in here."

Calliope followed her husband into the room. "Shut up, gigante. It looks festive. I don't want the baby's first images of Christmas to be a sterile hospital room."

"She can't even focus on the boob in front of her. You think she's going to remember this room?" Tox asked.

"I'll remember it," Emily spoke from her bed. "It's just the most thoughtful thing."

Tox stage whispered to Nathan, "Is she crying?"

Nathan leaned over and wiped her tears, then kissed his daughter on the top of her head. "Hormones, I think. She cried at a cough syrup commercial earlier."

"The wife had a cough, and the husband drove to the pharmacy in the middle of the night!" Emily defended. "It was sweet."

Deciding that topic had reached a natural conclusion, Nathan turned to his friend. "Is Miles with you?"

"He's on his way."

"I'd like to speak to you both when he gets here," Nathan explained.

"I'm here." Miles Buchanan loped into the room carrying a wooden rocking horse. "I figured the boys could use it until she's old enough. What's up?"

Nathan stood and walked over to the Buchanan twins. "You may or may not know that we haven't asked anyone to be godparents for our children."

Tox stood a bit straighter, sensing the follow-up.

"We'd like to ask you two to be godfathers to the boys. Miller to Jack and Miles to Charlie. Emily has already chosen her childhood best friend Caroline to be Charlie's godmother. Calliope, we'd like you to be Jack's."

Calliope sat on the bed and put an arm around her friend. "Oh Emily, I'd love to be Jack's godmother. Thank you."

Tox laughed. "Great, now they're both crying. Thanks, man. It is an honor." He clapped Nathan on the shoulder. "We'd be honored. Right, Mi?"

Tox and Nathan looked over at Miles, who stood still as a statue, his eyes glassy. He cleared his throat and stepped forward. "Yes, of course. Honored." Miles echoed his brother. "I'm going to grab a coffee. Can I get anyone anything?"

"Coffee, black," Tox requested.

Nathan withdrew his wallet. "I'll have the same."

"I got it." Miles turned away, set the rocking horse down, and hurried out the door.

"He's okay," Tox replied, seeing Nathan's puzzled expression. "He went from having no one to... us in just a few months. I don't think he realized what he was missing."

Nathan nodded his understanding.

"And what about daddy's little girl? Who will guide her on the path of life and, you know, teach her how to pick locks and get a fake ID?" Tox rubbed his palms together.

Nathan shook his head at the ceiling. "What have we done?"

"Hey." Tox held up his hands. "I didn't even mention boys."

Emily cut him off. "We're going to ask Chat to be this little angel's godfather when he gets back. He flew home to spend Christmas with his family. And of course Twitch, her namesake, to be godmother."

"Namesake?" Twitch poked her head around Tox's imposing frame.

"Namesake," Nathan confirmed. "Twitch, we'd like you to meet our daughter. Charlotte."

Twitch walked over to the pink bundle and gently pinched the baby's bootied foot. "You named her after me?"

Emily covered Twitch's hand. "Is that okay? We know you don't like to be called Charlotte, but we love you, and we love the name."

Twitch beamed through her tears. "Of course it's okay. I'm... well, I'm speechless." She ran a gentle hand over the pink cap of the now sleeping baby. "Hi, baby Charlotte."

"And you'll be her godmother?" Emily asked.

"I'll change all of her grades to As." Twitch laughed.

Nathan stepped up to the bedside. "What makes you think her grades won't be As to begin with?"

Steady stepped into the room, Ren followed. "Is there some sort of holiday today? I can't quite remember." Plucking the mistletoe from among the string of candy canes, Steady dangled it above his head. Bouncing his eyebrows up and down, he offered, "What do you say, Calliope? Spread a little Christmas cheer."

Tox growled. "Brother, I will lay you out."

"No?" Steady turned his attention to Emily. "What about you, Em? You up for a little smoochin'?"

"Brother, I will instruct Tox to lay you out." Nathan didn't bother looking up from his phone.

"So, no swingers in the group then. Noted." Steady walked over to examine the menagerie under the tree. "Any word from Cam?"

Nathan answered, "Just that he's with Evan. And he sounded very happy about it."

Steady bobbed his head. "Good." He beamed at the group and did his best Tiny Tim. "God bless us, everyone."

Nathan clapped once. "All right, I'm kicking everyone out. Maggie and Uncle Charlie are watching the boys, and Herc is picking up my mother at the airport in the morning. This is our nap window."

Miles appeared at the door with a cardboard tray of coffees, passed one to Nathan and one to his brother, then joined the goodbye hugs as the men shuffled out. Twitch stood from the bed.

"I love little Charlotte, Emily. Thank you."

Emily squeezed her friend's hand. "We love you. And it doesn't hurt that you have a great name."

Twitch stared at her sneakers. "And it isn't that I don't like my name. I do like it. It's just... Charlotte is different from Twitch, you know?"

Emily waited for her friend to look up. "You happen to be speaking to an expert on that subject. So yes, I do know."

Twitch laughed, "Right. I sort of have an alternate identity too, I guess. But mine isn't secret like yours was."

Nathan sat on the other side of the bed and gently lifted the baby from his wife's arms. He settled Charlotte into her bassinet with a kiss and returned his attention to his wife. He pressed his lips to the back of Emily's hand and tucked the covers around her as he spoke. "We love Twitch, and we love Charlotte. As long as you're happy, we're happy."

Twitch stood with a sad smile and promised to return the next day.

Emily snuggled into her pillow and spoke to her husband. "Do you think she and Finn will ever work things out?"

Nathan expelled a weary sigh. "I honestly don't know. He's never going to be the man he was. I guess the question that remains is what kind of a man will he turn out to be?"

"I hope it's a man who can love Twitch the way she deserves. That's my Christmas wish."

He kissed her forehead and lay down beside her. "We already got our Christmas wish."

Emily yawned. "Maybe we'll get two this year."

Nathan kissed his wife. "I'll tell you what I told Cam last week. Sometimes these things work out in unexpected ways."

CHAPTER FIFTY-TWO

Beaufort, South Carolina
January 9

Cam sat at the far end of the cherry wood table and drank in the scene. Nathan and Emily's dining room was illuminated by the candles flanking a centerpiece of white roses and vintage sconces emitting a romantic glow. Evan was on his right, her hand resting absently on his thigh. Calliope sat to his left, watching Emily tuck a pink blanket around the baby. He'd have to be blind not to see the longing in Calliope's eyes.

"Is anybody going to eat that?" On Calliope's left, Tox eyed the last piece of chocolate cake on the plate in the center of the dining room table.

Maggie Bishop had provided the cake—along with enough frozen meals to feed an army for a month—and taken the twins for a sleepover. Evan and Cam had brought dinner and wine. Calliope had arrived with flowers and yet another stuffed animal for baby Charlotte, and Tox had brought his appetite.

"It's all yours. I haven't eaten this much in months." Emily shifted the baby in her arms. "Thank you for bringing dinner, Evan. Everything was delicious."

"And the wine is exceptional. I wasn't familiar with your father's vineyard," Nathan added.

"Treasure Trove winery only produces about forty thousand cases a year. They also make a nice zinfandel along with this pinot." Evan held the wine glass by the stem.

"I can't wait to taste it." Emily followed the movement of the liquid in the goblet.

"A sip won't hurt." Nathan slid his glass to his wife. "My mum says a little wine in the breast milk does wonders for their sleeping."

Emily pushed the wine away. "Your mother also thinks martinis and espresso are two of the four major food groups.

"True." Nathan polished off the pinot noir.

Calliope forked a bite of cake from her husband's plate. "Evan, when are you heading back to California?"

Cam had been silent for the last several minutes, content to listen to his friends talk and overjoyed with how easily Evan had meshed with the group. She turned to him then and leaned closer. "I'm not."

All eyes shifted to them. Cam looked at Evan. "We want to be together."

"I'm changing my dissertation to focus on the antiquities of the Moors lost during the Crusades. Unfortunately, that means delaying my Ph.D. The good news is, I can work remotely."

Tox ran his fork along his dessert plate, gathering the last of the buttercream. "That's awesome." He pointed the tines at Cam. "Just you and Evan and Steady in that dilapidated beach house. It's a sitcom come to life."

"Not exactly," Evan clarified. "I'm a little more, um, practical than Cam."

"What Evan means is that she thinks it's crazy to move in together after knowing each other for six weeks, which, I might add, is exactly how long my parents knew each other before they were married, but I get it."

"Cam, you're my first real relationship."

"No *querida*. I am your *last* real relationship."

Cam looked up to see four sets of eyes on them.

Calliope pressed her temple to her husband's shoulder. "Wow. Gold star, Cam."

Nathan took the sleeping infant from his wife, switched on the baby monitor, and disappeared down the hall.

"So basically," Tox wiped the chocolate from his mouth. "You're going to blow a lot of rent money on an apartment you never use and stay with Cam every night."

"Wrong, " Cam corrected. "I'll spend every night at her place. We don't need Steady popping his head in every ten minutes to see if we want to binge-watch *The Mandalorian*."

"Evan, what's happening with the diamond?" Emily asked.

Sparked by the topic, Evan leaned forward. "The Panther's Eye was officially certified as the world's largest yellow diamond at two hundred and ninety carats uncut. The estimated value is two hundred eighty million dollars."

Tox gave a low whistle as Nathan walked back into the room and set a steaming mug in front of Emily. She tilted her head up to him, offering her lips, and he obliged.

"Well," Nathan commented as he took a seat. "That's quite a feather in your cap."

"What happens now?" Calliope asked.

Tox put his arm around his wife. "It won't be part of the crown jewels any time soon. It's probably already collecting dust in some government vault."

"I hope not," Evan said. "Part of the joy of being an archaeologist is sharing your discoveries with the world."

"Any news on Gemini March?" Tox asked.

"Nothing. Cam shared what information he had, but even with everything that went down in Mallorca, all it really amounted to was a well-supported theory. We weren't exactly holding a smoking gun," Nathan replied.

Calliope added, "Gemini March hasn't been seen. The tabloid rumor is that she's in rehab."

"She has intel on some extremely powerful criminals," Cam said.

"I gotta hand it to you, buddy. You unmasked an arch-villain, found a giant diamond, and got the girl. Not bad, considering you had no fucking clue what you were stepping into." Tox tipped his glass to his friend.

Cam rested his hand at Evan's nape. "Especially the girl."

Evan turned to Cam. "Dr. Emberton says we always seem to make the most wonderful discoveries quite by accident."

"He's right, *mi amor*. I found you."

CHAPTER FIFTY-THREE

Undisclosed location
January 19

The blacked-out Suburban traveled up the long drive and around the circular lawn. A statue depicting Venus and Mars crowned an empty fountain in the center of the grass. After pulling to a stop at the chateau entrance, the driver exited the car, moved to the back door, and escorted the dark-haired woman inside.

Jennifer Sorenson, the Deputy Director of National Clandestine Services, waited in the soaring hall wearing a black pantsuit and holding a tablet.

"The CIA needs better disguises. It looks like a rat died on my head." Gemini March pulled off the wide-brimmed hat and wig in one motion and dropped them to the parquet-tiled floor.

Sorenson ignored the remark. "Welcome to your temporary home."

The model glanced around, taking in the Renaissance portrait art and the grand staircase. "I hope you included a decorating budget in that deal of yours."

"I'm sure you can suffer through while we go over details and logistics, and the team gets your villa in Mallorca kitted out."

She inspected a marble bust at the foot of the stairs with a look of disdain. "I'm not."

The DDO waved over the suited man standing in the corner who walked to the center of the foyer and placed a black briefcase on the circular marble table. The man opened the case and the box within, then slowly pulled the cloth back to reveal The Panther's Eye.

"This should take some of the sting out of your hardship," Sorenson remarked.

Gemini ran her fingers over the smooth stone. "Well done, Director. The great and powerful CIA works their magic."

"Technically, the diamond belongs to you. That cave is part of the March Mining property. We just provided the Spanish government with some very good incentives to agree with that assessment," Sorenson said.

"Joseph will be so pleased," Gemini mused.

"I rather thought he would want the diamond for himself," Sorenson remarked.

"Nothing would bring him greater joy than seeing it dangling from my neck. Not in that hideous medallion, of course. Something a bit more tasteful, I think." Gemini pursed her lips in thought.

"If you say so."

Gemini ignored the director's sarcasm and gestured vaguely. "I assume there's a vault somewhere in this monstrosity."

The DDO nodded to the man, who secured the diamond and left the room. She gestured to her right. "Why don't we go into the dining room. We can go over everything there. The chef has prepared lunch according to your specifications."

"Fine," Gemini huffed.

Sorenson smiled then and spoke as she turned to walk into the next room. "Don't look so put out, Ms. March. The Conductor is about to become the CIA's greatest asset."

With a polite smile curling her lips and blood oozing between the knuckles of her clenched fists, The Conductor followed in her jailor's wake and murmured, "We'll see."

EPILOGUE

Miami, Florida
April 3

"Team leader, do you have a visual? Repeat. Do you have a visual?" Cam whispered into his comm unit from the bushes behind the large beach house.

The silence was infuriating. Finally, Tox spoke up. "Wait. I'm team leader? I thought you were team leader."

Ren chimed in, "No. We agreed in the van. You're team leader. Cam is Cam."

Now it was Chat's turn. "Tox has a point. Cam should be team leader. Maybe we should all have different nicknames for this op," he deadpanned.

"Excellent idea," Herc said from his perch. "For the duration of this op, I will be known as Thor."

"Guys," Cam pleaded.

Tox interjected, "Sorry, team leader. No, wait. That's me. Sorry, Cam. No visual yet. Oh, hey, did you guys know a fetus at four weeks gestation is the size of a blueberry? A baby the size of a fucking blueberry. *Just picture that.*"

"Dude, it's not like it's a miniature, blueberry-sized baby. It's still forming and shit," Steady chided.

"Is this what we have to look forward to for the next nine months? Fetus factoids?" Ren asked.

"Incoming," Tox announced from the van parked across the street.

Cam whispered into the comm, "I can't see a fucking thing back here. Herc, trade spots with me."

"So we're not a go with Thor?"

"Herc!" Cam yelled.

"Would you relax? I'm on the damn roof. You need to be on the ground."

Cam peered through the bushes and caught a glimpse of Evan's car as she pulled into the driveway of his grandparent's beachfront home. The car disappeared out of his line of sight.

"Target acquired," Tox confirmed.

Cam heard the front door open and his grandmother's loud Spanish as she greeted Evan. He couldn't catch everything she said, but he got the gist. She claimed she had been digging in the garden and had come across some pots that appeared quite old. She was playing her part well. Cam knew she would. His abuela loved a good scheme.

"They're entering the house. Heads on a swivel, boys." That was Steady. The guy could joke in the middle of a gunfight, but for this op, he was all business.

"Coming out the back." Ren took over surveillance.

Cam heard the screen door open and close and the two women laughing as they neared his hideout in the peonies. His abuela's voice carried across the flagstone patio.

"I was just working the soil in the garden when the trowel made a clink. I smoothed the dirt away, and there was this small pot. I didn't want to damage it, so I called you. What if it's some ancient Aztec relic?"

"It really could be, Mrs. Canto. You'd be amazed what people find on their property."

Evan was a mere three feet away when she knelt and began brushing away the dirt. "There does appear to be something here. It's broken in two."

Cam was a ball of nerves as he watched her lift the first broken half of the dime store pot from the ground. That's when she saw the weathered, red leather Cartier box.

"Oh my goodness, Mrs. Canto. I think you've stumbled upon someone's hiding place."

"That cannot be, nieta. We have lived here since we built this house."

Nieta. His abuela had called Evan, granddaughter.

He waited, knowing curiosity would get the better of her. After ten seconds that felt like ten hours, she opened the ring box.

"Oh my," she gasped. Then realization hit. "Oh my!" Her free hand covered her mouth.

Cam emerged from the bushes. "It was abuela's mother-in-law's ring. My great grandmother's from the nineteen twenties."

The Art Deco, emerald cut, yellow diamond was set in a platinum band with two baguettes, like tiny steps, on either side. His grandparents had saved the vintage ring for him.

When she still hadn't spoken, Cam came down beside her.

She laughed and cried behind her hand. "Oh, Cam."

"Evan, will you marry me?"

She looked up from the mesmerizing ring into his equally hypnotic eyes.

"You know, when we were searching those caves all those months ago, and you were undercover, or whatever you call it, you didn't think I knew you. But even then, I saw you, Camilo. I will always see you."

Cam pinned her with his gaze. "Answer the question, little mouse."

"Yes." She tackled him into the dirt.

"We are a go, people." Steady's voice carried from Cam's ear.

"Are you on comms?" Evan asked.

He removed the small device and held it between them. "I needed some moral support."

"Abuela, cue the band," Tox instructed.

"Can you boys hear me? There's no microphone?" There was a thunk and some scraping as his grandmother fiddled with the earpiece.

"We hear you. Go ahead and give Aarón and Kate the green light," Tox encouraged.

"Aarón, Kate? Can you hear me? She said yes!"

Music sounded from the tent on the beach. Cam took the box from her hands and slid the ring onto Evan's finger.

"You still sure about that big family?" he asked from beneath her.

"Yes. And very much looking forward to expanding it."

Cam rumbled into her neck, "Let's skip the party."

She kissed him. "Your friends are staring, and your family is waiting."

"Fine." He pushed to standing with Evan safe in his arms.

"But after the party, all bets are off." She ran her hand down the placket of his dress shirt.

The look he gave her had Evan's knees buckling, but Cam supported her, as she always did for him, and together, with a phalanx of imposing, protective friends surrounding them, they made their way down to the beach.

THE END

ACKNOWLEDGMENTS

Thank you to my editor, Peter Gelfan, for your invaluable assistance. I would also like to thank opinionated romance readers, Kara Horton and Dr. Mary Meyer, tech whiz, Henry Arneson, Steven Fox, Shari Stauch, and my mom, Shelley Johnson. Without your input, Buried Beneath would not be what it is. I also owe an enormous thank you to Ann-Marie Nieves and Suzanne Leopold, two women who went above and beyond to help a fledgling indie author.

Most of all, to you, readers, thank you for your continued support. Another book in the Bishop Security series is coming soon!

ABOUT THE AUTHOR

Debbie Baldwin is a successful print media and television writer. She is a graduate of Princeton University and the University of Virginia School of Law. Debbie and her husband live in Saint Louis, Missouri with their puggle, Pebbles. They have three children in college.

**FALL IN LOVE WITH NATHAN AND EMILY IN THE FIRST
BOOK IN THE BISHOP SECURITY SERIES, FALSE FRONT.**

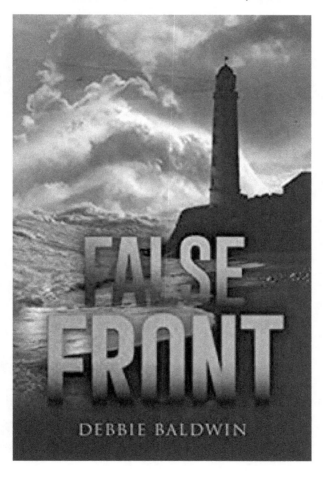

PROLOGUE

Two Years Ago...

Emma Porter looked bored. No surprise there. It was her standard expression—her failsafe. She, with some effort, avoided the imposing lighted mirror in front of her and kept her gaze on the screen of her phone. Her violet eyes, masked by colored contacts that turned them an unremarkable blue, glazed. It didn't help that the stylist was working his way around her head in a hypnotic rhythm, pulling long strands of honey-colored hair through his enormous round brush. He would have put her to sleep but for the incessant chatter. Sister, do you model? How has no one approached you before? Oh, they'd approached her.

She gave her standard reply.

"Nope, just in school."

She checked her phone again. A text.

We're good for Jane Hotel. I talked to my buddy. Bouncer's name is Fernand. See you at 9!

The exclamation point annoyed her. *You're a guy,* she thought. *Guys shouldn't use exclamation points when they text.* She'd probably end up dumping him over it. She'd done it for less.

"Big night tonight? It's a crazy Thursday. Are you going to that thing at Tau?"

"No. Just meeting a friend for a drink."

A friend? She guessed he was a friend. She'd met him twice—no, three times; he'd kissed her on 58th Street before she got into a cab three nights ago: hence the big date.

"A friend, huh? Sounds like a date."

"Yeah," Emma sighed, "it's kind of a date."

"So, no one special? No BF?"

"Nope. No boyfriend. Just a date."

"Well, I imagine the boys are climbing through your window, gorgeous girl."

She wanted to say *the last time a boy tried to climb in my window, security guards tackled him on the front lawn, as a leashed German shepherd bared his teeth at his neck while Teddy Prescott cried that he was in my seventh-grade ceramics class, and he just wanted to ask me to a school dance.* Instead, she buttoned her lip and checked her phone. Again.

"No, not so much."

"Well, my work here is done. What do you think?"

He ran his fingers up her scalp from her nape and pushed the mass of hair forward over her shoulders, admiring his handiwork. She managed as much enthusiasm as she could muster.

"Looks great. Thanks."

She grabbed her bag, left the cash and a generous tip—partly for the blowout, mostly for enduring her mood—and headed out.

The walk home was a short-ish hike. While Broadway up ahead was always jam-packed, the little Tribeca side street was surprisingly desolate. Scaffolds stood sentry, and crumpled newspapers blew across the road like urban tumbleweeds. Emma's footsteps clacked on the pavement, and her shopping bags swished against her legs. In the waning daylight, the long shadows reached out. Emma moved with purpose but not haste, running through the plan for the evening in her head. Across the street, a pair of lurking teens stopped talking to watch her. The jarring slam of a Dumpster lid and the *beep, beep, beep* of a reversing trash truck echoed across the pavement. Near the end of the block, a homeless man in a recessed doorway

muttered about a coming plague and God setting the world to rights. Emma forced herself to keep her pace even but couldn't stifle her sigh of relief as she rounded the corner and joined the hordes. A businessman let out a noise of irritation as Emma forced him to slow his pace when she merged into the foot traffic. Yes, this was better. She hurried up Broadway and headed for home.

Spring Street was insane. The stores ran the gamut from A-list designer shops to dive bars and bodegas. Beneath the display window of Alexander Woo, a ratty hipster strummed a guitar. In front of Balthazar, there was a hotdog vendor. The street was dotted with musicians and addicts and homeless and shoppers and tourists and construction crews and commuters and students. There was a French crêpe stand next to Emma's favorite Thai place that was next to an organic vegan café. It was like somebody took everything that made New York New York—the art, the diversity, the music, the food, the bustle, the noise— and jammed it all onto one street. The street Emma called home.

Outside her building, a group of guys from her Abnormal Psychology class was coming out of the corner bodega.

"Hey IQ, what's up tonight? Heading downtown?"

"Maybe."

"Martin's parents' brownstone is on Waverly. Party's on!"

"Okay, I'll try to stop by."

"Cool."

The guys in her class had started calling her "IQ" freshman year. She was flattered at first, thinking it bore some reference to her intellect. A few months in, she discovered it was short for "Ice Queen." That was fine with her too. Whatever.

Her elegant but inconspicuous building sat just down from Mother's Ruin, her favorite pub, and next to a heavily graffitied retail space for rent. She waved to her doorman, who rushed to help her with her bags.

"Hey, Ms. Porter. Shopping, I see."

"Hey, Jimmy. Yeah, just a few odds and ends."

He glanced at the orange Hermes shopping bag and raised an eyebrow but didn't comment.

"You want me to take these up?"

"Yes, please, Jimmy." She handed over the bags and pushed through the heavy door to the stairs, while Jimmy summoned the elevator.

As she climbed the seven flights, Emma felt pretty calm. It was just a date. People had them all the time. Normal people had them all the time. She was normal. Well, she was getting there, and this outing tonight was proof of that. She had met a cute guy. She liked him well enough, and he was taking her out. She was excited about it; well, the progress more than the date. Another box to check on the list. She could crow about it to her therapist next week. The guy, Tom, seemed excited too, based on the aforementioned errant exclamation point. That, and the fact that she had actually heard him high-five a guy over the phone when she'd said yes.

Her bags were waiting by the door when she emerged from the seventh-floor landing. She fumbled with her key and pushed the door open with her butt as she scooped her purchases from the hallway floor. As she walked into the small but tasteful apartment—well, huge and elegant by college standards but certainly low key for Emma—she was greeted by a squeal and then the vaguely familiar strains of Rod Stewart's classic, "Tonight's the Night," so off-key it was barely recognizable.

"Jeez, Caroline, could you take it down a notch?"

"Nope. Can't. Sorry."

Caroline Fitzhugh had been Emma's best friend since before they were born. That wasn't an exaggeration. Their mothers had grown up together, had married men who were themselves best friends, and were neighbors in Georgetown as newlyweds. The women were inseparable until Emma's mother crossed the line separating "life of the party" from "addict." Their pregnancies were well-timed. It gave the two women a chance to rekindle their friendship, and it gave Emma's mother a fleeting chance at sobriety. Their moms spent their pregnancies together, nearly every day for the nine months leading up to the girls' arrival. Well, seven months and three weeks—Caroline was always in a rush to get places. After that, Emma's family moved to Connecticut, Caroline's to Georgia, and the girls saw each other on holidays and trips. Caroline knew Emma *before*. Before what one of her shrinks had euphemistically referred to as "the event." Before she was Emma Porter. Before she was from a small town near Atlanta. Before. Caroline was one of a handful of people with that knowledge. She knew Emma, and she protected her with a ferocity that rivaled Emma's father. Tonight, however, was a different story. Tonight, Caroline was pushing her out of the nest. It's *time*, she had said.

Caroline popped a bottle of Veuve Clicquot way too expensive for pre-gaming, declaring a dispensation on Emma's father's strict alcohol ban, and poured them each a glass.

"One glass, Em, to loosen up."

Emma answered her with a sip.

"Go get dressed. The LBD awaits."

The "little black dress" to which she referred was the Versace black crepe safety pin dress. It was the sexiest thing either of them had ever seen. The sleeveless dress hit Emma mid-thigh and was accented with mismatched gold safety pins at the waist and hip. Caroline had bought it for Emma on her credit card to avoid any questions from her father. He was generous to a fault, but anything remotely provocative was frowned upon. Emma garnered enough attention as it was, and a sexy dress only upped the ante. Now the dress was laying on her bed next to a pair of strappy sky-high heels and a small box holding a pair of diamond hoops. *The outfit for the virgin sacrifice.* She laughed to herself, then stopped abruptly, surprised by the term her thoughts had conjured: *virgin.* It was a word she never used because it had no meaning for her. She hated the word because the status of one's virginity was inextricably linked to one's past, and she couldn't dwell on what she didn't know. Therapists encouraged her to embrace a term that expressed her "emotional virginity," but Emma never could think of one. Her shrink was not amused when she suggested "vaginal beginner" and "hymenal newbie," so they let it slide. She could be an actual virgin after all. The point was that it shouldn't matter, and if everything went according to plan, after tonight it wouldn't. She could pop her emotional and/or physical cherry and move on. At this point, she just wanted to get the damn thing over with.

They had hours before she had to meet Tom. JT, her driver and bodyguard, usually accompanied her out in the evening, but Caroline told him they were heading to a study group at a friend's in the same building, so he had the night off. She was on her own, and she was thrilled.

Caroline pulled up the zipper on the dress and bounced around to Katy Perry, while Emma sipped tentatively on the same glass of bubbly.

"Oh Jeez, Em, just drink it. One glass won't have you cross-eyed. It'll calm your nerves."

She was right. Emma was nervous. For obvious reasons.

Emma left Caroline at Mother's, their local bar, with some friends and ordered an Uber to head to the Jane Hotel. As Tom had said, the bouncer, Fernand, was expecting her. Not that she would have had any trouble getting in anyway—she never did—but that dress was like a VIP pass. The group of people waiting gave a resigned sigh almost collectively as Emma deftly moved past them and entered the elegant bar. Tom had a table he was guarding with his life, and she made a beeline for him. When a guy at the bar grabbed her arm as she passed, not hard, just enough to stop her, Emma paused, stared at the hand on her bicep, and then slowly looked up at him with a perfected impassive glare. Ice Queen indeed. He released her without a word, and she dropped into the seat across from Tom.

"Hey, Gorgeous. You look amazing."

"Thanks."

"I didn't know what you like, so I ordered you a white wine."

She rarely drank. Well, that wasn't entirely true. She drank in one of her self-defense classes. Jay, her instructor, had insisted that she know how to do some of the moves "impaired," as he put it, so he'd fed her three beers and then had her train on the mat. She'd thrown up all over him.

The wine did relax her, and they chatted effortlessly. It took Emma nearly an hour to polish off the drink, and when she returned from the ladies' room with a fresh coat of lip gloss, a second glass sat waiting. What the hell. It was a big night.

It took her exactly four sips and ten minutes to realize what was happening.

Emma wasn't normal. Her father, in an extreme effort to get control of their world, made sure of that, and at this moment, she was thankful for it. Most girls would think the subtle blur of vision and the slight wave of nausea were due to nerves or too many drinks. But she knew exactly what was happening. She reached into her purse and texted her panic word, "lighthouse," to JT, but he was off duty. It could take him hours. She took a calming breath, keeping her heart rate as low as she could in her panic.

"I'll be right back. I think I left my lip gloss in the bathroom."

"I'll go with you. You look pale."

"No, no, I'm fine. Just dizzy from the wine, I guess. I'm a lightweight."

She forced a giggle. That appeased him. He didn't know she knew.

"Okay, I'll be waiting."

"Be right back," she repeated.

Emma took deliberate steps. When she glanced over her shoulder, she saw Tom throw some cash on the table and pull a key card from his breast pocket. She needed to focus on making her way down the hall. She couldn't get help in the bar; a stumbling, slurring girl in a bar would only bolster Tom's ruse. There was an elevator at the end, but as she made her way toward it, she stumbled and realized that it was exactly where Tom wanted her. She needed help or a hiding place, and she needed it fast. Whatever he had slipped in her drink was strong. The symptoms were hitting her fast. She moved down to a janitor's closet. Locked. She started moving frantically hand over hand, keeping her balance on the wall, avoiding looking at the nauseating pattern of the wallpaper as it started to blur. Tom's footsteps were heavy behind her as he closed in. She got to another door, pushed it open, and stumbled into the room. A group of surprised suits looked up as she blinked at them with terrified eyes. The man at the head of the table stood.

"Jesus, are you all right?"

"No. Help."

She heard the man closest to her mutter, "she's wasted." The man at the head of the table moved like a flash. He was coming toward her, and she was losing her ability to discern whether she had put herself in more danger by stumbling into this room. He seemed to float toward her, and Emma started to shake.

"Not drunk. Drunk," she slurred. "Drugged," she amended. "Help."

"Jesus." He put his hands on her shoulders, and she instantly calmed. Emma tried to shake the fog out of her head, but it only got worse. When she looked up, she saw three of him. So, she looked straight ahead at his tie. A cornflower blue tie that hung between the open sides of his dark suit jacket. She grabbed it with both hands, crunching it in her fists. She tried to remember her training, but all that came out was a plea.

"Please."

He put his arm around her protectively and calmly spoke.

"It's okay. I've got you."

And with that soothing notion, she passed out in his arms, still clutching his cornflower blue tie.

Emma woke up nineteen hours later in a hospital room that looked like a suite at the Ritz. JT was standing at the side of the bed like a royal guard, a pissed-off royal guard. He felt responsible for her indiscretion; she could feel his anger and guilt. Her father dozed, ashen, in an upholstered leather armchair. The night was a bit of a blur, and she ran through a timeline in her head to catch up. She had as much of it recalled as she probably ever would. Other than the mother of all headaches, she was otherwise uninjured. When she lifted her arm, the one without the IV, to move an itchy strand of hair from her face, the final few moments before she blacked out came flooding back. There, in her hand, was the cornflower blue tie, still knotted, with the length of it dangling down her forearm. It was wrapped around her palm and knuckles. JT informed her with a perplexed smirk that the nurses gave up trying to pry it from her, and the man, who had not given anyone his name, had ended up pulling it over his head and wrapping it around her hand as they wheeled her away on a gurney.

Completely unconscious, she had refused to let the thing go.